D0974495

DATE DUE   4/18

ISBN 13: 9780692919835
Library of Congress Control Number: 2017908754

ACKNOWLEDGEMENTS

Foremost, I am indebted to my wife, Callee, whose work ethic is matched by her good nature, sense of humor, and positive attitude. I have tried for nearly two decades to make her cynical and pessimistic, but haven't even made a dent. She is an incredible mom to our daughters, Charlotte and Catherine, and is also a best friend who makes it all worthwhile. Despite her schedule, she was tireless in her efforts to help make this first novel the best it could be, and half of the plot points were hers anyway, so, thanks honey, I love ya.

To Mom and Dad, for everything. Thanks for being so commonsensical, and teaching us to see both sides. We couldn't have asked for a better upbringing.

To Jim and Cindy, for always being my advocate. A guy with long hair and a high school diploma asks to marry your daughter, and you say yes?

To family members, for reading through numerous versions, and for your suggestions.

Additional thanks to my youngest brother Tyler, who read *Sanction* with a close eye, and provided important input.

To Rink, for recommendations concerning several characters.

To Judy Newman and Josh Wilbur, who went well above and beyond, which gave me the initial confidence to soldier on.

To Luc Rioual, for his review and recommendations, which helped shape subsequent drafts.

To Stacey Donovan, for proofing a later version, and suggesting ways to make it more readable.

To Dr. Perri Klass, for introducing me to Lucy Cleland, and to Lucy, for her professionalism.

To Kathy Simpson, for furthering an early love of language, and literature.

Special thanks to Bret and Gina, for introducing me to Lynn and Cele Seldon, whose advice was instrumental in getting this book published sooner than not.

For my family

Tell men of high condition,
That manage the estate,
Their purpose is ambition,
Their practice only hate.
And if they once reply,
Then give them all the lie.

Sir Walter Raleigh

PROLOGUE

Cairo, Egypt
Summer 1946

*T*he doors of *El-Fishawi*, which by all accounts had
never closed since the fashionable café first opened
them in the eighteenth century, were shut. The din of
foot traffic and dust kicked in from the bustling open-air
souk in the bazaar district of Egypt's capital city might
have encouraged such a move on any other day. But that
morning, it was a precaution taken to safeguard the clandestine assembly of a group of men who were being hunted
worldwide in the wake of their failed war.

Mint tea had been served, and Haj Amin al-
Husseini readied his shisha. As he pressed tobacco into
a clay bowl and waited for the coals to heat, the Arab
leader of Palestine opened a weathered telegram he had
carried since the winter of 1943, when Germany's confidence of victory blazed across three continents as fast as

its blitzkrieg could carry it. The special missive had been sent personally from Reichsführer of the SS, Heinrich Himmler, who affirmed that a natural alliance existed between Nazis and Muslims. It had been a decade since al-Husseini had welcomed Hitler's cause as his own, and he smiled as he reread the note.

Al-Husseini glanced across the table at his friend and comrade in arms, Hassan al-Banna. The younger man nodded and lit the hookah he brought with him, fearful that British agents could too easily poison one provided by the café. As the honey-infused leaf began to take effect, the imam realized that it had been nearly twenty years since he founded the Muslim Brotherhood. And while his seminal manifesto on the need for jihad brought the former schoolteacher fame before the war, al-Banna knew his fledgling organization had struggled in obscurity until Nazi support pushed its membership from a mere eight hundred in 1938, to nearly a half million since. Many warriors heeded his call to action, and enlisted with the 13th Mountain Division Handschar. Named for the curved sword their ancestors had stained red in making the Ottoman Empire one of the most powerful in history, the Muslim regiment served as the first non-German division of the Waffen-SS, the armed wing of Hitler's feared Schutzstaffel.

Between intermittent pulls on ornate waterpipes, both men kept an eye on the kitchen entryway, in anticipation of the fugitive Nazi officers who would soon join them. Though the collapse of the Third Reich had abruptly ended their shared objective, al-Husseini and al-Banna were certain that it would be their kingdom which was destined to reign for a thousand years. Only it would be able to defeat the Kafir, their non-Muslim enemies. Only their Soldiers of God would be triumphant in establishing a worldwide Caliphate.

It was simply a matter of faith, time, and blood.

PART I

CHAPTER ONE

Youssef al-Zahrani sat beneath a pavilion in Hemlock Park and bit into a sweet pastry layered with chopped nuts and honey. He watched the small crowd already gathered, and wondered if any of them were aware that so many others had once laid claim to this land.

For a thousand years it had been the indigenous peoples that lived and warred along the Detroit River. Then came *les coureurs des bois*, who trapped, traded, and settled on Ribbon farms throughout the region. The French were finally driven from the

1

territory by Britain, who owned it for all of two decades until the New World English took violent possession as Americans. Waves of Europeans followed, and transformed the fringe outpost into an empire.

And now, al-Zahrani's people, who began as a trickle one century earlier. What was the difference between John Winthrop, the powerful seventeenth-century governor of the Massachusetts Bay Colony, and he, wondered al-Zahrani? Both had come to the New World to purify the rot that threatened their communities. Each yearned to build a "city upon a hill," which would emanate as a beacon of light across the world.

Who could deny the supremacy of his God? Not these people, for it had been their Founding Father, John Adams, who praised the founder of Islam as a seeker of the truth. It was in their Supreme Court where a likeness of Mohammad stood in honor as one of history's greatest lawgivers. It was their very own George Washington who became a favored epistoler of Mohammed ben Abdallah, Sultan of Morocco, the first ruler—and country—to recognize the revolutionary yelps of freedom from the fledgling nation.

Al-Zahrani saw himself as the father of his people, the new chosen. America was as much their rock as Plymouth had belonged to the Pilgrims. And the ripple from what he was about to cast into an unholy well would spread outward with devastating effect. Soon, he was certain, the name al-Zahrani would resonate alongside Winthrop and Washington.

"*As-salamu alaykum*, my brother," came a voice over his shoulder.

"And unto you, peace," answered al-Zahrani, diverting his attention from a small grove of trees across the park. He glanced at the man. "Did you bring it?"

Aabis al-Adheen nodded as he reached into a backpack.

"And you are set on this course of action? You were warned of the consequence the last time, yet you chose to ignore it."

"I've considered the risk," al-Adheen replied, "and it is one I am willing to take."

"Then the die is cast, my friend."

"It is cast." Al-Adheen smiled, and set down a wooden chessboard on the bench between them. "Your turn to select," he said, offering two closed fists.

"In that case, I choose your right hand. May it not smite me down on this most glorious morning."

Al-Adheen showed his palm. "Black again."

The men organized the ornate, hand-carved pieces on interlocking squares, and al-Adheen opened with queen's pawn.

"What do you have in store for me today?" Al-Zahrani asked as he played king's knight.

"All good things to those who wait." Al-Adheen pushed queen's bishop pawn.

Al-Zahrani thought he recognized the opening. "The Budapest Gambit?"

Al-Adheen smiled.

The imam played his king's pawn. "And what news of our London gambit?"

Al-Adheen considered the board before taking the piece. "The pawns are in place. They await our move."

Al-Zahrani pushed his king's knight into an attacking position. "Then let us move them."

"Yes, it is time. *Al-Hamdu lillāh.*"

"Praise be to Allah, indeed," al-Zahrani seconded the thought. "And to us, my friend."

CHAPTER TWO

London, England
Four months later

It was a bitter, wet workday for anyone looking to shake the lingering effects of the weekend. The live board at the massive railway complex in North London showed all tracks running on time. Uncommon for a Monday morning. Unusual, considering the waterlogged mob that overran the scores of domestic and international platforms of King's Cross St. Pancras. The combined system, which served as the terminus of several main lines, Eurostar, and half of all Tube routes in the city, was one of the biggest and most important transportation hubs in the U.K. Despite its crowd, the sounds of the station were dampened, far different from the buzz of other places far away and warm, where travelers fled in search of seacoasts and suntans.

It had been four months since Mohammad Imran Basha was activated, and almost two years that the twenty-year old student at Leeds Beckett University had dropped out while pursuing a degree in business. Born in London to Pakistani immigrants, the youngest of four raised in a poor, but loving, household, Basha had never given much thought to the teachings of Islam, radical or otherwise. Until he was eighteen, and a fresher at university. Until he met a sympathetic neighbor who worked as a counselor to struggling young Muslims, a mentor to those who felt foreign in the land of their birth.

After several months, the man introduced Basha to Abdul al-Faraj, formerly Devon Whyte Walcott, a Jamaican-born convert and radical imam who had arrived in England by way of Saudi Arabia fifteen years earlier. Basha soon joined a mosque near Finsbury Park, where his education truly began.

You feel like an outsider because you are considered one, he was taught.

These people do not want you in their country, he learned.

Their system has no interest in helping you succeed, he heard.

Such was drilled into his core until the message came to define Basha. And, he had been convinced, there was something the new convert could do to remedy the wrongs perpetrated against him and his people.

Basha's initiation soon moved outside the mosque. He memorized chapters of the Koran, hoping one day to become a *hafiz*, and became so proficient at reciting verse and doctrine that he was sent into local parks to recruit schoolboys younger than himself.

In the winter of 2011, Basha was sent to the Lake District, a rough-hewn picturesque region in the northwest of England. Promoted as fellowship and bonding sessions for young Muslims who felt displaced, the camp was in reality a terrorist initiation school aimed at training small cells to wage a holy war throughout the Western world. The budding jihadi exceeded expectations more than any other candidate, and was isolated from the main group for more advanced instruction.

Soon after, Basha was instructed to reapply to university, and reenter society under the pretense of a well-adjusted, happy lad, coming of age and completing his studies en route to a prosperous life and fulfilling career. An example of how a first-generation British-born Muslim could integrate and succeed. And Mohammad Basha, now known as "Mo," performed the role with exception, excelling at his studies, while playing the dutiful son, brother, and devoted partner to his new fiancé. In the summer of 2012, on the eve of the Olympic games in London, he was overjoyed to announce to his family a well-rehearsed lie, that he had been awarded a one-year fellowship to study medical science at Bahria University in Islamabad.

Nine months later, Basha returned home, schooled in guerilla warfare and sabotage. Skilled in firearms and bomb-making techniques. Proficient in violent jihad.

Weaponized.

To his handlers, Basha was the perfect recruit. He was a "cleanskin," someone completely off the radar of MI5, the United Kingdom's domestic, counter-intelligence agency. And as he descended a stairwell at King's Cross Station that morning, the only other people who knew of the coming carnage were in Dearborn, Michigan, and Cambridge, England.

Basha had traveled from Leeds to London one day earlier. He carried only the backpack in which the device would be concealed, its components preassembled, and one change of clothes. The young fanatic stayed at a cheap hotel in the

East End, with his plan to board the Piccadilly Line at peak time and detonate between Russell Square and the Circus, near the dead center of the city.

He would be successful, Basha had been assured by his handler, because it had been willed. His act, Allah's sanction, would send a message worldwide. It would be heard, and heeded, and others would answer the call. His confidence had grown after conducting several dry runs over the previous two weeks, using the same hotel and train route, and carrying the same backpack. The composite bomb, which Basha had learned to build in an al-Qaeda camp in Malakand, Pakistan, was a mixture of boiled hydrogen peroxide, sulfuric and citric acid, hexamine, and pepper. Wrapped in aluminum foil, it would be triggered by a nine-volt battery.

Basha awoke at first light that February morning. He ate nothing, and prayed until it was time to leave. It was a miserable day as Basha calmly retraced his practiced path, arriving at King's Cross shortly after 9:00 a.m. The target had been chosen carefully—the Piccadilly Line was one of the busiest in the Underground system, transporting over two-hundred million people each year. The deep level Tube was also one of the longest in the network, with half its stops below ground.

Basha moved behind a partition of commuters, and stood against a wall emblazoned with the ubiquitous red circle crossed by a blue horizontal bar. The train pulled in, and passengers cycled through in one chaotic, yet synchronized, motion. He pushed his way to the middle of a crowded section, and grabbed a support pole next to an elderly man and a pretty blonde woman, who smiled at him. Basha stared at her for one long moment, but did not return the gesture. And though he didn't know why, he forced his way to the other side of the car, and stood near the exit.

The doors were still open. Basha stared blankly at the *Mind the Gap* warning at his feet.

Suddenly, his own mind focused on an alternate ending, one in which the would-be jihadi would disembark the Underground and abandon the mission. And in that instant, his commitment and resolve, hardened by others, began to waver and unspool. Basha suddenly realized he could defuse the bomb and toss the pack into the Thames. He would disappear with his fiancé, and finish his studies elsewhere, perhaps America. The young man could grow old, and his large family would grow up to become successful doctors, businesspeople, and community leaders. He envisioned a peaceful death in his bed sixty years later, surrounded by his wife, scores of grandchildren and great-grandchildren, and whispering to himself, with pride and in peace, *Mashallah.*

What Allah wishes.

His entire existence, everything that Basha had become, but could yet be, teetered for one fleeting moment on the precipice.

The doors hissed shut and the train lurched from the platform. Basha decided that he could not wait, knowing he would ride the Tube to the end of the line, before making his way meekly home. He could not let so many people down. The young man from a loving family, full of promise and with a full life ahead, pulled the pack off his shoulder, peeled back the top pocket, and as he pinched the battery snap in place, quietly muttered, "*Mashallah.*"

CHAPTER THREE

King's College, University of Cambridge
April 30, 2015

The man ignored the image cast off a small mirror of the single-room lavatory in the Caffè Nero on King's Parade, the tourist thoroughfare that housed one of the most visited landmarks in England, the chapel at King's College, Cambridge. Though he rarely dwelt on his past, for what was the point, the man mused that his origin could be traced to an almost singular moment in history. The profession of those like him, the few who existed and enjoyed life beyond forty years of age, had been born in the last decade of the eleventh century, on the eve of the first Crusade to reclaim Jerusalem. It was from a fortified citadel, high in the mountains north of modern-day Tehran, that a militant polymath named Hassan al-Sabbāh created a secret society of radical converts proficient in a form of warfare the world had never seen.

The man disregarded the rattle of the handle and frustrated rap that preceded a muffled curse from beyond the door. The unique fraternity to which he belonged had long been maligned, even from the earliest days, when its adherents were viewed by many as a witless group of *hashasheen*, the Arabic term for "trouble-making rabble." Others saw them as *hashishi*, or "hashish abusers," the disparaging label Marco Polo attached to them centuries later. In reality, Hassan's operatives were highly disciplined and well trained, versed in the language and culture of the royal households they infiltrated and served. And they remained humble servants and trusted advisors, until the moment each of them struck with sudden and absolute vengeance.

The greater the success of his *fedayin*, the "men who accept death," the larger Hassan's shadow spread over the Persian Empire. Death at anytime and from anywhere became an unmistakable signature, and ensured that sultans who opposed his radical agenda, whether targeted or not, lived in a constant state of fear. Where this elite corps had once been dismissed as outcasts by the Egyptians and labeled as junkies by the Europeans, history recognized them as something else—killers of the highest order.

The assassin refocused on the present, and a small washroom in the chain coffee shop where he would finish his painstakingly meticulous prep. Though his skill rivaled those who had waged war from the shadows for a millennium, David Laurent was a collision of worlds. His physical frame and mixed complexion, tan and chiseled, with dark brown hair and deep-set hazel eyes, could have been mistaken as the result of a long weekend on the beaches of Mallorca. But, it also allowed the professional killer with an Apulian father and mother from Skopje, who was fluent in Arabic and Farsi, as well as French, Italian, and an array of Slavic dialects, to pass through the streets of Marrakesh with the same attention paid a corner rug merchant.

At forty-four, supremely confident and still operating at his peak, the elusive assassin had become the preferred weapon of an exclusive group who knew of his existence and could afford his services. Initial contact for potential clients originated with one man, an Albanian, who routed inquiries through a near labyrinthine string of digital dead drops. As Laurent took the assignments no one else wanted, or were capable of, the few he accepted paid handsomely, half on the front end, and with no time frame guaranteed for completion. When the target turned up inexplicably dead, the job was done.

The contract on Mohammad Haamid Ahmad, distinguished professor at King's College, Cambridge, had been offered to Laurent three months earlier. His preparation, habitually exhaustive, showed the Saudi scholar to be, among many things, a man as vain as he was connected. Born into wealth and privilege, Ahmad found his place in academia, and had been at the renowned university for nearly five decades.

After two weeks of shadowing his target, Laurent was fully acquainted with Ahmad's daily routine. He knew the professor would have already pardoned himself, to the accustomed irritation of his colleagues, from their bi-weekly meeting. As Ahmad made his way back to a large, ornately decorated office, the assassin calmly cycled through his own routine. *Three precise shots, an unmistakable grouping.* He tightened a King's College tie under a liturgical gown, similar to the cotta of a church acolyte, and donned a pair of black, designer, non-prescription glasses. *Followed by a direct train to London, and a quick stopover on the Strand.* Laurent finger-combed water through his hair, slicking it back nearly flat against his head. *Two days after the murder, when Scotland Yard's investigation began its descent into a maze of dead ends, he would be in Paris.* Laurent chambered a hollow point in his Heckler & Koch 9mm, fitted with a five-inch suppressor, and re-clipped the weapon into the waistband of custom-made wool-mohair trousers. His target would be preparing tea, and settling, for the last time, into a plush recliner.

Laurent exited the lavatory and visually swept the room for anything out of place. The coffee house held its customary fare, twenty or so patrons clustered around tables. Forty eyes cemented to electronic screens. The assassin smiled to himself. With the invention of smart devices, his anonymity was nearly assured even before setting foot in King's College.

Had anyone glanced up, though none did, they would have noticed—and ignored—a college member moonlighting with the chapel choir. Laurent moved fluidly between the chorus of heads bowed in one form of social media worship or another, exited the café and crossed King's Parade, and strode confidently through the gatehouse of the college. The porter on duty touched his brow, certain he had seen the man before, at evensong, making haste to make the first hymn.

Laurent casually circled the perimeter of the college's famed center court, and skirted the crowd that had gathered for evening service. He eyed the statue of its founder, Henry VI, standing atop a fountain, the only one paying any attention to the assassin.

That evening, the professor had plans to dine at Simpson's-in-the-Strand, a London staple so famous, that it served as the haunt of not just Sir Arthur Conan Doyle, but his fictional alter ego, Sherlock Holmes. Like them, Ahmad had become accustomed to the finer things in life, particularly that which could be openly flaunted. Laurent knew that the man's ego would allow him to remain in his office for only a short time after Laurent, posing as the proxy of someone with real power, failed to show for a meeting that had been prearranged.

The assassin moved into the darkness of a passageway along the inner wall of Bodley's Court, a semi-enclosed space bound by the Cam River and the Old Provost's Lodge, and waited.

His contract stipulated that Ahmad's death was to appear official in nature, something misinterpreted as a sanction likely carried out by any number of the usual perpetrators. The demand was unusual, as the overt assassination of such a prominent, and controversial, figure, was certain to guarantee an exhaustive and very public investigation at the highest level. In the end, Laurent did not care. Whatever his employer wanted the death to look like was not his cause, nor his problem. He was paid large sums of money to rid other people of theirs, and after that evening, the well-known scholar and vocal critic of the West, who sat alone and comfortably unsuspecting behind a walnut desk with a fine lacquered finish, would no longer be anyone's problem.

By the time Ahmad's body was discovered, Scotland Yard summoned, MI6, Mossad, or the CIA suspected, and Fleet Street at full frenzy, the killer known only to a select few would be long gone, one and a half million pounds richer, and lounging beneath a hand-carved pergola on the mountain-side deck of a safe house in North Tyrol.

Unbeknownst to the assassin in the shadows—a killer *par excellence*—the time had come to clean up more than just one loose link of a Tube bombing that had killed thirty-seven people and brought London briefly to its knees. Little could Laurent have suspected that he had indeed been chosen as the means to an end, one that would include not only Mohammad Ahmad, but his own.

CHAPTER FOUR

King's College, University of Cambridge
April 30, 2015

The freshman waved his wallet at the man standing beneath the stone gatehouse of King's College. The porter matched the student's detached participation in the daily ritual with a half-nod, but the boy had ignored him and barely checked his pace into the inner courtyard.

Neither had the doorman managed more than a passing glance at the second fellow, whom he assumed was a companion of the undergraduate. The lateness of the hour and dreary nature of the evening dismissed any notion to call him back and properly check his I.D. Hadn't the chap, a post-grad by his appearance, also brandished a blue university card? The porter wasn't certain, but he could let it go this time. Soon it would be high season, with tourists let loose on the city like the plague. His would be a keener eye then, with every visitor properly logged, provided they had cause to be at the college at this hour. If not, *thank you very much, and kindly be on your way.*

Sean Garrett shadowed the student long enough to stay any belated suspicion the staffer might have of the man who had just flashed him an expired Natwest banking card. As the pair reached the doors of the college pub, the same moment the student became vaguely aware of his surroundings, Garrett stepped around him and continued toward The Backs.

Evensong began to ring across the Front Court. Garrett frowned. His timing should have been better, but the train that brought him from London had twice been delayed. The familiar call to choral service would only encourage more people, *more potential witnesses*, into the college grounds.

Garrett was certain the undergrad had taken no notice of him, for he had not looked up once from his phone. As the student stumbled along the stone path, it was inconceivable to the *Cambridge Man* that it would be the famed institution which would ultimately give him a name, with no favor returned. The university's celebrated reputation would be left to the likes of Darwin, Newton, and Hawking. The boy's contribution would be little more than twenty-seven thousand pound sterling, and a running tab at The Eagle.

CCTV could prove problematic, considering there was one surveillance camera for every eleven people in the U.K., recording the image of the average Brit over three hundred times each day. But Garrett's long hair and beard, which would allow him to blend with the student population, would soon be trimmed and shaved, and provide an additional layer of protection during his exfil from England. Nevertheless, he wondered if there was anything about his appearance that might invite unwanted attention, and be recalled later. Like Raskolnikov's hat, he thought.

Garrett's arrival in England two days earlier had been carefully planned. He had disembarked a ferry from Calais under credentials that had since been discarded for his new cover, a travel writer from Canada. His hair had been washed back to its original color, and the green contact lenses he had worn since Geneva were tossed as soon as Garrett cleared passport control at the port of Dover. An overstuffed suitcase, which he had rolled around like some clueless tourist for the last twenty hours, now sat at the bottom of the English Channel.

He crossed the Cam River. There were few people out, to his surprise, and Garrett remained on the path near the Fellows' Garden long enough to gauge he was alone, before disappearing between two hedgerows. As he opened his backpack, Garrett began to run down a mental checklist, something that once would have been second nature, but which now required added concentration. He traded the oversized down coat he had worn into the college for a fitted black jacket and academic gown, which would allow him to mix with the more traditionally-minded students heading to the Hall for dinner.

Garrett shrugged off a gust of wind as he changed into dress shoes and knotted a King's College tie. It mattered little that it was late spring, for this was England, which at any moment could feel like February, so the old yarn went. This worked in his favor, because wearing gloves would not be considered unusual to anyone with the ensuing murder investigation who poured over the digital recordings of King's College cameras between 6:30 and 7:30 p.m. His transformation complete, Garrett removed a black backpack from the bottom of the blue duffle, and stuffed everything into it.

Control, he had to remind himself, was the key. Command your environment, and you could control the outcome. Slow down and limit the errors that incaution was certain to produce. Garrett switched his breathing to a four-box count, and focused. He wiped the nervous sweat that he recognized should not have so easily beaded on his collar, and mentally traced his steps, from the garden, back across the bridge and to the outer door of the Old Provost's Lodge. From there, inside the building and down a hall to an office near the last stairwell.

Garrett pulled out a Beretta 84 and chambered a round, complementing another twelve in the magazine. He screwed a suppressor in place and flipped on the safety, before pushing the pistol into his pocket.

You are not to kill him, he had been instructed. You are only to gather information and get out of Europe.

Garrett checked his watch. His timing was not coincidental, as security cameras would be less reliable when switching to evening mode, which would be automatic and anytime now. He also knew that the sensors of the specific model the college had installed were typically programmed to work without infrared at dusk to reduce glare, making them less sharp than in full daylight, or complete darkness.

Moreover, King's had been slow to modernize. Lights scattered across the college would detract from its ambience, or so the old guard had long argued. Keynes, Turing, and Walpole hadn't needed their evening strolls illuminated, and neither should lesser men who walked the storied grounds. King's had lost that battle after a string of simple assaults forced the hand of other colleges at Cambridge equally resistant to change. The newly installed chain of yellow-tinted lamps, which had not yet been turned on for the evening, gave off an aura of cheapness, Garrett thought.

He exited the Fellows' Garden, and fell into an easy walk along the graveled path that led back to the main grounds. The crosscut lawn was still fairly free of people as Garrett crossed the river, where an army of summer tourists would soon punt down the Cam, sip crème teas, and snap the exact same postcard photo of the backside of the famed sanctuary.

Three undergrads loitered on the bridge, but paid him no notice as he passed over. Two other groups, a combination of students and staff, moved in from random directions toward the Front Court. One of them looked his way, and let her gaze linger long enough to confirm Garrett's rugged handsomeness. He did not return her smile, but instead looked away, not wanting to encourage a second, more established, glance. Chapel would soon let out, and with it, whatever crowd that had gathered for the service.

Garrett knew that his target, Mohammad Haamid Ahmad, would have already returned to his office from a Fellow's meeting. The dossier listed the man as Saudi, though most assumed him to be Yemeni, as he had been raised in Sana'a. Born into privilege, Ahmad had moved from boarding schools in Switzerland to a BSc at the London School of Economics, and then to Merton College, Oxford, where he took two graduate degrees, in religion and logic. Ahmad touted himself, and was perceived by many, as a moderate, though Garrett knew otherwise. The professor had been at Cambridge for forty-nine years, a fellow of King's College for twenty of them.

It was moot whether Ahmad disclosed what he knew about the bombing of King's Cross Station fourteen months earlier, which had taken the life of Garrett's grandfather, and put his sister in a coma. He had already resolved to disobey his directive. Tonight, Garrett decided, would be Ahmad's last as a Fellow. His last as an esteemed academic and frequent BBC talking head. His last night of being anything.

Garrett planned to make the death look violent and personal, the work of the jilted or aggrieved.

The professor would remain undisturbed long enough for Garrett to travel from Cambridge to London, and then to Paris via the Eurostar. When the bullet-riddled body was discovered, he would have already disembarked a Delta connector at Nashville International, the second leg of an Air France transatlantic flight out of Charles de Gaulle. By the time Scotland Yard got the call, Garrett would be in the back of a Greyhound bus bound for Gatlinburg, Tennessee, via Knoxville. From there, a two-day hike into western North Carolina through a series of trails that split Thunderhead Mountain and Clingmans Dome.

Fourteen months of personal tribulation and an unpunished act of terror would be resolved that evening. As King's College was cordoned off, and the Metropolitan Police set to waste their time interviewing a queue of disgruntled colleagues and ex-lovers, Mohammad Ahmad would have met the death he deserved, and Sean Garrett would be home.

CHAPTER FIVE

Mohammad Ahmad donned a gray herring-bone blazer and settled into a Herman Miller chair, impatiently awaiting the arrival of his appointment. The widely feted octogenarian was not allowed to smoke in his office, but he had long ignored the rule, and lit up at his leisure. He cared little for the repeat complaints from students and colleagues. Neither did the college as far as he was concerned, for although Ahmad was given repeated warnings to at least curtail the habit, he refused, and nothing was ever formally pursued. That summer marked his fiftieth at King's. He was untouchable.

The professor cracked an office window and took notice of the time. It was nearly 7:00 p.m., and a representative of Saudi Prince Al-Ahmed bin Halabi, who was to personally deliver information regarding their meeting that summer in Dubai, was late by nearly fifteen minutes. Ahmad's rank as a world-renowned Cantabrigian, coupled with his family's longstanding influence in Yemen, positioned him well to represent the interests of the prince in England. And while the professor acknowledged the need to constantly subordinate himself to bin Halabi, he also recognized that his own power and reach warranted some measure of deference and respect. As such, Ahmad was certain that the reception he expected that July at the *Hotel Burj al Arab*, the world's only seven-star accommodation, would be well deserved.

Irritated, Ahmad glanced again at the ornate clock on the wall. This man, no matter who he represented, should have been instructed not to take advantage of the professor's time. He decided he would wait no longer, and packed up his chestnut-colored leather *Ettinger* satchel. As he rang his housemaid and reminded her that he would be dining that evening in London, Ahmad heard a rap on his office door.

CHAPTER SIX

Garrett advanced beneath the stone trestle outside the Old Provost's Lodge to the outer entry at the west end of the building. His return train to London, which he could not miss, was scheduled to depart in forty-five minutes. It was a tight window to elicit the information he needed, and whether he got it or not, Garrett would execute Ahmad with extreme prejudice.

He depressed the latch, but found the door locked. Garrett quickly thumbed open a Spyderco knife, and was set to slip the blade between the latch and jamb plate, when he noticed that a corner of the door had caught on the frame and not properly closed. He gave a firm push and entered the main hallway, which was dark. Garrett wondered if his intel was bad, and whether the professor had already left for the evening. It was then that he saw light filtering through the opaque window of a door at the end of the hall. He conducted a peripheral sweep of each side room and open space as he moved methodically toward Ahmad's office. Everything was quiet and empty, as expected, and Garrett slowed his breathing as he came square with the office door.

Suddenly, time slowed with a shattering sound. Garrett felt something glance off his chest as splintered glass covered his clothing. A sharp pain ripped across his neck, and a jagged fissure opened where the windowpane had been. Through the gaping hole he saw the professor, staring out with wide, wild eyes. Standing in front of Ahmad was another man, himself frozen in one fleeting moment of surprise. He held a large caliber weapon, and possessed a piercing look that Garrett could see had already begun to rapidly process every detail of the unfolding situation, organizing what was important, and committing it to memory.

Garrett refocused into real-time, and reacted on instinct. He registered a flash of movement as he spun from the doorway and turned a corner near the lavatory. He pushed through a door that opened to the rear of the building, and before it hissed shut behind him, heard three muffled, snapping sounds. The unmistakable report of a silencer. Garrett turned and looked back once, seeing no one, as he moved quickly away from the building and toward the back gate of King's College.

CHAPTER SEVEN

Secret Intelligence Service
Vauxhall Cross, London

The horizon over the River Thames continued to darken. The black veneer, forecasting a familiar mix of rain and gloom, also brought into focus a chalky residue that had settled between glass panes of one corner office on the eighth floor of MI6, Britain's Secret Intelligence Service. But before Banastre Montjoy could grouse about the waterlogged façade of West London, he could hear his grandmother admonish him. *The weather has nothing to do with it, my dear.* Perhaps not, he acknowledged, but it always seemed dreary of late in the city, and his view had become habitually dirty. His primary source of distraction the last few months, a hairline crack that slowly angled downward, reminded him of a negative earnings report from a FTSE exchange ticker. Stained, chipped, and in steady decline. Montjoy lifted his whiskey in toast. He and his window had much in common.

He would sometimes imagine the damage as the result of a bullet meant for him, fired from some secluded perch across the river, at Milbank. One of many failed efforts to eliminate the architect of the once highly valued *Dalmatia* program, an initiative that had propelled Montjoy to the corner office with the cracked view. But, there had been no assassination attempts, and little notoriety outside the confines of the Foreign Office of SIS Headquarters. In the end, showing premature flecks of gray and putting on enough weight to feel it, the head of Near East operations was tired. Tired of his office. Tired of the Service. After three decades and at fifty-four years old, just tired.

"You look tired, Monty," Gavin Abbot announced as he entered, addressing his boss by his nickname. The moniker was a foregone conclusion, considering that Montjoy's Christian name was Montgomery. And although his full appellation

made him sound like some scheming, bit character from a low-budget BBC miniseries, he had also
answered to Monty since childhood.

"You really should have those cracks mended,"
Abbot added.

Montjoy smiled, less in that the comment
could have applied to him personally, but because he liked Abbot's sense of order and his
"everything in its place" attitude. *The Service can't
properly function without either*, Abbot would argue every time he submitted paperwork to have
something fixed or improved around headquarters. And each time, the request would end up in
the *we've got more important things to tend to* stack,
somewhere up the chain.

Abbot reminded Montjoy of himself thirty
years earlier. Perceptive, clever, and most importantly, with a firm grasp of the bigger picture, the
young man had come to MI6 by way of his impressive tenure at GCHQ. A mathematical prodigy cut
from the Oxbridge mold, Abbot had worked for
the better part of four years at "The Doughnut,"
the moniker given to MI5's circular building in
Cheltenham that housed cryptography and signals intelligence. Prior, and after taking first-
class honors in mathematics at Cambridge, and
an MPhil with distinction at Oxford, Abbot
had landed at MIT, in Boston, on a Kennedy

Memorial Scholarship, where he completed his PhD in applied mathematics in only four years. From Cambridge to Cambridge to 85 Vauxhall Cross by age twenty-nine. Not bad for a lad from Birkenhead, Montjoy acknowledged.

"You know," Abbot offered, "I've never inquired as to whether it was inappropriate not to address you as 'Mr. Montjoy,' or 'sir.' I assumed you preferred your nickname because almost everyone calls you by it, even the junior staff." Before Montjoy could respond, Abbot added, "after all, your namesake is that of one of our most famous military leaders. Perhaps you would secretly enjoy the daily affirmation?" He was referring to Banastre Tarleton, one of Britain's excess of generals during the American Revolution, and after whom Montjoy was in fact named.

Montjoy smiled. He appreciated Abbot's penchant for historical comparison. "He lost, by the way."

"The War of Independence should have been a walkover. The brothers gave it away," Abbot replied, alluding to William and Richard Howe. "Tarleton was a genius."

Montjoy smiled again. No doubt Abbot's own rebellious persona prompted his referencing the war by its American moniker. "A 'genius'" Montjoy countered, "whose behavior encouraged nearly the entire backcountry to turn out against him by the end of the war."

Abbot waved him off. "There's no proof, other than the bleats of the losing side, that the Yanks had either surrendered, or that Tarleton ordered any massacre." He referred to the untidy slaughter of the defeated American contingent at the Battle of Waxhaws in 1780.

Montjoy moved in for the kill. "Nevertheless, and let this be a lesson, my boy. Even the slightest misstep in the war of perception can prove disastrous, no matter how competent your leadership, or battle plan."

Abbot paused to counter, but only shook his head and changed the subject. "Who gave you the nickname, by the way? Someone at headquarters?"

"My grandfather."

"The famous one?"

"None other."

Abbot remained quiet, hoping Montjoy might offer up more than he typically did about Sir Nigel Aldrich.

Montjoy did not, and instead took his own turn to change the subject. "Are you still dating that nice girl from Chelsea?"

"Oh yes," Abbot replied, "I've been dating her brains out for several months now."

Montjoy chuckled. In that regard, youth was definitely not wasted on the young.

"You know, you should get out and have some fun. Get a girlfriend—or what not." Abbot had added "or what not" because Montjoy had never married, and around the office, this fed the usual conjecture.

"I have one," Montjoy responded. "She's 18 years old, single, and gorgeous."

"Really, sir?" It was the first time Abbot had ever referred to him as "sir," and it made Montjoy feel surprisingly optimistic. "Always the last to know," Abbot shook his head. "Come on then, out with a name."

"Glenlivet." Montjoy held up a tumbler of expensive scotch. "Cheers, I say."

"Very good, Monty." Abbot laughed out loud, reverting back to his nickname, much to Montjoy's chagrin. Ordinarily, he would have followed with a subtle reproach to his boss' whiskey at ten in the morning, but did not that day.

A harsh knock reverberated around the office, and Montjoy frowned, having long since developed a keen distaste for boisterous interruptions. Before he could address the intrusion, the head of MI6 pushed through the door. Abbot quickly turned toward Sir Alex Moore.

"Sir," Abbot deferred, stepping back and nodding to the director.

Montjoy was slower to rise, but stood nonetheless. "Good morning, sir," he said cheerfully enough, though Montjoy could not recall a single time during his tenure at SIS that its chief had personally visited his office.

Moore neglected to return either salutation, as he glanced sideways at Abbot. "A word, Montjoy."

Abbot recognized his cue. "Yes, sir. Good day, sir," he said, and quickly disappeared from the office.

Moore watched him leave. "What's his name again?"

"Abbot, on loan from SIGNIT."

"Very good. Abbot. SIGNIT," Moore replied, momentarily detached from the aura that had long followed him around the halls of MI6. At eighty-eight, he was still sharp, but older than other heads of service had dared remain at post. Which meant that Moore was now swimming with the piranhas, and had put himself in danger of being chewed up and spit out before he chose to step down voluntarily. Like a washed-up Premier League gaffer, waiting on one last cup title for which he could take credit and retire gracefully. Moore was old guard, whose past exploits should have afforded him ample protection, if not for the generation of jumped-up, politically correct straw men that flooded their ranks. And make no mistake, Montjoy well knew, it would be them who would eventually make his boss redundant.

But Montjoy liked and admired Moore. He was the last bastion in the truest sense, one of the remaining few who had waged war against the Nazis, and after them, the Russians. Unlike the new lot, who puttered away in front of laptops only to play pretend agent to impress the two-drink tarts after hours, Moore hailed from a time when the game was played for keeps. He was cut directly from the mold of a quintessential English gentleman. The man was rumored never to have taken a drink, something Montjoy could not appreciate, but toasted nonetheless. They did share one Victorian trait. Like his chief, Montjoy never swore, and controlled his emotions to the point they were suppressed to the extreme.

Moore brought Montjoy's rumination to a full stop. "Sometime late last night, or early this morning, *Shepherd* was assassinated in his office at Cambridge."

Montjoy stared blankly at Moore for one long moment before muttering, "Fuck."

"An adequate assessment," Moore replied.

CHAPTER EIGHT

Central Intelligence Agency
Langley, Virginia

R obert Riley hugged a wall as he overtook a small group of staff clustered together and drinking coffee, a last-ditch delay tactic before the day kicked into high gear. The head of Europe Division for the Directorate of Operations, the clandestine arm of the CIA, kept his head down and walked quickly. The dispatch he carried, the reason Riley failed to recognize and return two salutations from colleagues, had been confirmed by a phone call to London ten minutes earlier.

It had been a week of setbacks, though the majority of them were minor and involved lower-level assets of dubious loyalty from the outset. Such was the nature, and risk, of the business. But *Charlemagne* was a different matter altogether.

Riley paused at the office door of his boss, William Scott, Deputy Director of Operations of the DO, and took a deep breath. He knocked once, and entered.

"Good morning, Robert," Scott said without glancing up from the file he was reading. "I'm in a stellar mood, mind you, so nothing you say or do will change it."

Riley said nothing, and only held up the communiqué at eye level.

Scott shook his head. "Still smiling, still happy, so you'll have to do better than that."

"Hence the reason Shakespeare performed his tragedies in the afternoon, after the comedies." Riley then announced flatly, "*Charlie* is dead."

Scott did not reply, though Riley watched whatever plans his boss had made for the weekend dissipate in one quick moment. Scott closed his eyes and rubbed his temple. "When? How?"

"Last night, give or take. Shot dead, apparently not by his own hand, in his office at King's College."

Scott suddenly slammed his hand down on the desk. The sound seemed to reverberate even after he stood and walked to the window, which over-looked the Potomac River. His secretary peeked around the door at the commotion, but he waved her off. Both men continued to quietly process the myriad problems they now faced, until Scott finally muttered, "Fuck."

"That pretty much sums it up."

"Where are *we* on this?"

"We have exactly *fuck all.* I've spoken to my counterpart in London, and as of twenty minutes ago, they don't seem to be faring any better."

"So they say," Scott replied. "Rees is Lindsay's lap dog. You know that sawed-off runt won't divulge anything unless you squeeze him. Get back on the phone and find out what he knows."

"I did, and he wouldn't budge. Something's not right."

"You're damn right something's not right. Our most important asset in Europe, and the Near East, for that matter, is murdered a month before we're set to launch *Operation Saltbush.* No chance that is a coincidence." Scott turned back to Riley. "Forget Rees. Get me Moore."

"He'll put you off as well."

"Better by him than some little pissant head of section." Scott gestured an apology of sorts. "Present company excluded."

"I could get on a plane. Bypass the lot altogether and talk to Montjoy."

"Montjoy—" Scott muttered. "He might be half-battered half the time, but he keeps his cards close to the vest, especially since he was unceremoniously yanked as Ahmad's handler."

"And our asset in-country?" Riley referred to John Campion, a former CIA operative he had worked closely with for two decades.

Scott shook his head. "Keep him on the fringe until we decide *if and when*. But I do want you on the next flight to Heathrow."

"Yes, sir."

"And Robert," Scott said as Riley turned to leave. "Find out what the hell happened."

CHAPTER NINE

Woodberry Down Estate
London

It was 3:00 a.m., the witching hour for cities that forced its pub-crawlers onto the streets before they were done drinking. Sean Garrett ascended a side stairwell in Woodberry Down Estate, a massive tenement structure in North London. Built eighty years earlier and billed as the estate of the future, the purpose of the project had been to clear out the city's hovel housing in order to centralize respectable, law-abiding renters. By the 1980s, all that had been managed was to turn single-row slums into a massive soviet-style ghetto, quartering thousands of low-income tenants.

Known as Seven Blocks by its residents, which only reinforced the impression of a prison ground, the tenement had provided Garrett cover since his last meal, the evening prior. He had sheltered long enough in one location, and needed to alternate his position before deciding on a next course of action. In more ways than one, Garrett found himself in no man's land. Considering the danger that a rough district like Manor House could present at any moment, he was also potentially chum in the water.

Garrett's phone began to vibrate, and he stepped further back into the stairwell as he answered it.

"What in the hell went wrong?" The voice on the other end of the line, which Garrett did not recognize, remained even-tempered, but still betrayed a measure of irritation. "And why didn't you make contact at the prearranged time?"

Both men were acutely aware that their conversation was bouncing across England. "Where is *Game warden*?" Garrett asked. The din of the street sounded above him.

"Where are you?" the man demanded, over-hearing the background noise. "Secure?"

"A payphone outside of Scotland Yard," Garrett responded sarcastically. "I'm on a disposable in the bowel of some council estate in Hackney."

"Then we won't need to worry about arranging your departure. You won't last the night there."

Garrett ignored the comment, determined to keep the exchange short. "The client's gone away on vacation."

"We damn well know that. You were instructed to assist with tourist information only—"

"I didn't book his trip," Garrett cut him off. "There was another travel agent."

The line remained silent for several seconds. "Then you need to arrange a get-away as well."

"No shit, and sharpish."

"Go to the rental," the man said, which referred to a designated location in Scotland. "A broker will make contact at the usual time."

"How long?"

"Within the next three weeks." *Three days, at 3:00 p.m.*

The line went dead before Garrett could respond, and it dawned on him that he was three thousand miles from home, or help.

He exited the sunken stairwell and moved quickly toward Manor House Tube Station. As he walked, he adhered to the laws of the street, head down, eyes up, and mouth shut. Garrett did not bear the look of a mark, those people who wandered through life as if they wore a flashing *please fuck with me* sign. But neither did he carry the physical demeanor of someone who would be guaranteed a wide berth. At just over six feet tall and with a fit frame that disguised his two hundred pounds, Garrett could travel with confidence, but not immunity, through a place like Seven Sisters.

As if on cue, he rounded a corner and encountered three yobs, English slang for violent, young hooligans. They encircled a trash bin, and were drinking something cheap and potent. As soon as Garrett appeared, they suspended their mindless banter and measured his approach. He knew that while the streets could be unpredictable, they were not without laws. There was a pecking order, like the jungle, and those just fledged tended to act with either the confidence, or caution, of youth.

The boys watched Garrett, unsure of his tier in the hierarchy. He checked his pace and eyed the group with a demeanor that could be interpreted as pissed off, crazy, or both. All three felons-in-waiting looked away, signaling they would be no trouble.

If it had not been a weekend, the borough would have been quieter. Moreover, the morning crowd would have soon been out, and the area overwhelmed with commuters walking, biking, and driving to work, or packed nuts to butts on public transportation. If there was a weakness of video surveillance, it was strength in numbers.

Garrett could have mixed with rush hour, which would have guaranteed him ample cover to disguise his size, shape, gait, and other markers that CCTV technology used to match specific individuals to time and place. Without the weekday crowd, Garrett would have to rely on the fact that because he was in a rough neighborhood, any number of cameras might be ripped down, or smashed and not yet repaired.

His immediate concern was a confrontation with some legless drunks, or, locals not so much seeking trouble, but certainly not looking to avoid it either. No sooner had Garrett cleared the estate and neared the Tube station, that he came opposite of two men who would not be backed down with airs. They fronted him as he attempted to move to one side, signaling that Garrett would not be fortunate enough to make it out of the area unchallenged.

Both men were cut from the sad typecast that littered London's poorer urban districts. They appeared to be in their mid-twenties, and one had close-cropped hair, while the other sported a shaved head with his hood pulled halfway back. Each had equally rough skin, and were decorated with the typical combination of tattoos and piercings. Both wore a dead look, and walked with a wide-kneed gait comically exaggerated by skinny jeans that were pulled too low on their hips. The taller of the two, slightly larger than Garrett, flashed a set of gold crowns, which rounded out the absurd stereotype.

"Wotcher, me old china?" asked the shorter of the two men. He used cockney rhyming slang, with *wotcher,* a contraction of *what are you up to,* and *china,* short for *china plate,* meaning *mate.* The working-class East End dialect, known for its glottal stop, double-negations, and elongated vowels, was difficult to understand under the best of conditions.

"A Billy Bragg with your skin n' blister?" chimed his partner, meaning *shag* and *sister.*

"Bollocks." *Nonsense.* "This one's a Perry," his buddy countered, as in *Perry Como, homo.*

"You've got the wrong guy," Garrett replied.

Hearing his American accent, the taller man jabbed a finger in Garrett's direction, sloshing his beer in the process. "He's not a Perry. He's a bloody septic." *Septic tank. Yank.*

Garrett had yet to break the gaze of the bigger fellow, the alpha of their little gang. "No," Garrett responded, his words now measured and deliberate, "I mean, you're fucking with the wrong guy." He was left with a singular option, one that had been predetermined the moment these two marked him. It was now simply a matter of when, and as Garrett had forced the moment, the inevitable was upon each of them. If he allowed the fight to come to him, his chances to quickly fend off the assault would be considerably decreased. His father had taught him the only way to respond in this situation was to hit first, and hard.

"Is that fucking so, Billy," as in *Billy no-mates,* meaning *friendless,* the smaller of the two men responded, as he flipped out a serrated blade.

"Out for a bit of Barney?" *Barney Rubble. Trouble.* His buddy smiled, his gold teeth more visible. "You've sure enough fucking found it." Both men then stepped toward Garrett.

Their first tactical mistake.

"I assume you are with those guys?" Garrett asked. He nodded to his right and at no one in particular, and said it in such a casual manner, that both men, accustomed to a certain progression of behavior at this point, stopped their advance in momentary confusion. The smaller of the two stupidly took the bait, and glanced in the direction Garrett had gestured. It was a natural response, similar to the mimicked reaction of catching someone at a half-yawn, or checking their watch.

Second mistake.

The other one did not look, but it didn't matter. Before his partner could correct his lapse of attention, Garrett launched himself. He did not use the typical head-butt, an action that lacked power. Instead, he fired his entire body into the man like a battering ram, through the bridge of his pierced nose. The impact cracked the man's neck back with such force that Garrett could hear his C vertebrae crunching against one another.

His friend reacted like most people caught unaware by such speed and violent action—he didn't. Instead, he stared dumbfounded for one long moment, the entire scene playing out before him in slow motion. By the time he recovered his presence of mind, Garrett had regained his balance enough to jab his left hand, fingers spread open, into the man's face. It was a maneuver meant only to disable, not debilitate. The man's response was involuntary, as he lurched off-balance and brought his hands up to protect the eyes. His midriff opened, allowing Garrett to step forward and slam his right fist into the sternum. The sheer force of the blow caused the man to drop the knife and recoil forward, his arms now unconsciously crossing to protect his midsection, as his diaphragm spasmed and his breath was knocked out.

Garrett snapped an elbow to the bridge of his attacker's nose, once more whipping the head backward. As the man brought his hands back to his face, Garrett thrust his heel through the man's knee, hyperextending the patella and tearing cartilage. His leg collapsed backward as the man howled in pain. He crumpled to the ground, simultaneously attempting to hold his face, stomach, and knee, next to his buddy, who was knocked cold and hemorrhaging from the nose and mouth.

"You fucking bastard," the man growled.

Garrett quickly scanned the area. No doubt these two idiots had mates somewhere in the estate. The courtyard between the rows of buildings remained quiet. He stood over the man, who was now rocking back and forth in the fetal position and quietly cursing to himself in a whining cadence. "You're all mouth and no trousers, mate." *All talk and no walk.* Garrett didn't wait for a reply as he stepped around the counterfeit street fighters and began to move toward the Tube station.

CHAPTER TEN

Savoy Hotel
London

David Laurent had not moved from the plush, Edwardian-style chair for the better part of an hour. He sat near a window and with the lights out in a suite at the Savoy. The assassin had lodged at the five-star hotel on the Strand only one other time, a decade earlier, and was aware that his repeat patronage flirted with a cardinal rule of a profession that seldom tolerated even the smallest miscalculation. But, as the Savoy had closed once for renovation since his original stay, Laurent reasoned that he was not officially in breach of the unwritten code.

He focused on the London Eye, the massive, carnival-like Ferris wheel located on the south bank of the Thames. With each gradual, thirty-minute rotation, backlit against a black sky, his own imagination turned as to what his next move should be.

Laurent knew that while the elimination of Ahmad was technically a success, the presence of a witness made the assignment a failure. In his line of work, a kill was either clean, or it was not. There was no middle ground, and no amount of excuse-making could change that. Nevertheless, the assassin was accustomed to perfection, and the more he replayed the events of Thursday evening, the easier it became to blame what had happened on bad luck.

Foremost, the behavior of the professor had been completely unexpected. The eighty-six-year-old had somehow managed the agility to remove and fling his shoe in one surprisingly quick motion. In much of the Arab world, this action is viewed as the highest form of insult. In Ahmad's case, Laurent knew it was nothing more than one last, desperate act of self-defense. The assassin had deftly sidestepped the makeshift weapon as it flew past.

The reaction was purely instinctive, but it wreaked the havoc that followed. The projectile had somehow smashed the window of the office door behind him, which exposed a stupefied, younger man. The witness, a witless graduate student by his bedraggled appearance, bolted before Laurent could shoot him. Left with only a moment before Ahmad could bring more attention to himself, Laurent executed him as instructed, two shots to the chest and one to his forehead.

Though the entire episode played out in less than five seconds, what was left in its wake was a litany of unpredictable complications. Laurent's only recourse at that moment, sitting alone by himself in the dark, was to second-guess every decision he had made over the course of the assignment. It was a completely pointless endeavor, but he did so anyway, if only to make himself feel better.

What happened was his fault, ultimately, though he was loathe to admit it. Laurent had broken a cardinal rule of his own, and had stupidly allowed someone else to partially dictate his course of action. He had been tasked with several, pre-agreed upon directives from his handler. Specifically, that the professor be executed in his office at Cambridge in a manner consistent with a professional assassination. Originally, there had been no time frame attached to the assignment, as Laurent would have never agreed to one. Until he received word that his employer was willing to pay an additional five hundred thousand pounds if Ahmad was killed on April 30.

And now the assassin cursed himself, not for the first time in the last twenty-four hours. He knew better. A long and successful career had taught him better. Allowing someone else even the smallest amount of say had the potential to create one problem that could spin out of control and into many. It was at that moment that Laurent recognized he had become too comfortable over a career of mistake-free assignments. What followed was a form of mild contempt that allowed greed to get the momentary better of him.

He laughed to himself, despite the situation, and recalled how surprisingly easy it had been to justify the lucrative stipulation. The day in question, April 30, was a Thursday. That particular day of the week happened to suit Laurent, for the assassin knew the professor had long demanded his Fridays and Mondays be free of any teaching and collegial obligations. The body should have remained undiscovered until at least the following Tuesday, the earliest time someone might have had reason to come looking for Ahmad.

Now, the gaping hole in the office door guaranteed the dead man had already drawn attention. Laurent should have had four days to leave England. He was now on the clock, as local police and domestic security were certainly in the process of choking out potential escape points one at a time.

On top of that, there had been a witness, for the first time in his career. Simply put, the man should not have been there. Laurent had ensured that the building was empty. He had turned off the lights and locked two entrance doors. But the irrefutable fact remained that a witness was *there*, standing outside Mohammad Ahmad's door at 7:05 p.m. on Thursday, April 30, and staring at Laurent through a bloody broken window. Someone had seen the assassin's face. That Laurent even existed was no longer only a suspicion.

What rotten luck, Laurent again lamented, as he reminisced over countless operations where he had left behind nothing but a dead body, a dead-end trail, and the best investigators in the world completely dumbfounded. He had been an apparition for twenty-five years, and then Mohammad Ahmad decided to throw one of his custom-made George Cleverly loafers.

Laurent's mobile began to ring.

He stared blankly at the flashing phone, though he expected the call, before finally swiping the green icon.

"Hamley's, how can I help?" Laurent offered the first half of a prearranged code by referencing

one of London's oldest and most famous toymak-
ers. He expected, *"Do you sell blue remote control
boats?"* the second half of the code.

"At least you can answer a mobile without
mucking it up," the voice on the other responded
sarcastically, having foregone the required predi-
cate response.

Laurent immediately recognized the voice as
from the man who had offered him the contract
on Ahmad three months earlier. He considered
hanging up, reasoning that, since the code went
uncompleted, it was necessary to protect everyone involved. But, Laurent was well aware that he
was still owed one million pounds. "The deal was
closed, as instructed," he responded flatly, keeping
to the protocol of ambiguity.

"Closed, apparently, with as much attention as
was bloody possible."

Laurent worried that his contact was skating
close to language that would flag their conversation for closer scrutiny by whichever spy service
might be eavesdropping on the call, which was all
of them. He measured his reply, considering how
to best inform the man that there had been a witness, who remained at large and very much a part
of the problem. It suddenly dawned on Laurent
that he'd cocked this up, but good.

"There was another party involved, with whom I will be in future talks to make part of the merger," the assassin coolly replied.

His contact remained silent for several seconds. "We need to meet in person, immediately, to discuss this negotiation. Are you still at the company?" *In the U.K.?*

"Yes, at headquarters." *In London.*

"Tomorrow. *Two days.* 4 p.m. Same place, at the water," the man said, which referred to a specific bench near the Round Pond in Kensington Gardens. It had been the location where Laurent had received the dossier on Ahmad. "I will meet you there, and advise about the acquisition."

"Understood." Laurent hung up, with no intention of making the meet. He wiped down the disposable, removed and snapped the SIM card in two, and broke the phone in several pieces. His train, a Eurostar bound for Paris, departed in eighteen hours.

CHAPTER ELEVEN

King's College, Cambridge

Roger Holland rocked back in the stylish chair and surveyed the crime scene once again, certain he had overlooked evidence that would have jumped out at him only a few years earlier. At fifty-five, with his birthday literally falling on the day he had received the call about a murder at King's College, the chief inspector from Scotland Yard knew it was there. There was always something. He just needed to find it. Then again, with his move to superintendent less than a month away, perhaps he did not particularly want to see the obvious. Better to coast into the promotion than risk a delay by being clever and opening Pandora's box on one last high-profile case.

But a renowned, widely-feted professor lay dead at his feet, and the Cambridgeshire Constabulary had "called in the Yard." And so, the famous detective whose reputation had long been staked on figuring out what others routinely could not, refocused his attention.

"Figure it out yet?" chimed the voice, always cheery and optimistic, from the entryway.

"Yes." Holland swiveled in the direction of Samantha Anderton and took the tea she offered. "Specifically, sergeant, that the cost of this chair would probably finance at least one month of my mortgage."

"Then count yourself lucky, because what you and Helen have been paying over the last twenty years wouldn't cover a closet in Clapham now."

"How London has changed," Holland muttered to himself. "To answer your question, outside of bugger all, we have one very dead Mohammad Ahmad, scholar of antiquities, who will now be able to more fully appreciate his field."

"Actually, I think he was a professor of logic."

"Then my joke wouldn't have worked," Holland smiled. "What have *you* got?"

"Between not much and nothing, I'm afraid." Anderton walked back to the pile of broken glass and the lone, slip-on loafer lying in the hallway.

"Someone from the cleaning service found him first thing Friday morning. Other than that, no witnesses, and all of three grainy seconds on CCTV of someone leaving the building, which might as well have been filmed with a Betacam, considering the quality."

"A beta-what?"

"I expected you'd know what that was, sir, considering your age. Happy birthday, by the way."

"There's the cheek," Holland smiled again. "I shouldn't think any witnesses will turn up, considering the professional nature of the professor's death."

"Which begs the question, has any one from the Security Service graced us yet?"

"Not that I'm aware, though as sure as it will rain this week, they'll turn up. But until MI5 do get involved, my piece of plastic," Holland held up his I.D. badge, "puts me in charge of having absolutely no idea what happened."

"Speaking of—" Anderton bent down over the shattered pane. "I should have thought you'd be sitting in some fancy recliner at the new HQ by now."

"Such is bureaucracy and molasses. For now, this one will have to do." Holland patted Ahmad's chair. "I need a few moments. Be a dear and clear the lodge."

"Of course."

Holland watched as Anderton examined Ahmad's shoe for another moment, before politely ushering out a handful of forensic staff still snapping photos. He turned his attention back to the professor's desk. Something wasn't right. Two well-placed shots to the chest and one in the forehead did not add up with the broken glass and an assumed professional killer caught on camera leaving the scene.

"Hello, Raj."

Holland recognized the voice without having to look up.

"Sitting down on the job again?" Ewan Healey, a counter-terrorism officer at MI5, leaned against the doorjamb and glanced around in his typically detached manner. Healey had called Holland by his nickname, which the chief inspector answered to more than his given. But as his grandparents had emigrated from India, and he was second-generation British born, Holland had been made aware that a few called him *Raja* behind his back, which he knew amounted to a derisive moniker. With Healey, he could never be certain.

"Ewan." Holland stood and extended his hand. "Glad to see MI5 sent their best man." If Healey picked up on the muted sarcasm, he didn't show it.

Healey pulled what amounted to a smirk across his fairly crooked teeth. He held out his hand rather than grasp Holland's, like some feudal monarch acknowledging a line of courtiers. Accustomed to Healey's manner, Holland took a step forward and firmly shook the limp offering.

"I see you've beaten us to it, yet again. Need I bother with any detective work, or have you closed the case already?" Healey responded with more than a hint of his own sarcasm. He took a handkerchief from a coat pocket and wiped his hand. "And speaking of *best man*, shouldn't you be somewhere else, Superintendent Holland?"

"For someone who's afraid of germs, you spend a lot of time around dead terrorists." Holland wasn't in the mood to so quickly defer, though with Healey on-scene, he suspected Scotland Yard would soon be taking a back seat.

Healey's background was not dissimilar to many at MI5. He hailed from the middle class, but just barely, and on the south end. The scion of a surveyor had overcome a slight stutter to become a constable in Manchester before moving to the Met, and then, the Security Service. Healey had worked hard to replace his local dialect, rough even by Mancunian standards, with the kind of proper accent that Holland thought made him sound like some aging BBC presenter on the verge of redundancy. Only a trained ear could catch the intermittent slip. Most, however, assumed Healey's crowd to be the Oxbridge lot, even though he had barely managed second-class honors in psychology from the University of Hull.

Healey had a reputation for his cold, detached manner, and an impatience in dealing with fools. Any time spent around the man gave the impression that he considered almost everyone to be one. But he was also extremely efficient, and with respect to Holland's own standing outside Scotland Yard, Healey seemed to more or less tolerate him.

"So, you've established Ahmad's death as linked to terrorism? Is that the Yard's official position?"

Holland shrugged indifferently. "I only see you when someone has blown themselves up, or there are cameras everywhere, so naturally, I assumed." Holland glanced at Ahmad's body, which still lay twisted and on its side, having crashed off the bookcase behind the desk.

"As far as we know, the professor was a moderate Muslim with nearly a half-century of distinguished academia behind him." Healey then added, "if Whitehall is privy to something we aren't—"

"I would suggest the same thing, considering your people were Johnny-on-the-spot with this case."

"We tend to take the murder of well-known foreign nationals quite seriously." Healey accentuated a hint of boredom. "And you know how much the Service always appreciates your help."

"Yes, I'm familiar with the routine, we do the legwork and you get the credit." Holland only half-joked.

"Something like that." Healey turned to leave. "We're going to poke around while you finish up here. I'll stay out of your pocket, but since I know you're itching to tidy this up and get on with your move, why don't you have that sergeant of yours coordinate with me directly."

"I'll be in touch," was all Holland replied, though Healey had already left the office.

Holland was in the process of shuffling through a stack of papers, when Anderton stuck her head back in the doorway. "Speak of the devil. Did they give us the boot?"

"No, but he requested to work with you personally."

"Really? Go figure."

"Somebody's figure has inspired him, and I doubt it's mine." Holland gestured at Ahmad. "I'll deal with Healey, until then, let's figure *him* out."

"You speculated it was clean and professional."

"Not clean." Holland pointed to the shattered door. "But definitely a pro."

"One who allows himself to be seen on CCTV?"

"That's what I can't put my finger on, but something definitely forced our man out in a hurry."

"Or woman." Anderton's voice trailed off as she winked at Holland. "Perhaps someone heard the commotion and came to investigate?"

"Then I should think we would have two outlines on the floor."

"There is something." Anderton reached into her pocket. "When you had me turn out the team earlier, I found this in the professor's shoe." The sergeant held up a small key. "The left one had a false heel, with this hidden in a small depression. The sole pivoted on a hinge, which was knocked cockeyed from being thrown through the door pane."

Holland held out his hand. "What do you make of it?"

"It looks like a safety deposit box key."

"Indeed." He turned the key over in his hand. On one side was a double-digit number, and on the other, six numbers written in three sets of two in black ink. He handed it back to Anderton. "Well done, and off you go. We need to turn Ahmad inside out. The receiver was off its base, so check his call logs. And find out where the professor did his banking."

"Yes, sir." Anderton turned to leave.

"And Sam—" Holland ran a finger across his lips. "Keep the key between us. For now."

CHAPTER TWELVE

Savoy Hotel
London

Andre Durand casually descended a stairwell that exited the Savoy Hotel through a rear delivery door. He had arrived two days earlier as Dr. Thomas Schweiger, a German architect from Munich. His presence in London, the third time he had been in the city on this kind of business, was the result of a contract that offered him five hundred thousand euros to eliminate one of his own. The term was one loosely applied, for to compare Durand to his target, David Laurent, would have been to underrate an assassin with more than one hundred kills to his credit.

A handful of these, and only those intended, had been high-profile and very public assassinations. A young magistrate, a rising star with *le Front de Gauche,* during a campaign stop in Avignon. A vice-president on *Der Oberster Gerichtshof,* Austria's Supreme Court, one month before she was to become only the second female President of the European Parliament. A British executive with NIBC Bank in The Hague, soon after he had turned Queen's evidence on the eve of what was billed as the largest money laundering trial in Dutch history.

Though the investigations technically remained open, authorities across the continent had all but given up, filing each quietly away as unsolvable. They had become cold cases before the first detective even arrived on-scene. And the unknown killer who a select few at Interpol suspected as being responsible for these, and a string of other, prominent deaths, had been given the name *Kharon,* after the spirit in Greek mythology who ushered souls across the river Styx and into Hades. *The ferryman of the dead.*

At forty-four years old, Durand was at the top of his profession. But the Dutchman was also acutely aware that in his line of work, even the smallest miscalculation could mimic a high-caliber bullet fired into the body. While the entry point would appear small and the damage minimal, the exit wound was almost always explosively large and fatal. In this case, Laurent's carelessness at King's College was a butterfly flapping its wings. Durand was the hurricane on the other end.

The irony was that the botched assignment was beside the point, for the termination of David Laurent had been planned and paid for one month earlier. The dossier given to Durand showed his target to be a seasoned killer for hire whose exact origin was unknown. It contained a photograph, and the alias under which he was operating in England. Twelve hours earlier, Durand had also been supplied with his target's exact location, the Savoy Hotel, in London. The information was far more detailed than the assassin was accustomed to, and in essence, would greatly reduce his time and effort in the field. Typically, it would take Durand weeks to locate his objective, establish a pattern of behavior, and determine when, where, and how to most effectively fulfill the contract.

One thing Durand was absolutely certain of. That any one person knew so much about the supposed elite assassin known as David Laurent, meant that someone wanted him dead for a very specific reason.

Upon arriving at the Savoy that morning, it took Durand less than an hour to ascertain Laurent's room number. Earlier, Durand had arranged for a parcel to be delivered same-day to the hotel, in care of David Laurent. He positioned himself near the front desk, rang from a lobby phone, and posing as Laurent, requested that the staff bring any deliveries immediately to his room. Once the package sealed with blue tape arrived, Durand casually followed the bellhop upstairs. When the young man stopped at the door of the single king luxury suite on the sixth floor, Durand, wearing a bowler hat and black raincoat and pretending to be the recipient, intercepted the messenger, as if their arriving at the same moment was coincidental. He thanked and tipped the fellow generously, and took possession of the empty parcel.

Unfortunately, the room Laurent had booked, undoubtedly an intentional choice, was a large, direct river view suite near the center of a long hallway. Its placement, too far from stairway exits, would not allow Durand a safe or efficient range to target Laurent in the hotel itself. He considered his own behavior were he in the same situation, and was certain that whatever time-frame Laurent planned to leave England, he would stay at the hotel no longer than one night. Durand decided to take a vantage point which offered an easy approach to a set of doors near the delivery dock. It was through one of these that Laurent would likely exit, and, as it was nearing check-out time for the Savoy, it would be soon.

Durand need only wait.

CHAPTER THIRTEEN

David Laurent finished loading a small backpack. He had been careful over the last fifteen hours to touch only what was absolutely necessary in his hotel room. Twenty years of practice had reduced his presence to almost nonexistent in any location he stayed. Never fully close interior doors so they could be manipulated with elbows and feet. Palm faucets to ensure that not even partial fingerprints would be left on handles. Never drink from provided glassware in order to limit trace DNA. Touch almost everything with a personal article of clothing, never something from the hotel.

The Scottish Police Services Authority had recently begun perfecting a method to detect latent fingerprint ridge impressions on flexible fabrics. Known as *vacuum metal deposition,* the technique coated an item in an enclosed chamber with evaporated gold. Heated zinc then applied to an area would affix itself to the film in sections where fingerprints were not present, leaving remnants of whatever imprints remained. The process worked best on garments with high thread counts, such as sheets from luxury hotels like the Savoy. While the technology could not be relied on even a minority of the time, Laurent took no chances. He used bedding and towels as little as possible, and even then, thoroughly wiped down or rinsed off anything he had come in contact with.

He glanced at the clock on his bedside table. His train, an early afternoon Eurostar out of St. Pancras Station, was due to depart in less than three hours, and would take just over two more to reach Paris. Laurent planned to take his Business Premier seat only a few minutes before the train embarked, and would now be traveling as a French tourist returning from an extended vacation on the southwest coast. His new cover, Thomas Martin, statistically the most common first and family names in France, had been created one month earlier when the attorney from Nice entered England through Birmingham International, in order to establish a footprint in the U.K. The name David Laurent, which had served the assassin well over many assignments, would finally be laid to rest alongside Mohammad Ahmad.

Laurent decided he would walk the two miles to the station, and avoid the notoriously unreliable British public transit system. In Switzerland, commuters routinely complained when trains were even seconds late, hence the maxim that watches could be set by Swiss transport. Any attempt to synchronize a timepiece by English train timetables was risky, as it was not uncommon to arrive at a station and discover that an entire leg of a trip had been cancelled altogether at the last moment.

He decided on a route that passed the British Museum, and Russell Square, which would allow him one final look at some of the city's more desirable tourist attractions. He would not be back in the country for some time, if ever. Laurent conducted one final sweep of his room, knowing he could never again patronize the Savoy. Pity. He opened his room door and scanned the hallway. The assassin moved cautiously to a corner stairwell that would take him to the alley behind the hotel.

CHAPTER FOURTEEN

Heathrow Airport
London, England

Nasir Hajjar peered through a rain-slicked porthole of the Gulfstream as it rolled toward its terminus at London Heathrow. Haji, as he was known to a select few, in particular, the Saudi prince who owned the private luxury jet that had flown them from Riyadh, reminisced as he surveyed the familiar landscape. He couldn't count how many times he had taxied across this same wet, black tarmac since his days as a student returning for term at the Imperial College of London.

Hajjar smiled as he considered how much he had gained since then. Twenty-five years earlier, he had become accustomed to deplaning a cramped, musty cabin, accentuated by stained pastels and dim yellow lighting, for an even more congested Piccadilly Line bound for Gloucester Road Station. Hajjar could still remember the posh flats he by-passed in South Kensington, en route to his dingy, shared room near Bayswater, which made him feel as if he'd never disembarked the plane or the Tube. How far he had come.

Prince Al-Ahmed bin Halabi smiled at Hajjar as the plane was wheel-locked at its gate. Normally, only attendants, advisors of his inner circle, and members of the Saudi royal family were permitted to travel with the prince, but he often made an exception for his close friend of over two decades. He could vividly recall how the young Yemeni had saved his life on a London street when bin Halabi was a graduate student at Oxford. The two became fast friends, and while Hajjar had come to be considered part of the extended family, his true value was as a man who quietly fixed problems for the prince.

Bin Halabi frowned as he stood and assessed what needed to be done to bring the aircraft to a standard more suited to his wealth and rank. He had recently spent a considerable sum to renovate the cabin, which included fancy décor and new furniture, as well as reinsulation to decrease internal noise from eighty to sixty decibels, the difference between a garbage disposal and electric razor. He realized that he could not expect to upgrade his Gulfstream to the caliber of those owned by his better-positioned and wealthier relatives, which included a five hundred million euro Airbus commissioned by his cousin, next in line for succession. Nonetheless, bin Halabi still considered his small, outdated plane noticeably unbefitting his status. He lamented how far he still had to go.

"*Takbir.*" The prince uttered a retrained exaltation as the pilot shut down the engines.

"*Allahu Akbar.*" Hajjar returned the sentiment, still focused on what lay behind him, and beyond, the window.

The prince gestured to his contingent of bodyguards, a sign he wished for privacy. The armed men ushered bin Halabi's servants from the plane in order to ready the hired limousines. The pomp and fanfare of the prince's many travels were always greater and more ostentatious than his small entourage warranted. But that was the point.

Hajjar sat impassively, his imagination still affixed on his past. He fondly recalled his first week in London, fresh off graduation from the prestigious Sana'a International School in Yemen. He was seventeen, smart and handsome, and had already traveled extensively throughout the U.S. and Europe. His father insisted he attend the University of Science and Technology in Sana'a, but Hajjar was set on continuing his studies abroad. With the patriarch making good on his threat to cut him off financially if he left, the son set out for England with little more than bare-bones funding from Imperial College, and a fierce desire to succeed on his own.

He could still remember how determined he was to pursue a demanding joint business and engineering degree. The professors, impressed with his acumen and inquisitive nature. The scores of Western women he bedded, so many of them intoxicated by his soft Middle Eastern features and sharp wit. The two medical students he murdered in his second year.

Hajjar had just arrived for the start of term and was out celebrating with friends, when a small contingent of pub-crawling graduates decided to have an unprovoked go at him. He pretended to meekly laugh it off at the time, like an unschooled provincial recently emerged from the dusty backwater of some former British protectorate. The primary instigators eventually let him be, but did not notice the man who quietly shadowed them home. Hajjar slashed each of their toff throats, the first one slowly, while the second watched in a terrified panic, gagged and bound to a chair. The grizzly massacre sent shockwaves through the college community, who had since set up a scholarship in honor of the dead students. Hajjar had once donated one pound anonymously to the fund, a congratulatory gesture to himself.

Everything changed during Michaelmas term of his second year. Hajjar had just settled a tab he could not afford, when he heard the unmistakable sound of gunfire. With everyone diving under tables or frozen in fear, he ran to the tavern door. Lying on the sidewalk was a well-dressed, younger man of Middle Eastern descent, protected by an armed contingent in a high-caliber exchange with several assailants. Hajjar watched as three of the bodyguards were gunned down, having killed only two of the attackers. The remaining assassin, himself a young Arab, was wounded, but alive, and left with unfettered access to his high-value target.

Without thinking, Hajjar rushed the gunman, who was so fixated on the student curled up on the pavement, that he blocked out everything in his periphery. Hajjar slammed into the man at full speed, who dropped his weapon and crumpled to the ground next to his intended target. As shocked bystanders looked on, Hajjar grabbed the gun and shot the would-be killer several times at point-blank range.

By the time police and TV cameras arrived, Prince Al-Ahmed bin Halabi, ninth in line to the House of Saud, was in full PR mode, heralding his fellow exchange student as a national hero of Saudi Arabia.

Hajjar finished his studies in greater fashion than be began them, and during his remaining two years, was brought before the royal court in Riyadh several times to be honored by the King. Bin Halabi declared them life-long friends, something Hajjar perceived as genuine. And it was. After graduating with first-class honors from the prestigious university, the prodigal son returned home to a forgiving father, who received him with open arms and even wider purse strings.

The country that Hajjar returned to was far different than the Yemen his forefathers had controlled. His great uncle, Ali Abdul Hajjar, had served as personal advisor to the imam between the world wars. The ruler and his reforms were popular, in particular among Jews, who enjoyed increased rights and protection during his reign. Ali Abdul was deft in the manner he counseled the imam, advising him to decree a ban on all weapons in Sana'a, at the same time he was importing guns and armaments illegally from Nazi Germany.

Hajjar's great uncle was also a natural at languages, speaking a variety of Arabic dialects, as well as French, German, English, Italian, and Hebrew. This, combined with a natural charisma, allowed him to move fluently between lucrative business transactions throughout the Arabian Peninsula and Europe. Ali Abdul had become a wealthy man by the time the imam was assassinated, and he was forced to flee to Mandatory Palestine.

Hajjar's grandfather, Muhammad Ali Hajjar, also hailed from Socotra and was raised in South Yemen. The port region was governed as part of British India until his sons, Hajjar's father and uncle, were born, the same year the province became a British colony. The world they came up in had become an amalgam of East and West, and where secular courts, not Sharia Law, dictated legal disputes, both Muslim and European. By the time Hajjar was born, South Yemen had been decolonized, and the federation that flourished under British protection had collapsed to become the People's Republic of Yemen, a region hardened by communist resolve.

His father and uncle recognized they could become powerful men by utilizing their position to play warring interests against one another. And divide and conquer they did. While both men purported to support the more moderate faction of the South Yemen Civil War in 1986, they funneled guns and money to the hardline opposition, who eventually won the conflict. Along with the newly appointed ruler, the Hajjar brothers were two of the few men of position to survive and benefit from the victory.

Hajjar was fourteen years old when the war came to an end, and he watched as his father and uncle, who saw the writing on the wall with the wane of Soviet aid, deftly negotiate the process of pre-unification with North Yemen. Four years later, by the time his father had been appointed Minister of the Interior in the unified Yemeni government, Hajjar began school in England. His brother and cousins were determined to follow their respective fathers' wishes, however, and joined the Yemeni Republican Guard, thanks to the connections of his uncle, the new Minister of Defense.

Upon returning from England, Hajjar began intelligence training with the General Intelligence Directorate in Jordan, as well as military exercises with the country's Joint Special Operations Command, both courtesy of his family connections, and his relationship with bin Halabi. Over the course of five years, the amateur homicidal sociopath was converted into a professional killer, with connections at the highest levels of the international clandestine service community.

By the time bin Halabi was appointed Deputy Defense Minister, Hajjar had returned from Jordan, and moved into the inner circle of the prime minister of Yemen. Both he and the prince quickly realized that neither could pad their wealth at an acceptable pace while in official government positions. Bin Halabi informed his ruling cousin that he wished to leave his post as a regional governor in Saudi Arabia, at the same time Hajjar resigned from his position as chief security advisor in Yemen. The prince, with Hajjar at his right hand, founded EuroPenninsula Investments, a company offering business and investment guidance on three continents.

While bin Halabi used his contacts and business acumen to make the corporation a successful venture, Hajjar created assetless shell corporations and dummy charities to secretly front illegal business deals, as well as funnel money to terrorist factions throughout the Middle East. The organization that benefited most directly from his covert funding was AQAP, al-Qaeda in the Arabian Peninsula. An offshoot of Osama bin Laden's primary terrorist network, it operated primarily in Yemen and Saudi Arabia, but was able to expand its sphere of influence thanks to anonymous donations from Hajjar. It mattered little that one of the network's main objectives was to oppose bin Halabi's House of Saud, nor did Hajjar take issue with AQAP's attack on his own uncle's defense ministry in Yemen.

The company became so successful that bin Halabi expanded his dealings deep into Europe, and in particular, England, a country with a growing Muslim population. For the last decade, the primary middleman for many of bin Halabi's business ventures had been Mohammad Ahmad, a well-connected, but now very dead, professor at the University of Cambridge.

"Haji."

The reverberation of his name a second time broke Hajjar's concentration. He turned from the window and smiled at the prince. "Yes, your Highness."

"Do you remember the day?"

"Of course," he nodded. "Each time I come back to England."

"*Al-Hamdu lillāh*," the prince exclaimed, "for what you did that day."

"Praise be to Allah, and EuroPen," Hajjar answered. "What news of the professor?" Word had reached them almost immediately after Ahmad's death, and soon after, bin Halabi had secured a meeting with Baldwin Davis-Banks, deputy commissioner of Scotland Yard.

The prince weighed his response. "Allah wills many things, my friend, and it is not our place to question it. Who is that movie star you are so fond of?"

The prince referred to Hajjar's favorite Western actor, and he recognized that bin Halabi's cryptic response was a subtle hint that any thought on delving deeper into the subject should be shelved.

"Clint Eastwood," Hajjar replied.

"That's right!" the prince clapped his hands together once, and laughed. "And what is that line again? Of all you quote, it is my favorite."

"*Deserve's got nothing to do with it.*"

"Indeed," the prince responded, as he stopped smiling.

Hajjar wondered whether the professor's death was a good, or bad, turn for the company. Ahmad's assassination was as suspicious as it was ill-timed, considering the lucrative contract the man had brokered between EuroPen and an Arab-controlled export company in Liverpool, a deal set to deliver a seven-figure profit over the next five years.

Hajjar was also aware that the professor had, of late, become rather self-assertive as EuroPen's primary factor in the U.K., something bin Halabi had grown considerably less confident in. An audience with the prince had been arranged in Dubai that summer, to ensure that Ahmad understood the nature of their relationship. Someone had obviously decidedly to be more demonstrative in advance of the meeting.

The prince again interrupted Hajjar's thoughts. "I will be traveling to Liverpool tomorrow, to assure our new partners that Ahmad's death will not impact the timeline for the North Sea project. I will be back in London in a few days' time for a sit-down with the new deputy commissioner at Scotland Yard. It will be interesting to hear what they have learned about the murder, or at least, what they choose to divulge. In the meantime, I want you in Cambridge, and London. Use your contacts, and find out what you can, quietly. I will also meet with Danesh this week, after which, you and I will coordinate."

Hajjar considered the man the prince had referenced, a contact he had never met, nor been allowed to vet, but whom bin Halabi had known and utilized for nearly as long as Hajjar had known him. "Do you trust this man?" Hajjar asked, not for the first time.

"He is Saudi born, English raised, and influenced by money," bin Halabi smiled, "so, yes."

Hajjar did not respond. The prince clapped his hands together again and laughed. "My friend, you should be more trusting."

"You employ me not to be, so I shall continue to earn my paycheck."

"Let me worry about Danesh, and the dead professor. *Ahmad, Allah Yerhamo.*"

"Somebody put his soul to rest, that is for certain," Hajjar answered, as he stood to escort the prince off the plane.

CHAPTER FIFTEEN

Savoy Hotel
London

The remaining lorry exited the access road behind the Savoy. Checkout time was midday,
and Durand expected his target to depart the hotel soon, and by way of one of its back exits.

As if on cue, a delivery door opened slowly in-
ward. David Laurent surfaced for a moment, before
stepping back into the shadow of the entryway to
surveil the compact lane. Durand had worked this
moment out carefully. He had initially considered using a silenced rifle from distance, but while the shot
would be quick and easy, even when suppressed, a

long gun could draw attention. It would also require additional time and effort to conceal and discard. Durand decided to earn his payday at close range.

He decided on a weapon he had created, a small canister that fired a burst of fine mist from an atomized nozzle. The mixture was a potent combination of platinum and iridium, and would kill Laurent within minutes. It was similar to the method the Bulgarian Secret Police used to assassinate dissident writer Georgi Markov in London in 1978. Using the sharpened tip of an umbrella as the delivery system, an assassin jabbed a ricin pellet into Markov's leg as he crossed Waterloo Bridge. Markov felt the prick, and even witnessed a man picking up the umbrella, but thought little of it at the time. Three days later, Markov died in a city hospital.

Durand had perfected his system over several years and multiple assassinations. The device was a straight tube that was designed to look like a cigar, with the firing mechanism in the form of a small button at the base of the weapon. At the moment of contact, Durand would simply raise his wrist, as if checking the time or preparing to take a puff on the cigar, and depress the trigger with his thumb. The discharge, which delivered a small but lethal dose directly to the mucus membranes of the nose and mouth, was silent and nearly invisible. Potency was such that immobilization was immediate and death imminent. And because the interaction was not violent enough to elicit any noticeable reaction from the victim, it would appear to any passerby as if someone had simply stumbled and fallen over.

The most difficult part of the assignment would be to get close enough to Laurent. Assassins dealt with the possibility that anyone could at anytime pose a threat, and were, as a result, always alert. Crowded environments needed to be vetted quickly, and the majority of people dismissed. Durand knew Laurent would not exit until he was certain the alley was clear of potential danger. Dressed in a smart business suit, carrying an expensive satchel and talking on a phone, Durand would be assessed as a businessman on his way to lunch, and ignored.

While Durand's approach would appear seemingly random, his movement at the time of attack would be virtually unnoticeable. Though Laurent might be aware that something had happened, he would be unable to react, or get help quickly enough to counter the effects of the toxin. Before police could even begin to locate potential witnesses to the mysterious death in the alley, the Dutchman would be moving through Heathrow International, an hour's flight from Zurich.

It was time. Durand flipped the safety cap off the trigger and carefully twisted the top of the cylinder a half rotation, exposing a small opening. He stepped out from his place of concealment and began walking down the alley, toward Laurent's position.

Durand began a feigned mobile conversation, laughing loudly in order to draw attention to himself, all the while stealing glances at the entryway. The door remained open, and while he could no longer see Laurent, the assassin expected him to emerge at any moment.

Thirty feet. The entire operation would be over in ten seconds. His heart rate notched up slightly, as Durand prepared to step into the opening and engage his target. He slowed his breathing, and concentrated. Time seemed to draw out as he came level with the exit.

It was empty.

Durand suddenly realized that he had focused too intently on the lane in front of him for the length of his approach down the alley. He quickly glanced over his shoulder, and his eyes betrayed the slightest hint they registered the lapse of judgment as a bullet snapped from Laurent's silenced HK 9mm into the bridge of Durand's nose.

Laurent causally stepped over Durand, reentered the Savoy, and closed the door behind him.

CHAPTER SIXTEEN

King's Cross Station
London

The automated voice at King's Cross Station requested that Inspector Sands report immediately to the operations room. Sean Garrett recognized it as code used by public transport throughout the U.K. to signal an emergency, or potential threat, on the premises. The point was to alert station staff without panicking travelers, regardless of the fact that the majority of people in public venues throughout the world had long been conditioned to ignore loudspeakers and their typically incoherent announcements.

If Garrett had cause for alarm, it would not be because of a possible fire. The violent murder of a Cambridge professor, still the lead story across much of Europe, was playing on almost every TV in the station. Leaked pictures of Ahmad's body had already been published, and it was also reported that the killer had been caught on CCTV leaving the scene. Though there had been no official corroboration from Whitehall, one news outlet speculated that the release of a photo was imminent.

Garrett stood, withdrawn and alert, behind a locked rack of luggage trolleys near platform nine. The lead cart, which required one pound to release, had been jammed in at such an angle that it rendered the remaining stack unusable. Several overpacked travelers had discovered this only after depositing coins and yanking violently, to no avail, on the first cart. Nearby, another stream of tourists rotated through and snapped selfies with Harry Potter's half-trolley cemented into Platform 9¾.

The Flying Scotsman would take four hours to reach Waverley Station, and Garrett again considered whether he should abandon the meet. Staying in London to determine how to safely get himself out of England was, on one hand, more logical than trotting the length of one country and into another to do it. But, to remain in proximity to where the entire effort to establish what had happened at Cambridge was concentrated, and to attempt to leave the U.K. on a set of credentials that might be compromised, was equally risky.

Garrett knew he was left with Hobson's choice, and boarded just before his train was set to depart. He took his seat in a standard car farthest down the track, near the engine, and watched as last-second commuters jammed into sections nearest the station, unfazed that luggage racks crammed like a Tetris puzzle signaled a packed car. He mused that Europeans seemed to have abandoned the concept that humans required any modicum of personal space, traditionally eighteen inches, in which to feel comfortable. Americans, on the other hand, having grown spoiled by four hundred years of unlimited room, had expanded their comfort buffer well beyond a foot and a half.

For the English, who packed fifty-five million people into fifty thousand square miles, it came down to the simple reality of space constraints. North Carolina, Garrett's home, and the ninth most populous state in the U.S. at just over ten million, was three thousand square miles larger than the whole of England. Perhaps Europeans living in the aftermath of the Black Death viewed personal space differently than their twenty-first century descendants, he considered.

Garrett's thoughts turned back to his journey. He had no idea who or what to expect in Edinburgh. The meet was to take place at the northeastern end of Princes Street Gardens, the large botanical park in the shadow of Edinburgh Castle. The green space had once been little more than a boggy marsh that served as a natural defense for Old Town. When the area was drained in the nineteenth century, city planners discovered that the long-standing habit of castle occupants casting their human waste over the walls and down the steep grade had created one of the richest and most fertile grounds in Edinburgh.

Garrett was to wait on the east side of the Scott Monument until approached by a man in a blue jogging suit, who would inquire whether he knew anything about the massive Gothic structure dedicated to Sir Walter Scott, one of Scotland's favorite sons and among its most recognizable novelists and poets.

Look back, and smile on perils past, the writer had long ago penned.

We'll see, Garrett thought.

CHAPTER SEVENTEEN

Clapham Junction Station
London

The mob of early morning commuters that massed along the platform edge waited impatiently for the next train bound for Waterloo Station. David Laurent leaned against a kiosk and finished a black coffee. With one departure every thirty seconds, Clapham Junction was the busiest track in the world, and like many throughout London that morning, it was standing room only. Soon the South Western Main Line would arrive, and overfilled cars would spill out through the crowd waiting to cram into what few spots opened up. It reminded Laurent of a large, chaotic game of musical chairs.

As he weighed his options, Laurent's paranoid surveillance jumped between commuters and the platform around him. It had been fourteen hours since he had killed the man sent to kill him. He had not recognized his would-be assassin, and since the man's face had been blown apart, neither would anyone else.

As he feared, the broken office window had already begun to spiral out of control. If Laurent wanted to get out of England, and this predicament, he would need to act quickly. He had to separate what he knew from what was assumed. He could not compartmentalize what had happened. Most people did this on a daily basis, ignoring reality in favor of their own biases.

William of Ockham, the fourteenth-century Franciscan philosopher, would dictate his next move. *Pluralitas non est ponenda sine neccesitate.* The fewer assumptions made, the better. When confronted with competing theories, the most straightforward was usually the correct answer. Simplicity was the razor. Laurent knew he must map his way backward. One day since he had arrived at the Savoy. Two weeks since he had entered England. Three months since he was contracted to kill the professor. Somewhere along that path lay the answer. Follow the twine, and he could extricate himself from the labyrinth.

Simplicity was the razor.

What was most troubling, was the glaring fact that he had been compromised. The dead assassin behind the Savoy was the end of that thread. At its beginning was the only person connected to Laurent. But, the Albanian had long been kept at a distance, operating as a handsomely-paid proxy. Even if the man had been swayed by greed or coerced by some other means to betray him, it was out of the question that he could have given away Laurent's location in England, particularly at the hotel, as the reservation had been arranged only forty-eight hours prior.

Laurent had already acknowledged that his stay at the Savoy violated protocol, but there were over seven hundred hotels in the Greater London area. It was impossible for anyone to have found him under a throwaway alias based on one night of business a decade earlier. No one was that good, or lucky.

The dead end brought Laurent back to the dead assassin. He had first become aware of the man's existence thanks to chance, a completely random encounter in the Savoy lobby. As Laurent finished up a late breakfast, the front of house manager asked him whether he expected any other deliveries during his stay. If so, the man promised to personally see that they too were brought to his room.

Laurent knew immediately. Someone was aware that he was staying at the hotel, and had used a clever method to discern his room number. The ruse would have been successful, so too the ensuing kill, if not for the attentiveness of one employee. The man's professionalism was Laurent's good providence. At the time, he was able to turn the assassin's tactic back on itself by finding the porter who had delivered the package.

I say, old chap. I seem to have misplaced the outerwear I had on earlier when you delivered a parcel to my room. Has anyone turned anything in?

The bowler and the black overcoat?

Both, I'm afraid.

I'll check, sir, and let you know.

Laurent assessed his situation. The assassin knew who he was, where he was, and presumably what he was. And, he had been able to successfully pass himself off as Laurent, albeit to an unsuspecting staffer in a quick exchange in a hallway, which indicated that he was likely of similar age, height, and build.

The man was good, a professional. But, second-guessing worked both ways. Laurent was certain that his pursuer would expect him to wait until checkout to depart. The man wouldn't waste any time or effort attempting to figure out where his target might go, he only needed to ambush Laurent at some point after he left the hotel. Which meant that he was ready and within striking distance, and, positioned in the most logical place to follow and intercept Laurent, the access road behind the Savoy.

At checkout, Laurent had exited the Savoy through its front entrance and circled back to the hotel, from the river. It took him nearly ten minutes of cautious surveillance to finally spot a man wearing a black coat and hat, tucked into an alcove at the end of the rear alley, and clearly monitoring the back of the hotel. He was well-placed to engage Laurent, but poorly situated to avoid detection should someone be looking for him. The man assumed, incorrectly, that no one would be. He should also have changed the outfit he had worn earlier.

Negligent.

Laurent then reentered the Savoy and moved to a delivery door, propping it open with an information guide he had taken from the lobby. He waited a moment, and then quickly exited the hotel and repositioned himself behind the assassin. He watched as his would-be killer left the alcove of rubbish bins and began to advance up the alley, talking on a mobile. The feigned conversation was a tactical slip, for while the assassin banked it would mitigate suspicion, it served to distract him as well. So too did the satchel on his arm, which would hinder access to a gun, should he need it quickly. His third mistake was in concentrating too intently once the door had been opened. In their profession, being too inexperienced or too seasoned could carry the same risks.

By the time the man realized he had been derelict in keeping intermittent tabs behind him, he was under the bridgeway that connected the two buildings from above. Laurent had been able to make a quick approach and kill shot, with the momentary darkness of the overpass shadowing him from CCTV cameras, which were positioned in groups of three at either end of the street. Laurent's assassin had committed several small mistakes that compounded into one moment of carelessness, which proved fatal.

Laurent refocused on the present, and watched as passengers swarmed the train that would have taken him to St. Pancras. Originally, he planned to depart immediately on a return Eurostar train to Paris, whose first leg had been paid for and ridden one month earlier from Gare du Nord. His secondary avenue of escape was to hole up in a cottage in Wales, and depart the U.K. on a British Airways flight two weeks after the assassination.

Laurent now recognized that neither was a viable option. He would have to find another way out, and had spent the entire night trying to determine where he should go, and how he would get there.

The doors of the train shut and it pulled away from the station.

Laurent was back where he started. Considering what had almost occurred at the Savoy, he had only a few viable avenues of escape, and each posed an equally high risk. The next train to Waterloo could get him, as Thomas Martin, to Birmingham International. He could be in Austria by lunch, and at his safe house outside Kitzbühel by afternoon tea. *If that location wasn't compromised.* Or, he could stay on the move, and hope to outlast whatever security measures were being put in place in England. *If authorities weren't already looking specifically for him.*

Every course of action was overshadowed by an "*if*," which meant prison, or worse.

Another option was to make the meet that afternoon, which would amount to the single, stupidest decision he'd ever made, if his employer was behind the assassination attempt. Unless they were not, in which case his handler represented Laurent's best option for getting answers and getting out.

He was giving himself a headache.

Reduce the problem to its simplest denominator.

Laurent made his way out of the station, and plotted how to control the Kensington meet.

CHAPTER EIGHTEEN

The Security Service
Thames House, London

Alastair Clarke watched the Traffic Management Unit steadily clean up two wrecks that had occurred on Lambeth Bridge. The head of A Branch had allowed his attention to wander well away from MI5 for the better part of an hour, when a lorry trying to avoid a cyclist sideswiped an oncoming car. Several other motorists careened off one another near a roundabout at the bridge entrance, and interrupted what, for Clarke, had been a pleasantly unfocused train of thought. A messy

Monday morning for commuters, but for everyone else, an agreeable May day in Milbank.

For the moment, at least.

Clarke had been summoned to the office early in preparation for what would likely be a very long week. The murder of a prominent professor at Cambridge was beginning to spiral into an international mess, and both Scotland Yard and the Security Service were already playing catch-up to determine what had happened.

A knock resonated from outside Clarke's office, and he knew who it was immediately—his head of section A1 always rapped on the secretary's desk on his way through the outer foyer, rather than wait at Clarke's door.

Maitland Murphy smiled from the entryway. "Morning, sir. Do you have a moment?"

"As many as you need, Matt, come in," Clarke gestured, calling Murphy by his nickname. He had spent the better part of his childhood in the States, and as the Yanks could never quite get his name correct, Murphy had left England as Maitland, and returned as Matt. His mother remained the lone holdout, refusing to use the American moniker.

Clarke liked his head of technical operations, including eavesdropping and video surveillance. Murphy did his work quietly well, and without pretense. He was one of the few under thirty years of age who didn't saunter around Thames House like some privileged schoolchild privy to a secret. After A levels, Murphy had decided to head back to Massachusetts for college, earning a degree in statistics from Boston University, before returning to the U.K., and Durham University, where he completed a masters in mathematical sciences.

His application to MI5 would have been filed away and likely forgotten, if not for Murphy's score on the SIAT, the test that measured security inspection aptitude. He possessed an uncanny ability to detect faces, objects, and events that were unusual or out of place, and over the last five years, Murphy had moved quickly up the ranks. His dogged work a year earlier in singling out two unassuming travelers at Gatwick Airport for further scrutiny had been instrumental in preventing a planned attack on the Great North Run in Newcastle.

"There is something I want you to see," Murphy said.

"I'm all eyes."

"Footage from CCTV, near Woodberry Down Estate, early Saturday morning around 3:10 a.m." Murphy cued up several clips taken from two cameras.

Clarke watched as a lone man came into frame and was accosted by two others, whom he proceeded to put down, rather violently.

"What am I looking at?"

"A fight, sir."

Clarke smiled at Murphy's habit of focusing on each detail in linear progression. "You've got a punch-up in one of the roughest boroughs in London? Perhaps we should file it with the other rare footage we have of tourists taking photos at Buckingham Palace?" he added good-naturedly.

Murphy smiled. "Quicker to the point?"

"It is Monday."

Murphy clicked on another photo taken from CCTV footage, which had been close-cropped and enlarged. "I isolated this shot," he noted, manipulating the monitor with a few clicks. "Here, for a moment, a light reflects from somewhere to the man's left, illuminating his face. This is right after the unsub torpedoes the larger guy." Murphy liked to use the term unsub, *unknown subject*, which he had no doubt gleaned from American television, although no one else around A Branch used it.

The quality of the photo wasn't ideal, and its perspective was too angled to hope for a hit from facial recognition software. But, it was good enough to tell that the man appeared to be in his thirties, and fairly rough, though not Manor House rough.

"Impressive, Matt, but I'm assuming there's a reason I should be more impressed."

"There is." Murphy pulled up another set of stills. "I was able to isolate individual frames from another batch of footage that came our way yesterday."

Clarke compared the photos side by side. "It could be the same man, but one is taken at dusk, and the other after dark. It's inconclusive."

"Maybe a sixty percent match. But look at the man's neck, just below his left ear. I've blown it up." A third set of photos appeared, both enlarged and with sharpened contrast.

Clarke strained. In both shots, there was what appeared to be a similar dark mark. He looked closer. Possibly the same blemish.

"Okay, maybe I'm somewhat more certain," Clarke acknowledged. "Where's this second set pulled from?"

"Cambridge. Thursday night, from cameras outside the building at King's College where that professor was shot."

Clarke stood and studied both photos closely. After another moment, he slowly nodded his head.

Before Clarke could say anything, Murphy declared, "I'm isolating multidirectional feeds from cameras at the girls' school, the parish church, Goodchild, and Seven Sisters, to see if we can narrow down which direction he traveled after the fight."

"Good work, Matt. Keep me up to speed, and get this over to Ewan Healey's office."

"Right away."

Murphy hurried from the office, and Clarke turned back to the window. One smash-up had been cleared, and a pair of flatbed trucks were sorting out the rest of the cars near the roundabout.

He considered his next move carefully before calling to his secretary. "Marissa. Please get me Banastre Montjoy over at Six."

CHAPTER NINETEEN

Hyde Park
London

Laurent sat over a half-eaten tea biscuit in The Magazine and watched tourists dart across the only thoroughfare through Hyde Park, one of London's largest and most popular public grounds. The fashionable restaurant, in which he had spent the last two hours, was situated near The Serpentine, the large body of water that bisected nearly the entire park. It was almost four o'clock, and the meet with his handler was thirty minutes out and a half-mile away.

The assassin pondered the wisdom of his move. Once he had decided to make the meet, Laurent had made his way to Waterloo Station in order to use it as his base of operations, at least for the next twelve hours. He had purchased his third change of clothes in two days, and now carried only a small backpack.

Laurent settled his check and left the eatery. The assassin exited near the Italian Gardens, boarded a half-empty Tube at Lancaster Gate Station, and rode one stop. He reentered Hyde Park, and made his way to the Queen Victoria Statue, near Kensington Palace. Laurent feigned interest in the memorial dedicated to history's second longest-ruling female monarch, while he eyed the Round Pond, which was directly in front of him, and crowded with sightseers. An amalgam of nationalities wandered by, part of a guided group, and he mixed in with several stragglers as they strung their way around the water. The combination of languages sounded like white noise, and drowned out the tour in English.

Laurent spied the set of benches. On one of them was his contact, well-tailored in an expensive suit, with black hair and light, Middle Eastern features. He was wearing a red scarf and reading a copy of *The Times*, though Laurent could tell the fellow was doing anything but that. His eyes, shaded by sunglasses, were taking in everything around him.

Laurent continued with the tour group and past the bench. Several students stopped to snap photos of a red lifesaving buoy affixed to a pole near the pond, allowing the assassin to move behind his handler and onto the walkway that led to the center of the park. He concealed himself in a small stand of trees, far enough away to remain inconspicuous, but sufficiently close to follow the man once he abandoned the meet after Laurent failed to show.

Twenty minutes later, his contact stood, and with the newspaper folded under his arm, removed his sunglasses and took one last look around. He began to walk slowly in the direction of Kensington Palace, glancing back over his shoulder only once. Laurent exited the grove and moved parallel to the man as he continued toward the residence of the British Royal Family, weaving his way through tourists and goose shit, both of which littered the path.

Laurent increased his pace and made contact with the man just as he, and the students, all merged at the intersection of the pond walk. The assassin fell into a casual pace behind his handler, before stepping deftly next to him. "Don't turn. Keep walking."

The man did not break his stride, and only nodded. He rotated his head slightly in Laurent's direction. "You're late," he mused. His English accent was one he had clearly worked hard to perfect.

"Did you send the man at the Savoy?" Laurent oriented both of them to keep the pace and direction of the tour group, who were still chattering and laughing, and blithely unaware.

"I haven't a clue to what you're referring."

The man's confusion came across as genuine, Laurent thought. Or maybe he was a professional liar like Laurent was. Like they all were.

"The other assassin."

The man did not answer.

"Did you?" Laurent pressed.

The man paused a moment before answering. "And if we had, would I not feign stupidity?"

"I won't ask a third time, old son." Laurent steadied his HK, which was concealed in the folds of his jacket.

"No, we did not."

Laurent lowered his voice. "Walk toward the Hilton Hotel. If you do anything unexpected, I will leave you dead in this park."

"Indeed," the man responded.

Laurent was uncertain how to interpret the response as they approached Bayswater. He suddenly perceived that he might at any moment feel the silent impact of high caliber from distance. He braced. The hair on his neck bristled, but the air remained still. Laurent brushed off the anticipation, and the sense of alarm, and continued to walk the man toward the park exit without looking back.

CHAPTER TWENTY

Edinburgh, Scotland

Princes Street teamed with energy, as an un-relenting surge of tourists and traffic kept the main shopping district animated with noise and movement. Early planners of Edinburgh had kept the south side of the avenue almost entirely free of buildings, which provided an unfettered panorama of the castle, the Mound, and Old Town. Other than the Royal Scottish Academy, the only structure on the garden-side of the mile-long boulevard was the Scott Monument, located directly across from the Old Waverley Hotel.

Sean Garrett stood by the window of his corner room, which afforded a direct line of sight to the meet location. It was scheduled to take place in fifteen minutes, and Garrett now gave it even money he wouldn't make it out of the U.K. without seeing the inside of Belmarsh Prison as a Category A, Exceptional Risk Offender. Or worse.

He pulled the shade down, and prepared to leave the hotel via a side stairwell. As the hall exit door near his room had been banging open and closed all night, he wouldn't need to look very hard to find it. Edinburgh boasted a population of almost five hundred thousand people, and another four million annual visitors, and nearly that number seemed to be out and about.

Garrett stepped onto Princes Street. The late afternoon was already dimming gray, and it was getting colder. He blended with the mass of shoppers and sightseers who moved in tandem along the main boulevard, before shooting directly across the busy road. He entered the gardens, and walked slowly toward the benches that bracketed the statue. Every seat was occupied, but no one stood out in a dark tracksuit. Garrett glanced down the gardens and toward the shopping mall, where a line of tourists waited their turn to snap photos alongside a bagpiper, looking zombified and playing for small change.

A middle-aged man approached Garrett, dressed in a black jumper, but continued past him and towards the Balmoral Hotel. An elderly couple with a thick Glaswegian accent asked a woman to take a photo of them with Sir Walter in the background, but the confused tourist only smiled, and stared at them as if they spoke another language. Two taxis nearly collided at a one-way split near Waverley Bridge.

Twenty minutes passed. No man in a blue tracksuit.

Twenty minutes later, Garrett crossed back over Princes Street and reentered the hotel.

CHAPTER TWENTY-ONE

London

Laurent and his contact entered the Hilton. With a century behind it, the iconic building boasted features unique to an establishment its age. In Laurent's experience, this meant patrons could expect to trade location and convenience for smaller rooms and fewer amenities.

They passed through the lobby, and Laurent found a table along the rear wall of the hotel bar. He chose a seat opposite the entryway, and was surprised when the man dropped his hat and scarf on the table, and casually sat with his back to the door.

"I must thank you for choosing such a convenient spot, for I am lodging here."

Laurent only nodded, an ambiguous response that suggested he knew, though he did not.

"Contrary to what one might suppose, the rooms are very comfortable, quite spacious."

Laurent said nothing, but continued to monitor the exit while keeping his periphery on his contact.

The man lowered his voice. "Perhaps we could both agree to pocket our concealed pistols, and engage in a civilized conversation."

Again, Laurent did not respond.

The man added, "If my people wanted you dead—"

"I'm not worried about your people."

"Neither was the professor," the man replied with a hint of irony. "I could have had you shot at the park."

Laurent was quick to respond. "Not before I would have killed you."

"Perhaps, but now I've put down my gun." The man held his hands up to chest level and jiggled them for effect.

Laurent left the HK in his lap, and rested his hands on the table.

The man broke the silence. "We need to know what happened."

"I killed the man sent to kill me."

"No, at Cambridge."

"I killed the professor."

"And?"

"And I completed the job I was hired to do," Laurent answered flatly. "I assume the second half of the payment, including the bonus, has already been wired to my account."

"You were hired under the assumption that you work alone," the man noted with a tinge of sarcasm, referring to the witness. "You are a professional, yes?"

"What happened was an absurd stroke of bad luck." Before the man could respond, Laurent asked, "if you did not send the assassin, who did?"

"If we did, it would mean we hired two people who failed to complete their assignments as contracted." He then added, "you have a problem."

"One that begins with who betrayed me."

"No, that is where it ends. Have you asked yourself how this assassin knew to find you at the Savoy?"

"Of course."

"All of the other bits, the alias, your phone and travel itinerary, could have been discovered only by—how did you put it—a stroke of absurd misfortune. But the Savoy? Impossible, no?"

Laurent knew his credentials and phone were virtually untraceable, and that his movements had been well disguised for the last two weeks. He shook his head. "Everything is a dead end."

"Then you have a big problem."

Laurent knew what the man alluded to, and if the NSA or MI5 were involved, he was dealing with the biggest problem possible. "There is no chance that someone drew a bead on me by happenstance." His voice took an accusatory tone. "Someone tipped them."

"Clearly we did not supply any intelligence agency with the identity of the assassin we contracted to kill a renowned Cambridge scholar."

Laurent eyed the man. The only way anyone could have located him was to have trapped and traced his mobile, which would have been nearly impossible, considering he had used it only once, to coordinate Thursday's meeting with the professor a week earlier. Since then, it had been hidden in a London Tube station, and forwarded all calls to a second disposable he carried.

"MI5 have no dossier on you, as far as we can tell. But we do know they have compiled one on the man who interrupted your little meeting with the professor." The man pulled an envelope from his jacket pocket and waved it. "Your witness."

Laurent was surprised. "Who is he? How did you get this?"

"We don't know who he is," the man replied, ignoring the second question. "But as of this morning, we do know he has traveled to Scotland." He slid the folder across the table. "This man has seen your face?"

Laurent nodded.

"Then we *both* have a problem."

Laurent opened the seal and peered in without removing the contents. It contained a mobile phone, and a grainy photograph of what looked to be the man from King's College.

"He saw my face, but he doesn't know anything more," Laurent assured his handler.

"He saw your face and he knows that Ahmad is dead. If MI5 get him, then neither of us will be safe. You can be assured that the quicker you find and eliminate this witness, the better it will be for all of us. After which, we will also satisfy the second half of your contract."

Laurent canvassed the lobby. Better to follow and shoot this man and take his chances. But Laurent could not be certain he wasn't alone.

The man stood to leave. "If you succeed in Scotland what you failed to do in Cambridge, the money will be wired into your account, and you won't hear from me again. And I can also assure you that you won't leave London alive if you choose the option you are clearly contemplating."

Laurent did not respond.

"Since our little meeting last March was too brief for formalities, please allow me. My name is Danesh." He gathered his coat and scarf, and donned his hat. "I will be in touch."

CHAPTER
TWENTY-TWO

Secret Intelligence Service
London

Banastre Montjoy stood in the eighth-floor lift and wearily eyed the keypad before pressing level six. It was late afternoon, and he had been *summoned* to William Lindsay's office. That was the silly little word Berwyn Rees had used in his silly little note, delivered to Montjoy's office an hour earlier. For nearly thirty years, the head of section had been called, invited, requested, and *if you pleased* to meetings, but never had he been sent for like some nineteenth-century Dickensian clerk mustered to refill the coal bin in the foreman's office.

Fortunately, when he received the missive, Montjoy was three fingers into an eighteen-year-old, single malt whiskey from Highland Park. It was remarkable how well heather, cherry, peat, and vanilla could temper a summons.

William Lindsay was deputy chief of MI6, and his ascension through the service hierarchy had been as much the consequence of political allegiance as meritocracy, a rule that was typical to most intelligence services. But, he had come up with the old guard, and Montjoy had long acknowledged that Lindsay was not wholly lacking when it came to the managing of his heads of section. He had afforded Montjoy considerable leeway as Mohammad Ahmad's handler, and kept him in the loop after *Dalmatia* was moved out of Near East Section five years earlier.

Berwyn Rees, on the other hand, head of Europe Section and Lindsay's unofficial number two, was a scheming little hack who Montjoy thoroughly detested.

The lift came to a stop, and Montjoy nearly collided with Rees as he attempted to enter the car without looking up. The man was half a head shorter, and though ten years younger, was already losing his hair.

"Montjoy." Rees greeted him with a murine smirk as he stepped back. "I hope you are having a nice evening. So good of you to join us."

"My apologies for running behind schedule," was all Montjoy replied.

Rees beckoned Montjoy down the hallway with an embellished sweep of his hand. He followed the diminutive subordinate to Lindsay's office, where Rees announced their arrival like some bepowdered footman at a Victorian ball.

The deputy chief did not immediately look up, nor offer any kind of salutation, and Montjoy did not expect him to. But neither did he expect the other men who stood behind Lindsay's desk. Robert Riley, head of European Division at NCS, and Rees' equal at the CIA, Montjoy knew at arms-length. Beside him was John Edgerton, CIA station chief in London. Montjoy nodded at Riley, who, unlike Lindsay and Edgerton, had glanced up, though he did not return the silent acknowledgement.

"I hope you are having a nice evening, Montjoy," Lindsay finally said.

"Yes, sir, considering."

"Considering what?" Rees snapped.

Montjoy paused, calculating his response. Lindsay had a bad habit of allowing Rees to dictate meetings. What he was most curious about was why he had been called into in a mix of high-ranking Yanks without warning.

Rees did not wait for Montjoy to reply. "We would like to know—"

"We?" Montjoy inquired, knowing he needed to keep his counterpart off balance.

"Yes, *we*—" Rees hissed, visibly irritated at the interruption, "would like to know what you know concerning Ahmad's death."

Everyone in the room had drawn a bead on Montjoy, who sensed Rees taking pleasure in what he thought was coming.

Montjoy was caught off guard, but did not show it. "Meaning?" he responded after a measured pause, quickly weighing his options.

"Meaning," Rees shot back, "you got the call about Ahmad before anyone else, yet chose not to notify us immediately. Why?"

Ahmad's body had been discovered by a member of the King's College cleaning staff Friday morning, who alerted a passing professor, who notified Robert Adcock. Adcock, a provost who had made his way up the college hierarchy over a thirty-year period, remembered that a quiet, but promising, undergrad three decades earlier was himself, at least at one point, on the rise through the ranks at MI6, so Montjoy got the call. The problem was why he had sat on the information when Moore visited his office Friday afternoon. Now Rees was calling him out in front of his boss, and the Americans. Montjoy looked at Lindsay for some semblance of support, but the deputy chief only stared at him impassively. "I—*we*," Montjoy corrected himself and glanced at Rees, "wanted time to properly evaluate the situation—"

"How bloody long does it take to determine that a shared asset has been murdered?" Rees interjected, glancing at Riley and Edgerton.

Montjoy suppressed his irritation, at Rees personally, as well as the implication that SIS suddenly considered Ahmad, whom Montjoy had recruited and run, a mutually beneficial asset. Lindsay was out of bounds for allowing the meeting to progress in this manner. Robert Riley was an important colleague, particularly standing next to Lindsay as William Scott's proxy in a matter of such importance. SIS and the CIA had long shared a special bond, and a great deal of intelligence over the years. But despite the fact that Ahmad had been run out of both agencies, certain aspects of intelligence nonetheless warranted discretion. This was one such time.

Rees did not wait for Montjoy to respond to his redundant query. "Your delay cost us valuable time in which the killer could have been cornered and caught." Rees looked at Lindsay, who still said nothing. "Not to mention," Rees continued, "the

CIA could have assisted in the effort, had we been informed immediately." He should have stopped there. "Care to guess where Langley got their initial intelligence on this?"

"I imagine the same place you typically do, Berwyn, the telly," Montjoy calmly replied. He sensed the Americans stifle a laugh at Rees' expense, who shot him daggers. Rees struggled to counter, and Montjoy glanced at Lindsay.

The deputy chief stepped in for the first time. "What Berwyn is trying to suggest, is that, as an important asset of our collective organizations had been assassinated, perhaps it would have behooved both services to be in the same lane right from the gate."

An important asset? Try our most valuable informant in four bloody decades. Before Montjoy could respond, Rees sought to regain his footing. "You ran Ahmad for two decades."

It was a clumsy effort, and Montjoy took advantage. "Which begs the question, considering the professor was your man of late. Assuming, that is, you are aware of what's going on with your own assets."

Rees bristled again, and Lindsay, who sensed where the conversation was heading, cut him off. "Gentlemen, we need to focus our attention on an expedient course of action."

Rees again jumped into the mix. "Which I will personally oversee."

Montjoy noticed Lindsay say something quietly to Riley, who in turn relayed it to Edgerton, who nodded. It was clear to Montjoy that Rees had brought him in to serve as a scapegoat where the bungled communication with Langley was concerned. But that was incidental. Somebody was attempting to use Montjoy as cover.

"That will be all, Montjoy," Lindsay said, ending the meeting. "We will convene again tomorrow morning. Good evening."

Montjoy glanced again at Riley, who was shuffling the same papers he had been reviewing when Montjoy arrived. Rees gestured toward the hallway, and Montjoy turned to leave.

"Don't stray too far, old boy," Rees smirked as he shut the door.

Montjoy rode the lift back to his floor, and his waiting tumbler of scotch. He wasn't sure what was in play back in Lindsay's office, or how it would end. He was certain, however, of one thing. Where it began.

Rees.

CHAPTER
TWENTY-THREE

Rees shut the door loudly behind him as he reentered the office, causing Riley, Edgerton and Lindsay to look up simultaneously at the sudden noise.

"He's become a liability, William."

Lindsay furrowed his brow and gave a slight shake of the head as Rees circled behind the desk to where the group was still studying the intelligence splayed out before them.

The deputy chief turned to Riley and Edgerton. "Gentlemen, could I impose on you to give us a moment."

"Certainly," said Riley. Both men eyed Rees as they moved toward the door.

Rees smiled. "Sandra will see you to the conference room. I'll be along shortly."

He closed the door, again firmly, as the Americans left the office, and turned as abruptly.

Before he could speak, Lindsay cut him off. "Mind yourself in front of the Yanks, Berwyn. While we might apportion certain intelligence to our counterparts, we need not betray all our secrets."

"Montjoy is a walking breach of security. His stumbling up here half-battered is a beacon of the service's tireless inability to clean its own house."

"Regardless, we need not openly give them cause to question the efficacy of this office."

"The man's mere presence does that. That plonker has become an embarrassment."

"Might I remind you that the 'plonker,' as you put it, was a highly-decorated navy man."

"Whatever he's done is because of his name. Montjoy wouldn't be anything if his grandfather wasn't Sir Nigel Aldrich."

"Lineage only goes so far. I would mind what liberties you take in front of him. It is your neck you stick out—"

"It's his that should be on the block."

Lindsay said nothing, clearly lost in his own thoughts for a moment.

"And *Shepherd*?" Rees changed the subject.

"Yes—*Shepher*d—" Lindsay muttered to himself.

"Montjoy might be head of section," Rees noted, "but how much intelligence did Ahmad produce when he ran him? And *Dalmatia* had begun to bleed out before I took it over."

Lindsay regained his equilibrium. "*Dalmatia* produced more intelligence and asset acquisition in the Near East than any other program we've run out of SIS—while Montjoy ran it, I might add."

"I agree, *produced*. Montjoy has been resting on that laurel for too long. He needs to go, and if not soon and quietly, then it will be much louder, later on. I know the agency has a history of tolerating self-destructive behavior so long as it is contained to the self, but Montjoy—"

"I will deal with Montjoy in my own time," Lindsay responded curtly. "Until then, keep him isolated while we manage this bloody mess."

"With pleasure," Rees replied.

CHAPTER
TWENTY-FOUR

Southend-on-Sea
Essex, England

The briny scent from the mud flats along Hadleigh Ray Strait greeted Nasir Hajjar as he exited Gulshan Tandoori, an Indian restaurant a half-mile walk from Southend Victoria Station. His train, set to depart at the top half of the hour from Southend-on-Sea, would get him back to Liverpool Street just in time for a midnight meeting with his London supplier.

Hajjar had been in the seaside resort town for just under twenty-four hours, not nearly long enough to tend to his business. But, because he was meeting a proxy who represented his stake in the drug trade in southeast England—a venture Hajjar had undertaken without the prince's knowledge—he'd needed to keep his visit short and to the point. Which included cutting the throat of his go-between, who had skimmed off an incoming cargo of heroin from Turkey. Two of the man's associates, made to witness the murder, got the point.

Hajjar disliked dealing with the Turks, who had been running opium from the days of the Ottoman Empire. And since their modern counterparts controlled almost ninety percent of the heroin trade in Britain, he was left with little choice. It would have been less profitable and more dangerous to traffic directly through the cafes along Green Lanes, where foreigners were barred and the bulk of product moved. And because he was savvy enough to give a wide berth to the Bombers and Tottenham Boys, and other major drug players in London, as well as bin Halabi, who would condemn his venture, Hajjar was content to dabble on the fringes of a minor outfit that controlled sections of West Essex and East Kent.

His side business in drugs nearly equaled what he earned smuggling immigrants through the

Albanian gangs. The *Mafia Shqiptare* controlled the lion's share of the illicit sex trade in the U.K., and trafficked enough Balkan women to keep the brothels in Soho turning a fifteen million pound profit, per year. Hajjar complemented the supply of naïve runaways from Montenegro, Albania, and Romania, who fell prey to smugglers promising freedom and a green card, with older teenage girls from the Middle East. Over the last decade, the *Shqiptare* had allowed the Turks to profit off their prostitution racket, while the North London cartels turned a partial blind eye to the drug routes run by the Albanians. Between the two, Hajjar was in the process of making a small fortune.

He glanced at his watch, a Calatrava from the Genevian watchmaker Patek Philippe. It had been gifted from the King of Saud after Hajjar saved his nephew's life two decades earlier. While the cost of the Swiss timepiece was exorbitant, its value was immeasurable, and Hajjar had refused to replace it with other watches he had acquired over the years.

With his train set to leave in the next hour, Hajjar had enough time to find an open Wi-Fi signal. He had arranged to make contact with bin Halabi following the prince's meeting with Scotland Yard. The informal sit down had been extended as a courtesy to bin Halabi, considering that the murdered Cambridge professor was a subject of the Kingdom, as well as personally connected to the House of Saud. Ultimately, it was a fishing expedition on both sides, the prince to determine what the Met had learned of the killing, and they, to discern how much information could be disclosed to appease bin Halabi.

Hajjar casually but closely monitored both sides of the avenue as he neared the McDonalds on high street, near the University of Essex. The American fast food chain was relatively quiet, but it wouldn't have mattered if *Carnival* suddenly erupted. Operating in war-torn regions had taught Hajjar that safety was an illusion. Over the years, he had dispatched a handful of targets in broad daylight and on quiet city streets. Each of them blithely unaware as their final moments ticked down to the microsecond that brain matter and a bullet exited their frontal parietal lobe.

Hajjar slowed his entry into the restaurant long enough for the glassed façade to reflect what was behind him. The filth-streaked door had been propped ajar by a rolled-up magazine, and a stream of cold air whistled through the opening. Blackened grout on the foyer's tiled floor made its way around the registers and into the kitchen, past the counter clerk who was doing her best to ignore customers. Hajjar conducted a second visual sweep of the dining room and outside patio, and moved to an unoccupied table near the front exit.

Hajjar, rightfully so, had become paranoid that someone could too easily hack the details of EuroPen's business deals, so he had created a method to mask online communication, both with the prince, but especially, his own terrorist connections in Yemen. The process nearly guaranteed the anonymity that was necessary to remain as far removed from cyber oversight as possible. While no method was foolproof, his was far more effective than techniques popularized in movies and the media. Most of these were so easily bypassed, that one might as well email an invitation to intelligence listening stations.

Digital drops were especially susceptible to electronic eavesdropping. One technique, in particular, saved unsent conversations as drafts, to be accessed by shared users on cloud-based accounts. As no emails were transmitted, the perpetrators assumed they left no virtual tracks. For nearly a decade since the method had been successfully employed by al-Qaeda in planning the 2004 Madrid train bombings, software networking companies had created intercept technology that forwarded unsent messages left in the folders of targeted addresses to shadow accounts set up and monitored by the NSA, and GCHQ.

The key, Hajjar knew, was to ensure that the ISPs he used were ones which had not been tagged for closer scrutiny. To do this, new laptops were purchased on a regular basis. Batteries were removed so that the device would not transmit a traceable signal, while prearranged email addresses were created and used in public places that offered free, open internet.

Once at a cyber meet location, batteries were reinserted and computers powered on for the first time. Network software was downloaded that utilized onion routing, which anonymized internet presence by bouncing activity through thousands of relays across the world. All communication was further masked with a PGP data encryption program, which jumbled messages between sender and receiver. When the online session was complete, the battery of the laptop was again removed, and the device discarded.

Even if an intelligence service was savvy enough to isolate a single-use throwaway account for deeper scrutiny, and untangle layers of relays and encryption, by the time any team could be dispatched to signal locations, Hajjar would be long gone.

A footprint of a footprint.

He could stay one step ahead of the Americans and the British by turning their over-reliance on complex snooping techniques against them. Much the same way low-level insurgents in the Gulf War had bested similar monitoring techniques by transmitting signals from mopeds that stayed constantly on the move. Ultimately, the strength of high-tech Western spy services would become their weakness.

Hajjar booted up his laptop, and watched several oversized patrons enter the fast food restaurant. He did not possess the typical Middle Eastern opinion of Westerners, as that of infidels and Zionists. That type of hyperbole, he knew from living in England long enough to enjoy its excesses, was ineffective. But he did view them as lazy, indifferent, and undisciplined.

Only a people in the throes of moral decline would allow themselves to be freely monitored by their own spy agencies, who in turn documented every facet of their lives. Email, Skype, Facebook, internet searches, phone calls, texts, financial information, health records, educational background, essentially, everything that was said and done was being recorded, catalogued, and stored on massive, multi-exabyte Cray computers in Utah.

The masses were indifferent to the ramifications of such intrusion, believing that, as they had nothing to hide, there was nothing to fear. Other than governments whose very nature it was to be distrustful and duplicitous. And if their leaders were of the same mindset of Cardinal Richelieu, who four hundred years earlier boasted he could find reason to hang the most honest man in France from any one paragraph he penned? Or Lev Beria, head of Stalin's NKVD, who famously asserted, *show me the man and I'll show you the crime.* Hajjar reasoned that a people who so clearly took their freedom for granted, were destined, and deserved, to lose it.

He inserted a new thumb drive into an inexpensive Acer laptop purchased the day before, and transferred preloaded PortableTor software. He accessed a webpage, signed into the disposable account, and saw one unread message waiting. Hajjar opened the attached document, and with a smartphone he had purchased earlier, snapped a photo of the file.

Hajjar sent a return email with the word, "unsubscribe," a reply that the message had been received and read. He exited the McDonald's, and continued down high street toward the Southend Pier, which, at well over a mile in length, was the longest in the world. Hajjar only needed the first hundred meters, where he discarded the laptop into the Thames Estuary.

On his phone, he opened the screenshot captured from the computer. It was a message from the prince.

Must meet. Tomorrow. Time and place of acquaintance.

He turned, and began to make his way back to the station. The prince meant the Gloucester Arms, in London. Hajjar had saved bin Halabi's life outside the pub twenty-three years earlier at just after seven in the evening. The prince had tasked Hajjar with conducting his own investigation, quietly and behind the scenes, into Ahmad's death. They were not supposed to make contact again for one week, but that night, bin Halabi was calling for a meeting that directly violated the strict protocols Hajjar had long put in place and relied upon. He quickened his pace.

Something was wrong.

CHAPTER TWENTY-FIVE

Secret Intelligent Service
London

Berwyn Rees was still fuming as he walked to the conference room where Riley and Edgerton waited to be further debriefed. He was furious foremost at Montjoy, running off at his gob during the meeting, which only added to the CIA's perception that MI6 was allowing certain inmates to run the proverbial asylum. The man had made him look like a fool in front of the Americans. And what was Lindsay's reaction? *Keep him isolated*, whatever the bloody hell that meant. Montjoy was as good as tits up, and had been for the better part of five years. The same period Rees had been orchestrating his gradual removal from anything to do with *Dalmatia.*

Moreover, the man was a drunk, and if he weren't the scion of one of MI6's most respected vice chiefs, he'd be a drunk on leave. A dismissed head of section whose only exploit was one he had stumbled into by happenstance while a young operative under Geoffrey Charlton. Montjoy had ridden coattails off the massively lucrative operation that had sprung from the intelligence supplied by Mohammad Ahmad for too long. Why Lindsay was content only to cordon Montjoy off like some curious bystander at the scene of a wrecked lorry was lost on Rees.

Now he had to deal with the Yanks. They had anchored themselves to Ahmad a decade earlier, running him as *Charlemagne,* with the "cooperation" of MI6. Over the last five years, the professor had obviously begun to cater more to the CIA, who seemed far less willing to reciprocate where their highest-level intel gleaned from Ahmad was concerned. Now they showed up with hat in hand, suddenly willing to band together like the best of mates. Put the old team that won the war back on the pitch.

Bullocks.

"Robert. John." Rees said as he entered the office.

"Good of you to humor us on such short notice," Riley replied, without glancing up from the file he was reading.

"My apologies on the lateness of the hour—"

Riley interrupted him, "I see you're still taking your cues from Montjoy."

Bloody Montjoy. Rees seethed, but did not show it. "You'll be coordinating through my office on this one."

"What do we know so far?" Edgerton asked.

There is no we. You have nothing. Rees opened a binder and laid out the same photographs of Sean Garrett they had been viewing in Lindsay's office. "*We*," Rees accentuated, "believe this to be the man who killed the professor."

"Any idea who he is?" Riley asked.

"We don't know yet. We've run him through our system and nothing hits. It's not the best angle or quality for facial recognition, but it should have pulled up something. It hasn't. This photo here," Rees pointed to the one from Saturday morning, "was taken off CCTV near Manor House. He was involved in a punch-up with a couple of local ne'er-do-wells. He mashed them up pretty good. They're both still in the hospital."

"We would like to talk to them."

"You're welcome to, but it's a dead end. Both men claim they were victims of an attempted robbery as they left a nearby pub. They say the man was an American. That's about it."

Riley showed no reaction, but Rees caught him stealing a subtle glance at Edgerton. "Anything else?"

"MI5 have segregated all mobile phone communication from the weekend within a four-block area of the altercation, and came up with a call placed ten minutes earlier. Scotland Yard was referenced, and the computers tagged the conversation for review." Rees pushed several stapled sheets across the table. "It was a fairly nondescript exchange, on the surface discussing some sort of trip, which we believe to be code for something else. We isolated both mobile numbers, and put a trace on each signal. One routed to a dead end in London, but the other was emanating, as of three hours ago, from Edinburgh."

"That it?"

"For the moment, but we will send your way whatever we get."

"That would be appreciated, Berwyn," Riley said, suddenly more deferential and accommodating. "Can you shoot this over to our London office right away?"

"Of course."

"We'll run it through NGI." Riley referred to the FBI's state-of-the-art billion dollar upfit of its biometric center in Clarksburg, West Virginia, which included a prototype facial recognition program. "Let's sit down tomorrow and see where we are."

"Of course," Rees said again, as he stood and shook hands with both men. "Good evening."

"Yep," was all Riley replied.

Rees left the meeting gobsmacked. Riley had taken the intelligence too casually, considering the absolute sodded-up situation in which both services now found themselves.

Something wasn't right.

CHAPTER TWENTY-SIX

It was late evening, and the last river ferry service had departed Vauxhall St. George Pier. Montjoy sat in his office with his back to the Thames and assessed what he knew. Aside from the obvious, that *Shepherd* was dead and most certainly *Dalmatia* would not be far behind, there was an orchestrated effort to circle the wagons where Ahmad's assassination was concerned.

Earlier that day, Montjoy had received a call from Alastair Clarke, at MI5. For anyone who might have listened in, the chat was cordial and served as catch-up. For those who liaised between SIS and the Security Service, Montjoy and Clarke enjoyed a co-operative working relationship. Few were aware they had become fast friends thirty-five years earlier as Royal Marines stationed together in the Balkans.

Shortly after the conversation, Montjoy received two photos from Clarke's office. They showed a man leaving King's College at the time Ahmad was murdered. Likely the same man who was involved in a street fight near Manor House early Saturday morning, and whose mobile phone had been tracked, and was still transmitting, from Edinburgh, Scotland.

The same photos Riley, Edgerton, and Rees had been studying on Lindsay's desk, but had chosen not to divulge to Montjoy.

Abbot knocked on the office door and entered, carrying a folder. "Good evening, Monty."

"That depends. Do you have it?"

"One favor called in and two tickets for Sunday's fixture at White Hart Lane later, yes."

Abbot handed Montjoy the file and stood back with his arms folded over his chest.

Montjoy ripped the seal and emptied a bundle of A4 paper and one flash drive onto his desk. "Who did you go through at SIGNIT?"

"One analyst only, who shall remain nameless, for your sake and hers. She didn't ask who was asking, and I didn't tell her. She'll likely connect the dots, but these are only a few pages of line usage details from the thousands she processes on any given week. Just a jumble of numbers to her."

"Indeed," Montjoy replied, as he looked over the first few pages, lined with neatly stacked columns of ten digit combinations, mobile phone numbers, to and from.

"Care to enlighten?" Abbot asked cautiously.

"Not at the moment." Then Montjoy added, "for your sake and hers."

"Perhaps—"

"Thank you, Gavin." Montjoy glanced towards the door.

"Yes, sir," Abbot replied, clearly disappointed. "Anything else?"

"Not at the moment."

Montjoy watched him turn and leave. He smiled, knowing that Abbot was likely more irritated at giving away football tickets for the Chelsea match at Tottenham, than having put his neck out. Montjoy turned his attention back to the ream of numbers. When he realized he couldn't muster the punch to turn the pages, much less focus on what was splattered across the paper like incoherent binary code, Montjoy did the next best thing. He poured himself another whiskey.

If only everything that came across his desk went down so easily.

"Rise and shine."

Montjoy heard the voice reverberate, as if through a tunnel. He pulled himself off his desk and became immediately aware of both Abbot, and a lingering headache. Worse, Montjoy noticed that he had failed to finish his scotch, which was now an undrinkable, watery mess.

Abbot, always subtle in his rebukes, added, "hard work demands a kip now and then."

Montjoy forewent the faint smile he typically flashed when Abbot waded in to comment about his drinking. He needed to refocus, and discarded the near empty fifth of Highland Park, as he shoved the intelligence from A Branch onto a shelf behind his desk.

"I need you to collect everything we have on *Shepherd,* and *Dalmatia.*"

"Everything?"

"Yes, every bloody scrap," Montjoy replied irritably. To counter Rees' gambit meant circling what wagons he had left.

Abbot had already turned to leave, when Montjoy added, "and Gavin, strictly back room on this one."

"*No words but mum,*" Abbot replied, quoting Shakespeare as he disappeared around the doorjamb.

Montjoy wondered if he was aware that the duchess to whom the famous words were uttered, was ultimately betrayed and banished.

CHAPTER
TWENTY-SEVEN

Edinburgh

The booking hall of Waverley Station was crowded. David Laurent had arrived that morning from London, and for the better part of the day, mixed with travelers searching out journey times on the main digital board. Standing under the natural light that filtered through the massive, glassed rotunda in the center of the complex, the assassin sipped a coffee and reread a newspaper he had purchased at W. H. Smith.

Laurent's mind wandered momentarily off his assignment as he admired the mammoth structure.

Waverley was a mix of old Victorian and new modern, appropriate in that it split Old and New Town Edinburgh, and, covering one hundred thousand square meters in the heart of the city, was one of the largest depots in the U.K., second only to Waterloo. Having passed through countless stations around the world, he had come to appreciate the distinct culture of most of them. The great ones each had something special to offer, but for Laurent, Waverley bested them all.

He finished perusing his copy of *The Scotsman* for the third time, and once again exited the station, this time through Waverley Mall. After the unpleasantness in Cambridge and London, Laurent recognized that in order to regain momentum and get himself cleanly out of the U.K., he needed to tighten his environment. He was lucky to have outrun the misfortune at King's College, and outlive his mistake with the Savoy, but knew he would not be afforded a third chance.

Prior to leaving London, Laurent had booked a room at the Bonham Hotel in Drumshuegh Gardens, Edinburgh, under the name Thomas Martin. The assassin then checked into the Café Royal Hotel in the West End of London as David Laurent. After paying for the suite in full, he purchased a one-way flight on Air Berlin, London to Prague, also as Laurent, scheduled to depart Stansted Airport in three days. If any intelligence service was truly on to him, the dead-end trail would deter their attention long enough for

Laurent to deal with his target in Scotland, and get out of the U.K. under his new alias.

He had also severed the direct link with his handler from Kensington Gardens. Two hours earlier, Laurent had purchased a preloaded, pay-as-you-go phone, and concealed the one given him by the man called Danesh behind a ticket machine attached to a support pole in the middle of Waverley Station. He had charged the battery full, set the ringer on silent, and programmed the number to be forwarded to his new throwaway mobile. He could now receive calls without having to worry about transmitting his exact location. If anyone were capable of unraveling the layers of his misdirection in England, they would not find Laurent at the terminus of a traced line in Edinburgh.

Seventy-two hours. That was the length of time Laurent had given himself to find and eliminate his witness from King's College. He had not killed so many and become rich only to die in Scotland before he could retire and enjoy that wealth. If he did not hear from his handler in that time, or find the man on his own, Laurent would take the car he had hired and parked near Grassmarket, and drive to Glasgow. From there, the man who would now go by the name Thomas Martin, would catch a ferry to Ireland, hop an Aer Lingus flight to Brussels, and disappear for good.

CHAPTER
TWENTY-EIGHT

London

Sam Anderton walked along the fringe of St. James's Park, within sight of 10 Downing Street and in range of a construction crew that had been repairing a broken water main for the better part of a week. The Metropolitan Police sergeant was directly connected, albeit from a distance, to one of the most recognized front doors in the world. Her grandmother was a second cousin of Winston Churchill, and one of her earliest memories was of being shown a photograph of the prime minister flashing his famous V sign outside the residence in 1943, while her grandfather proudly reminisced that their family was personally linked to that moment in history.

Anderton thought about flashing her own sign at several workers who had taken a break to let her know, loudly and once again, that she had not gone unnoticed on her daily walk to work. At twenty-eight, the sergeant was exactly where she wanted to be, her parent's dream for her notwithstanding. She was tall, nearly six feet, and her blonde hair and olive-toned complexion, the byproduct of an English father and Welsh mother, allowed her to be mistaken for any number of European nationalities. The confident boys at university had used that assumption to chat her up, and Anderton often used the fact that she spoke fluent German and French to her advantage more than a few times during those years.

After taking a degree in law from the University of Warwick, which gave her mother great pride and her father even greater hope, she immediately joined the National Fast Track Programme at the Metropolitan Police Service, much to her parent's chagrin. But it was not Anderton's intent to pursue a career at Scotland Yard. She saw it as a stepping stone to her ultimate goal, Interpol.

She had risen quickly through the ranks, and had already received considerable accommodation by the time a widely respected chief inspector brought her under his wing. It was with Roger Holland that she really began to earn her stripes, and his intuition that she could eventually become a top-notch inspector was soon proven well-placed. He also became a second father of sorts, so much that she trusted Holland enough to divulge that her ambition was not the police headquarters in London, but Lyon, France.

The rain had let up momentarily, and Anderton decided to walk the entire distance to headquarters rather than jump a Tube line. She would not miss the chaos of the Underground because she knew she would find it at work—the Met was in the process of moving, and in a perpetual state of disorder. The older staff complained about having to leave an iconic location where they had spent an entire career, while the younger officers were irritated at being the ones who were expected to do much of the heavy lifting.

Holland smiled as Anderton entered his office, something her congenial boss did no matter the time of day or mood he was in. The whole of the West End could be ablaze, she once told him, and he would still be cheery. Holland had answered with, "*A man's as miserable as he thinks he is*," quoting Seneca, the Roman philosopher.

"Good morning, Sam."

"Hiya, chief. What news?"

"That's my line, mind you, but since you asked." He handed her several sheets of paper that constituted that day's early briefings. "Have a look."

Anderton skimmed the report while Holland continued his limping effort at packing boxes, all the while muttering to himself.

"This came from GCHQ?"

"MI5 confirmed that the number was triangulated to a housing estate near Finsbury Park on Saturday. The person they believe made the call was involved in a fight shortly thereafter, and it is the same man who was caught on CCTV leaving the building that housed Mohammad Ahmad's office at Cambridge, near to the time he was killed. As of yesterday, the mobile was transmitting from Edinburgh."

"Where are we on this?"

"Everyone is hustling teams here, there, and everywhere. The coordination, like always, will come later."

"Who's taking the lead?"

"Everybody, now that we have one," Holland replied. He had stopped packing, and was shuffling through a set of files on his desk. "I want you to concentrate all your efforts on Ahmad."

"And the key?"

"The key, I think, is the key."

"I mean, have you mentioned it to Healey?"

"I will if it goes somewhere. For now, he is busy chasing this new lead, and the press. Though, if I had to guess, I'd wager his office is ready to close ranks."

"And if he does?"

"Then we'll end up reading about what happens, like everyone else," Holland replied. "Sam, I need you to take lead on this, while I manage the investigation from here. It will allow me to put Healey off, if need be, and afford you leeway to investigate without MI5 lording over our shoulder."

It was the first time Anderton had been given the point on an investigation, and she smiled. "Yes, sir."

"We're on the clock, mind you, so off you go. Find me something that everyone else has ignored or dismissed."

CHAPTER
TWENTY-NINE

A Hackney carriage, London's ubiquitous version of a taxi, motored past Robert Riley and sprayed a wall of dirty street water onto the sidewalk. He was one block from Bloomsbury Square Gardens, the city's oldest square, and five minutes from a meeting with two men he had handpicked to accompany him before he departed Langley. The SOG operators had flown in on separate commercial flights, which had landed twelve and fourteen hours, respectively, after Riley's official arrival on a government Gulfstream V aircraft.

The Head of Europe Division for the Directorate of Operations had just come from a meeting at Grosvenor Square with John Edgerton, CIA station chief in London, which followed a debriefing with Berwyn Rees at MI6. It was clear Rees had not been completely forthcoming where Ahmad's murder was concerned, and Riley could gauge William Lindsay's undersized pit bull well enough to know that he suspected the CIA was withholding information from them as well.

Riley also knew that the circus surrounding Ahmad's death only added to Edgerton's headache of a week, during which time he had been thrust back into the middle of an ongoing pissing contest between U.S. intelligence services battling for control of operations in Britain. Central Intelligence had long been responsible for appointing their station chiefs, and had been tasked with oversight of data at rest and intelligence on the ground. The National Security Agency was in charge of intercepting and managing data in transit. Langley wanted more leeway to move into Fort Meade's cyber territory, while the NSA argued that, because it was much larger and had more of a physical presence in England, it should be given jurisdiction over all covert activities in the country.

In the meantime, the CIA's most important Middle East asset to date was lying in a freezer in South London, while the trail of his assassin got even colder.

After thirty-five years with the CIA, and nine of those with the Directorate of Operations, Riley had come to appreciate the complexities of his own position, as well as the necessity of the SOG. The Special Operations Group was part of the Special Activities Division, itself a department of the DO. One of its primary purposes was to carry out intelligence gathering and paramilitary operations where the government did not want to be seen as directly involved, and where plausible deniability could be later claimed. The type of covert action Riley knew to be paramount for protecting national security.

It had not always been the case. He had been recruited into the agency three years after Gerald Ford signed Executive Order 11905. As a New England born and bred political science major fresh out of Dartmouth, Riley had fervently agreed with the president's attempt in 1976 to rein in the rampant lawlessness of certain factions within the intelligence community by banning, among other things, political assassinations.

Over the last three decades, the tidy corner of Riley's early black and white idealism had been replaced with a nearly borderless gray expanse, governed by a moral relativism that he recognized was necessary to keep the playing field remotely level and safe. Which meant dealing with specific problems away from oversight, and killing certain people off the books.

Over the same period, Riley had become intolerant of the politicians who parked themselves on the sidelines and remained willfully ignorant of the need to operate with this mindset. It was an outlook that was intellectually dishonest and detached from reality, and one that routinely spread through the halls of power like an airborne sickness. The irony was that the same people who loudly opposed profiling young, single Muslim males, were the first ones to decry how a group of Saudi jihadists were able to fly two Boeing 767s into the World Trade Center. Give any of them the choice to fly on a plane where everyone had been "unfairly" profiled by their standards, compared to one where spot security checks had been conducted, and Riley knew which flight each of those hypocritical bastards would choose for themselves and their families every time.

Riley entered the square and walked past the statue of Charles Fox, famous Whig supporter of the patriot cause during the American Revolution, to a small bench opposite a large group of children on the playground. He opened a copy of *The*

Times, but kept an eye rotating between park entrances. Almost immediately, two men entered the south gate, each scanning the area as they walked toward him.

"Sir," Brian Bishop said, as he stopped several feet away and continued to monitor the square.

"Bishop. Ward," Riley answered, as Travian "Tre" Ward nodded.

The two operators were among the best SOG had recruited over the last decade, and both had come out of JSOC, the Joint Special Operations Command. JSOC, itself a component command of USSOCOM, United States Special Operations Command, had been formed in the wake of *Operation Eagle Claw,* the disastrous failure to rescue hostages from the U.S. Embassy in Iran in 1980.

Based out of Fort Bragg, JSOC's purpose was to study, plan, and execute special operations worldwide. Its most dangerous and covert assignments fell to the Special Missions Units, which regularly recruited its operators from the Army's Ranger and DELTA units, the Navy's DEVGRU— formerly Seal Team Six— and the Air Force's STS. The SMUs were tasked with classified direct action around the world, and were nearly as secretive as the Special Operations Group. Both units served as the president's private end-around to endless committee delays and partisan political dithering, and JSOC and SAD/SOG had on occasion combined its forces, including *Operation Neptune Spear*, which had located and eliminated Osama bin Laden four years earlier.

Brian Bishop was cut from the traditional operator mold, and hailed from exactly where one would assume by his manner, appearance, and lingo, Southern California. He had grown up bent on following in the military footsteps of his father, two older brothers, and one sister. After graduating from the Air Force Academy, intent on becoming a pilot, Bishop had instead navigated toward pararescue. After three years as a pararescue jumper, which included commendation for his actions at the Battle of Takur Ghar, during the invasion of Afghanistan, he began basic training to become a combat controller. Two years later, Bishop earned his scarlet beret, and had been with the 24th Special Tactics Squadron, attached to AFSOC, Air Force Special Operations Command, for seven years.

Tre Ward had been a JSOC DELTA operator attached to the mission to kill bin Laden, and the DO had recruited him in the wake of its success. With an utterly unique background—born to a mother from the bayous of Louisiana who was raised in Guyana, and a father from Wales who was brought up in South Africa—Ward had grown up outside of Georgetown, South Carolina. He was certainly the only student in the entire state, if not the country, who was fluent in French, Spanish, Afrikaans, Welsh, and Scottish Gaelic. He excelled both in the classroom and on the football field, and accepted a full scholarship to play cornerback at the University of South Carolina. Four years later, having bypassed two seasons in which he was projected to go no later than the third round of the NFL draft, Ward graduated summa cum laude from the Honors College, and joined the army the next week. He breezed through the Ranger Assessment and Selection Program, and after three years with the 75th Ranger Regiment, was recruited into the 1st SFOD-D. Six months later, he graduated from the Operator Training Course, and just fourteen months into his Delta career, was recruited by the NCS into its Special Operations Group.

Like many operators who reached the highest echelon of Special Forces, both men carried themselves with a controlled, but predatory, resolve. At sixty years old and nearly thirty pounds overweight, Riley admired the skill and discipline of the men he sent around the world to destroy and kill in the name of peace.

Today, Riley needed his operators to quickly and quietly locate a man whom British Intelligence was in the process of isolating as the assassin of Mohammad Ahmad.

Riley handed Ward an envelope with five photos of Sean Garrett. Two were copies taken from the King's College and Manor House cameras. Three others were computer-manipulated likenesses that Langley had simulated of Garrett with long hair and no beard, short hair and beard, and short hair with no beard. Also included were GPS geolocation maps that pinpointed Garrett's movement between London and Edinburgh, as well as two disposable phones.

"Target is coded *Acolyte*. Operation is *Whiplash*," Riley said as he donned a pair of sunglasses. "Teams are in place in Edinburgh and London, and you will coordinate through an agency asset, a man named John Campion, who will make contact once you are in Scotland. Assuming we get *Acolyte* in country, he will be debriefed at the safe house in Glasgow, and flown out of Perth."

"And operating under the assumption that *Acolyte* will be noncooperative once we locate him?" Bishop asked.

Riley paused a moment. "Then you do your job, but he leaves with us one way or the other."

Bishop nodded, as Ward slipped the folder into his backpack.

"Gentlemen, I cannot stress the need to roll everything up and be gone before our English counterparts get too far down this rabbit hole," Riley said. "Find him."

CHAPTER THIRTY

Edinburgh

It was nearing midnight. Garrett sat by the window of his room at the Waverley and watched the driving rain mix with the lights from the base of Edinburgh Castle, which cloaked the medieval fortress in an ominous black and orange glow. The weather hadn't so far dampened the spirits of late night Edinburghers, and the revelry kept Princes Street animated, and him awake. He had not moved for the better part of the evening, having missed dinner, but not several glasses of Irish whiskey. The vigilance had made Garrett tired and hungry, and he decided to leave the hotel and walk the city in order to clear his head.

The temperature had dropped into the upper forties, though the wind made it feel considerably colder, and Garrett drew the collar closed on a new coat as he stepped outside. A day earlier, he had tossed the outfit that had been imprinted on cameras from Cambridge to London to Edinburgh, for a pair of dark jeans, a black cashmere sweater over a white t-shirt, Doc Martin boots, a black vest, and a Millerain waterproof down jacket.

A tram passed as he crossed Princes Street, and several students banged on the window, yelling something in a drunken stupor. The rain continued to blow in sheets as Garrett sought momentary shelter beneath the portico of the Royal Scottish Academy. He joined several late-night revelers, including a mixed group of middle-aged women who were dressed like they worked at the Burke and Hare, a gentlemen's club near Grassmarket. The establishment was named after the famous team of serial killers who operated in Edinburgh during the early nineteenth century, ultimately murdering sixteen victims and selling their corpses to a local surgeon before being caught.

One of the women, more than a little lagered, teetered close to Garrett.

"How much to rent you till morning, luv?" she asked, nearly falling over as she grabbed his arm.

Hen night out.

Garrett played along. "Early birds out for a big worm?"

"Cute and clever," a friend chimed in. "Come on then, let us borrow a kiss. I promise I'll give it back."

"I'm certain I can't afford it," he joked, wondering what either of them might indeed give him. The jest was lost on both the women, and Garrett prepared to bid them goodnight when the one he was supporting suddenly tipped over backward. As her friends moved in to help, Garrett used the momentary confusion to slip down a side staircase and exit the portico.

He headed into New Town via the Mound, a steep grade that separated Princes Street and the Royal Mile. Wanting to avoid the main thoroughfare, Garrett instead cut through Milne's Close, one of the city's numerous, and iconic, narrow stone passageways that fed directly to the high street. He looked for a fish and chip takeaway, but doubted he would find one so close to the posh shopping street that ran from Edinburgh Castle to Holyrood Palace, the residence of the British Monarchy when in Scotland.

Instead, Garrett stopped at Deacon Brodie's Tavern, and ordered a ploughman's sandwich. The establishment was a typical Edinburgh pub, the quintessential Scottish experience. Like so many eating establishments across the U.K., it had been refitted to cater to a clientele that demanded better quality than had long given the island its poor culinary reputation. The recent influx of diverse nationalities allowed Britain to better compete with its European counterparts, and it was no coincidence that the national dish of England was not bangers and mash, nor Yorkshire pudding, but chicken tikka masala, an Indian dish.

While the tavern fare might not have been unique, its namesake was. William Brodie, the inspiration for Robert Louis Stevenson's *The Strange Case of Dr. Jekyll and Mr. Hyde*, remained one of Edinburgh's most notorious citizens, of any era. A respected cabinetmaker and city councilor by day, Brodie was a womanizing cad, thief, and gambling reprobate after hours. He used his skill as a lock and key repairman to rob the residences of Edinburgh's wealthiest families, until he was finally caught, convicted, and hung before a throng of forty thousand onlookers in 1788.

Garrett paid for his takeaway, and headed back up the Royal Mile. As he downed the ham, cheese, beetroot and rocket sandwich, he considered his options. With his contact a no-show, they were limited. He could travel back into England in the hopes of clearing initial security checks at Heathrow on his original credentials. If he was lucky, Garrett would be back in the States by this time tomorrow. But, it was an incredibly risky gambit. If his identity was compromised and his passport flagged, he would be detained, and authorities would make short work of him. Garrett could offer no alibi, nor any viable explanation of his movements for the last seventy-two hours that would stand up to scrutiny. He doubted MI5 would buy that he liked to travel to London and wander around tenement housing in the middle of the night, beating up local troublemakers.

He could chance traveling to the European mainland via train, which would free him to move between most countries without having to brandish a passport over each new border. The problem was the U.K. was not part of the Schengen Agreement, which governed unfettered travel throughout the Eurozone. Garrett could step off the Eurostar with no issues in Paris, but he would first need to clear passport control in England. Even if he happened to make it out of Britain, and Europe, there was no guarantee his credentials would get him back into the U.S. Moreover, he would be forced to buy a last-minute ticket with cash, which would set off warning bells across the known universe.

Garrett finished his meal and was back where he started, Milne's Close. He glanced up the Esplanade, toward the entrance of the castle. The street was empty, with the exception of a lone figure walking towards him at a weave, and singing in a low, incoherent baritone. Garrett stepped aside to let the man stagger past, when he suddenly wavered unsteadily and barreled into him. Garrett threw out his hands to support both of them, as the man mumbled a disjointed apology.

"Heads up!" Garrett protested, as he forcefully attempted to right the man and turn him back onto the sidewalk.

"Leave it out!" the man bellowed, wildly flailing his arms and cursing.

Garrett stepped backward to leave the drunk to his business, which was certain to include retching everywhere at any moment. In a flash, the man spun, too fast for his age and too agile for his state of inebriation. He shoved Garrett into the shadow of the passageway, in from the rain and out of view of the street. As Garrett attempted to regain his balance and counter the man's lunge, his heel clipped the corner of the cobblestone threshold. He slipped and smacked his head against a corner of the stone archway. Everything went black as Garrett fell back into the darkness of the close.

CHAPTER THIRTY-ONE

The sound echoed around the cold, wet confines of the close. Garrett rolled toward a state of semi-awareness, his ability to focus dulled by the ringing in his ears. He heard the voice again, more clearly this time, whisper at him in a gravelly tone.

"Wakey wakey, my dear."

A thump to his midriff partly knocked Garrett's breath out, but jolted him back into full consciousness. Standing over him, silhouetted by what small light filtered down from the entrance of the tunnel, was a man who looked to be in his sixties, but was likely a decade younger. He was dressed smartly, in dark trousers, a white button down shirt, and a long beige raincoat with the collar turned up. His hair was slicked back and full, but thinning, and he had a noticeable scar that ran several inches down from under his right earlobe. In one hand was a semi-automatic pistol with a suppressor attached, and in his other, Garrett's Beretta.

Garrett thought to ask the man who he was and what he wanted, but knew that the query was clichéd and pointless. Heavy rain pounded the stairway where it met the sidewalk, and sounded like the after-hours white noise of an outdated television, drowning out everything around them.

"Who are you—?" Garrett asked anyway.

"And what do I want?" the man cut him off. "That's a stupid question to ask someone holding two guns."

Garrett pushed himself partially upright as the man stepped back and surveyed the entryway of the close. Garrett's faculties had cleared enough to better assess his situation. "I assume you're not here to shoot me, or you would have done it and been on your way."

"Then why am I here?" John Campion asked sarcastically, "leveling a Sig on someone who wanders around like a confused git when its cats and dogs out? You should have known the Scott Monument was a bust within five minutes."

Garrett understood. Dismayed at his own laxity, he made an attempt at levity. "You're supposed to be wearing a blue track suit."

"So I was told." The man was American, though Garrett thought he could detect an inconsistent British inflection in his speech.

"You're CIA?"

Campion laughed. "I'm M.I.A. The one they call when dealing with a class A cock-up."

"I assume you're referring to this goatfuck of an operation. It was compromised the moment I set foot in King's College."

Campion ignored the comment. "We need to know what happened with the professor."

Garrett recounted everything that had occurred since he arrived in England up to that evening, paying specific attention to details surrounding the timeline on either side of Thursday's events.

When Garrett finished, Campion added, "you left out the part where I got the jump on you like some ingénue on prom night." Before Garrett could reply, he added, "be at the original meet location tomorrow at midday, with a recent photograph." Campion handed him a phone. "Single-use only."

Garrett took it, and stood.

Campion turned to leave. "Get out of Edinburgh. I'll ring and let you know where to pick up your new credentials. And I shouldn't have to tell you to stay the fuck away from very public, public houses like Deacon Brodies."

Garrett ignored the reproach. "My gun?"

The man flashed the Beretta. "You mean this toy?" Instead, he handed Garrett his Sig Sauer P250, a .45 caliber. "Don't hurt yourself," he said as he moved down the steps and back toward the Mound.

Garrett pocketed the powerful handgun, and then called after his contact. "What do I call you?"

Campion thought for a moment, and then said with a laugh, "Deacon."

CHAPTER THIRTY-TWO

Secret Intelligence Service
London

"Have a seat." Montjoy gestured to the burgundy Churchill leather chair opposite his desk. Abbot could not remember having sat in it once in his four years at MI6. In fact, he was certain he could count the number of times he had done something other than stand in the same, thread-worn spot in front of Montjoy's dark mahogany desk when the business of the day brought him to the office.

The stack of documents, folders, and photos which had been gathered on Ahmad's murder were sorted into haphazard piles that Abbot assumed was supposed to constitute some semblance of order. To him, it looked like a paper bomb had detonated. He desperately wanted to send Montjoy away so he could properly organize the disaster.

Montjoy glanced up and smiled, having noticed Abbot eyeing his desk. "It's like a horrid itch you can't scratch, isn't it?"

"No, I'm fine," Abbot smiled back, lying. "I'm sure there's some method to your madness."

"Not really, because there's no particularly good place to begin." Before Abbot could suggest the obvious, Montjoy caught him off guard. "Why don't you tell me what you know about *Dalmatia* that you shouldn't, and I'll fill you in on the rest."

Abbot measured his response, unsure of how his boss would react to what he had gleaned over the years. "*Shepherd* is a highest-priority asset, and I'd guess from all the commotion over the last week, that Ahmad is, or was connected to, said asset."

"And *Dalmatia?*"

"Assuming you're not referring to the ancient region of Croatia on the Adriatic Sea, I assume it's part of *Shepherd*."

"Well done." Montjoy hoped he would be able to keep Abbot on permanent loan from GCHQ, but doubted it. The young man was on a higher track. "It's the other way around. *Shepherd* preceded

Dalmatia, but *Dalmatia* ultimately became the umbrella for all intelligence that originated from *Shepherd.*"

"So the professor is *Shepherd?*"

"Was," Montjoy corrected. "And with him dead, it's likely *Dalmatia* will soon follow."

"Why?"

"Because the lion's share of intelligence we gathered under *Dalmatia* was through Ahmad."

"And the significance of the name?" Abbot asked. He knew British Intelligence had a tendency for cheek when it came to the naming of some of its programs. During World War II, MI5 ran a counter-espionage operation that involved turning German agents from the *Abwehr,* the Nazi counterpart of British military intelligence, who had been apprehended in England as deep cover spies for the Fatherland. Under John Cecil Masterman, the *Twenty Committee* employed the Double-Cross system to great success over the course of the war. The name was derived from the Roman numerals, XX, for double-cross, hence twenty.

"*Dalmatia* is derived from the Illyrian word *delme,* meaning sheep," Montjoy answered, referencing the Indo-European language spoken in the Western Balkans. "And the shepherd provided us considerable amounts of high-value targets, assets, and intelligence for almost three decades."

"Was no one worried that somebody might discern specific operations based on clever operational names?" Before Montjoy could respond, Abbot asked, "don't you think the Germans would have been smart enough to figure out what the *Twenty Committee* was, had they known its name?

"They did know, and didn't figure it out. Often, the most obvious answer is exactly that, too obvious. Think, *The Purloined Letter.* The natural tendency in this business is to assume your enemy thinks like you do. Psychologists call it mirroring. The Germans, as German as they ever are, couldn't imagine such temerity."

"I don't think much has changed. The other day I was looking to purchase a new rucksack online, and narrowed my choice between an American pack with an adventurous name. The other was a German brand, which was advertised as, 'Medium Black Backpack.'"

Montjoy laughed. "And which way are you leaning?"

"The overpriced option with the fancy title, of course," Abbot admitted, grinning. "And the American contingent I saw earlier?"

"There's a clever lad," Montjoy replied. "Approximately ten years ago, we got word that Langley was also using Ahmad. They, of course, claimed that it was he who had approached them."

"We've been running Ahmad jointly with the Yanks?" Abbot was surprised. "Not terribly ideal for keeping secrets, either his, or his identity."

"Apparently not, considering the events of last Thursday night."

"You handled *Shepherd*?"

"I recruited Ahmad, and ran him until recently. After he was kicked upstairs, I continued to oversee a few bits and bobs, but Lindsay's office managed the top assets Ahmad gave us."

"And Rees?"

"Lindsay took operational oversight with Rees managing the show behind the scenes. I got the corner office."

Abbot sat back, processing what Montjoy had told him. "So, what now? What are we looking for?"

"Any connection that will lead us to his killer."

"To the man on CCTV?"

"If he's involved," Montjoy responded.

"Regardless, who most wanted Ahmad dead?"

"Aside from everyone he's double-crossed, or anyone who might have suspected him as a mole?" Montjoy mused. "Half of the Middle East, I should think. The man had ever-inflating notions of self-importance. We warned Ahmad, but he fancied himself untouchable. He might have been killed for that reason alone, and not for any leaks that sprung where *Shepherd* or *Dalmatia* were concerned."

"He's dead now, so the ultimate leak has been plugged, and not in our favor."

"Less mine than the Service's," Montjoy speculated. "Before it was transferred out of Near East operations, *Dalmatia* had begun to experience a lag where high-value intelligence was concerned. We were reduced to a handful of lower-level assets and a few small, clumsy terror cells that likely would not have been successful because of their own incompetence, but certainly nothing worth parading before the chief."

"Any chance Ahmad turned, or curried favor, with Langley, while providing us bugger all?"

"That period overlapped the time that Berwyn Rees was promoted to head of section, and came on board where *Dalmatia* was concerned. I suspected that Ahmad had begun playing both sides against the middle, and suggested as much, but it went nowhere. Since then, Lindsay has essentially allowed someone who couldn't turn an asset if it set up shop in our lobby wearing a 'For Sale' sign, to run our most prized intelligence coup since the war."

"You and Rees have never been that chummy, eh?"

"An understatement, mate. There are plenty around here who fancy themselves the cock of the walk, but most truly have the best interest of the Service, and Britain, at heart. Berwyn Rees, on the other hand, would absolutely bugger MI6 if he thought he could get ahead, even in the slightest."

"He's done well for himself. How so far so fast?" Abbot asked.

"You've heard of Sir Radford Sinclair Rees?" Montjoy queried, referring to one of England's more famous World War II heroes, also Berwyn Rees' grandfather.

"Of course."

"First rule of the Service, have a name and a fancy pedigree, and you're halfway to picking your office."

"Which accounts for why I'm in the closet down the hall," Abbot mused, only having an Oxbridge background, but no well-known lineage.

"Bob's your uncle."

"And he's not famous," Abbot joked. "What now?"

Montjoy turned his attention back to the mass of papers strewn over his desk. "We backtrack through all of it, and I mean every last file."

"So, I can organize all of this beforehand?" Abbot asked, almost pleading.

"Knock yourself out, my boy."

CHAPTER THIRTY-THREE

London

The phone rang several times before the call forwarded automatically to a secure line. The man who answered waited several seconds before speaking.

"Yes?"

"It's me," John Campion replied. A moment of silence followed before he added, irritated, "*Flower-fucking-down.*"

"I see you've added a middle name." Though the man joked, referring to the expletive Campion had inserted into his cryptonym, he was clearly displeased with the security slip.

"I met with your boy," Campion said flatly.

"And?"

"And I doubt he'll make it out."

"You are sure?"

"As certain as I am tired of bloody codenames and secure lines."

The man on the phone sighed, and silently shook his head at the disclosure. "Have you sorted out his recall?"

Campion glanced through the phone booth window at approaching headlights that slowed where Horseferry Road met Regency Place, in southwest London. The car rumbled by, an OAP at the wheel. "In process."

"What news of the party crasher?"

"General only, subject and scene. Are you in London?"

"For the moment."

Campion caught sight of his hazy likeness cast off the dirty glass of the booth, littered with half-torn sticker adverts for Soho prostitutes. He had called from one of the few remaining bright red British telecom boxes left in the city. One of the last reminders of what England used to represent, during a time when everyone in play understood the risk, and anted up a personal stake. When all of this sodding well meant something. But since the Wall came down, well-bred and well-read had been replaced by empty suits propped up behind fancy desks, where notions of leadership were reduced to kibitzing over shoulders. Many for whom the CIA motto, taken from John 8:32, *And you shall know the truth, and the truth shall make you free*, was little more than something scripted in sand, easily shifted to suit.

Campion stared beyond the reflection of the man he long believed was impervious to the disillusion, and saw nothing on the other side.

"I say, are you still—"

"I'll brief you when we meet. You know the time and place," Campion said as he hung up, not waiting for a reply.

CHAPTER THIRTY-FOUR

Glencoe, Scotland

Garrett sat in the back of an empty CityLink bus as it skirted Loch Lomond. He had taken an early train to Glasgow's Queen Street Station, and changed to an express coach that connected central Scotland to the Highlands. He could have opted for a faster journey on a Scotrail direct to Crianlarich, but this route, through the Queen Elizabeth Forest Park, helped to remind Garrett of a happier time, on trips to South Ballachulish in an old Peugeot with his parents. For many years, he had sought to dilute the memories, but now they flashed at him like still shots that seemed of a different person from another life.

He had rendezvoused with Deacon earlier that day, and delivered the photo as directed. The new passport picture, taken at a digital tourist booth at Waverley, showed Garrett with much of his beard gone, and with shorter hair, pulled behind his ears. He had been given a new throwaway mobile, and had hidden the one he'd been carrying since Cambridge behind a kiosk near the main ticket hall in the station.

As the bus rolled through the Scottish Highlands, he let his thoughts drift back to Ahmad, murdered by a man slightly taller than Garrett, with hair his color, and deep-set hazel eyes. He could still envision the scene at King's College, though it felt like looking through a pinhole into a 3-D diorama. The assassin, standing in front Ahmad's desk, held a large caliber pistol. The professor, partly obscured by his killer, had thrown something in self-defense. The actions of both men were superimposed upon one another. When Garrett attempted to bring one image into focus, the other blurred, like a visual illusion that altered when the angle was changed.

What he did know was that a well-known Cambridge professor was dead, and the plot behind the murder, as far as the media was speculating, was movielike, and nothing short of Machiavellian. The mainstream news continued to parade out one "expert" after another, anonymous sources seated behind shadow screens and fueling the frenzy as to what Ahmad might have been, and who very much wanted him dead because of it. Officials from several Middle Eastern countries insinuated that the assassination represented a veiled declaration of war against Islam, while the only comment from Whitehall was its customary, "no comment." The average bystander on high street, always mesmerized by the shiny object in the shop window, remain transfixed, at least until the next sensational story.

And then there was Sean Garrett, one of two witnesses to the murder, who was on a bus heading to the Highlands to take care of something he should have dealt with a year earlier. He only hoped that she would be home, alone, and would understand.

CHAPTER THIRTY-FIVE

London

The lights on the Golden Jubilee Bridge mixed with an unusually thick fog that blew off the Thames, shrouding the overpass like a scene from *Bleak House*. Berwyn Rees glanced at his limited edition matte black Submariner. One of only fifty produced, it had cost him. His success in chatting up the twenty-something slappers in late-night clubs made it worth its weight in sterling, though Rees assured himself that he didn't need a rare Rolex to get laid. The timepiece was merely an accessory to be admired after a night out on the pull for MI6's deputy chief in waiting.

He checked the time again, getting more agitated by the second. Leighton Churchill Thackeray, long-standing MP from Chelsea, was late. As usual. Rees desperately wanted to give the man five more minutes and then walk, but was able to placate his emotions enough to recognize that how high he ascended at SIS depended on how he played the game. If Rees was to be left a chair when the music stopped, he needed Thackeray. The Service was top heavy. Everyone knew it, and calls from the *cut this and chop that* coalition were growing louder, something the pols across the river would eventually have to address, considering that the demands for an election were becoming more audible.

His wandering attention was interrupted by a voice that hissed his name from behind. Rees spun, the wrong way, and comically turned full circle before coming square with Thackeray. The man towered at six foot five, and in the silhouette of the bridge, looked almost as tall as one of its suspension cable-stays. In any environment, Leighton Thackeray cast a long shadow.

"Good evening, sir."

"Quite. Straight off a Turner canvas." The MP then quipped, "or some absurd American film over-embellishing English stereotypes." Before Rees could comment, Thackeray decided to dispense with any additional small talk. "What news of the investigation? Are the Americans involved?"

Of course they're bloody involved, ad nauseum. "Nothing new. We've got a photo off CCTV of a man we believe to be the assassin, and yes, the Yanks are front and center."

"I imagine like a new pup that's discovered its pecker. And who, might I ask, is this man from King's College?" The MP pulled a pack of Dunhills from his wool overcoat and thumped the carton on the back of his hand.

"We don't know yet. We've run his photo, but nothing jumps out in the system. We suspect the same bloke was involved in an altercation in Hackney two days after the professor's death, and we've isolated a conversation he had with someone in London. The subject of the call was coded and of little help, and the receiving phone was untraceable. However, we managed to keep a fix on the suspect's mobile, and we believe he is in Edinburgh."

"And the Americans are privy to this?"

"As of two days ago."

"Is it wise to keep Langley so close?"

Rees contemplated. "They're certainly keeping something from us, but I don't think they know what happened."

Thackeray took an extended drag on his cigarette. "Do *we?*"

"Not yet, sir, but soon."

"It's a dangerous game you're playing, considering who's involved. You're certain you won't be hoisted by your own petard?"

"Quite."

"Let me rephrase my question, Berwyn." Thackeray stepped closer, which caused Rees to back clumsily against the railing of the bridge. "Whom, and what, do I personally need to be concerned about, at this point in time?"

Rees regained his balance. "Nothing, sir, and no one."

Thackeray stared Rees down for several seconds. "Perhaps you are waiting for someone to state the obvious," he continued acerbically. "Allow me. The point man for our little enterprise has been killed, violently, in his office at Cambridge, in what appears to be a professional assassination. You have no leads, save for a photo of a man you cannot identify. Langley, who considered Ahmad to be one of their top assets, appears rather *non-*nonplussed with everything you've given them, and journos from the BBC to the *bloody* deep blue sea, are drafting potential Pulitzer acceptance speeches." Thackeray paused. "Need I go on?"

"No, sir."

"Do you have any suggestions, or should I assume you'll continue to wander the halls of MI6 with a limp dick in your hand."

Stop meeting in public and having these inane conversations. "I'm on it, sir."

"Who else has been apprised of the situation?"

"At this point, only Lindsay, and the team from Langley, are privy. Moore is involved, but on the fringe."

"Where I expect he normally wanders these days," Thackeray mused.

"A team has been dispatched to Edinburgh, and two others have been tearing apart the professor's life in Cambridge and London. All files are being sent directly to my office, and so far, nothing that implicates you in anything."

"*Us*, I think you mean." Thackeray cast a sideways glance at Rees. "Ahmad kept something besides that damned letter. That, you can bet your Sunday wager on."

Rees hesitated. "There is something else."

"There always is," Thackeray laughed to himself, taking another pull on the Dunhill and blowing a ring out beyond his hooked nose.

"Someone we reduced to a minor role, but at this point, I can't say how minor."

"Who?"

"Head of Near East Section. He recruited the professor and ran him early on. His name is Montjoy."

"Banastre?" Thackeray queried. "I knew his grandfather."

Rees didn't respond.

"Well? Is he involved?"

"He could be," Rees suggested with hesitation, and then added, "if need be."

"Indeed." The MP threw his cigarette on the ground and twisted it out with his heel as he turned to leave the bridge. "Keep me informed."

"Yes, sir."

"And keep this sodding mess away from my office."

CHAPTER THIRTY-SIX

Ballachulish, Scotland

The coach slowed to a stop short of a round-about near the confluence of two Highland lakes. It was not scheduled, but considering the bus carried only a few passengers, the driver obliged Garrett's request to alight on the outskirts of South Ballachulish. The sparsely populated and picturesque region was one bypassed by many tourists in favor of better-known bodies of water boasting pre-historic plesiosaurs. But, because Ballachulish was situated along the main thoroughfare that bisected the Grampian Mountain

Range and the Northwest Highlands, a sufficient number of travelers paused en route to give the village an economic pulse.

Garrett began to trek along the main road, making his way to where Lochs Leven and Linnhe conjoined. He spied the Ballachulish Bridge, which split counties Argyll and Inverness-Shire, and recalled stories from his mother of a time when the family house in North Ballachulish was accessible by ferry only. By the time Garrett was six, his earliest recollection of traveling to visit his grandparents was via a newly built steel overpass that spanned the narrows. He smiled at the memory of his younger sister christening it the Green Monster, arguing that Loch Ness shouldn't be allowed exclusive rights to lake legends, and at least theirs could be seen.

He also remembered being twelve, and of his father taking him to the site of the Appin Murder, one of Scotland's most infamous unsolved assassinations. Together, they had walked the same wood where Collin Roy Campbell, a Hanoverian appointed estate factor, was shot in the back in the aftermath of the Jacobite Uprising.

An innocent man was hanged here, he could hear his father say, *less because of his suspected complicity in a murder, and more the result of political leanings. Never underestimate the forces beyond your control that conspire against you,* he was pressed to comprehend, standing on the same hill where James Stewart had been gibbetted, predominately because he'd fought alongside Bonnie Prince Charles. Although the lesson was lost on him at the time, he remembered being so mesmerized by the murder that became the inspiration for one of Robert Louis Stevenson's best-known novels, that Garrett read *Kidnapped* three times.

He considered climbing the overlook behind the Ballachulish Hotel to revisit the ghost of his father, and *Cnap a' Chaolais,* the site of the hanging, but decided that his limited time urged him elsewhere.

It had been one year since he'd last seen his grandmother, briefly in London, with the remainder of their scattered family who had mustered from the proverbial four corners for his grandfather's belated wake. She remained that day as he had always remembered her, stoic and full of quiet resolve. Before the bombing, he had visited Scotland throughout his teenage years, trips that were never dull, with everyone entertained by the Churchillian wit of his grandfather, and the Highland wisdom of his grandmother.

The last time he had seen the house, his grandparents were in the process of upfitting it to become a small lochside bed and breakfast, offering all of two double rooms. To compete with the excess of inns scattered along the lochs, his sister had implored them to create a secure website to accommodate online bookings and credit card payments, but they adamantly refused, content to pencil in phone reservations at all hours and on good faith. With his grandfather's death and his sister's condition unchanged, Garrett wondered how their grandmother could manage much of anything, least of all a small hotel. He had broached the subject of skipping at least one tourist season after the bombing, or shuttering the inn altogether, but she would hear nothing of it.

It was late afternoon and he passed several hikers, likely returning from Glen Coe, arguably the country's most scenic vista. Formed by an ice age glacier and hardened volcanic ruins, the horseshoe-shaped glen sat in the shadow of the mountains, and boasted the highest peak in the U.K. Garrett knew it well. Once, alone in winter and anchored high up on Ben Nevis, he had nearly been swept off the North Gully by an avalanche.

He paused at the south end of the bridge and looked out over Loch Linnhe. The multitude of lochs, inlets, and small islands made the Argyll coastline longer than that of France, and he could smell the sea air blowing along its banks. The saltwater lake was situated directly over the Great Glen, a strike-slip fault that ran from near the Shetland Islands through Donegal Bay in Ireland, and into the North Atlantic. It had been the site of several minor magnitude quakes that had struck the region several years earlier. He had paid them scant attention at the time, but as they had occurred almost two years to the day before the King's Cross bombing, they suddenly came into focus each time Garrett thought of his grandfather and sister.

He quickly crossed the bridge and cut over Old Ferry Road, in order to skirt the loch coastline and avoid the main thoroughfare. The wind picked up and the temperature dropped as he moved below the tree line. A few boats were moored near Bishop's Bay, bobbing in unison like stoppers set for red fins. The soft sand line forced Garrett to traverse the remaining quarter mile along the road that would take him to his grandmother's doorstep. He rounded a sharp bend and caught sight of the familiar whitewashed stonewalls and double chimney, jutting just higher than the tree line surrounding the house.

It had been a fishing lodge a century earlier, and sat abandoned for nearly thirty years before his grandparents purchased and fully renovated the ramshackle house. But now it was small, quiet, and quaint. He could see why some tourists preferred it to the more well-known and perpetually crowded inns along the town-side of the loch. Garrett climbed the winding stone pathway that led to the front door, and saw that his grandmother had affixed a small sign that announced, *Campbells still not Welcome.* The warning hung as a humorous reference, albeit only because it was three centuries later, to the perpetrators of the *Mort Ghlinne Comhann*, the massacre of the Macdonald Clan that took place near Glencoe in 1692, in the aftermath of the Glorious Revolution.

The small, graveled pad next to the lodge was empty. Garrett walked to the front door, which was open, and rapped several times on the screen. He heard a voice chime from the kitchen, "Come in!"

Garrett assumed his grandmother was expecting guests, and stepped through the foyer into the small, comfortable sitting area. Both the coat rack and umbrella bin were empty, and he caught the scent of her favorite evening fare, haggis. Garrett could stomach the traditional Scottish dish that contained the liver, heart, and lungs of a sheep, but just barely. Most Highland inns offered the pudding wrapped in a sausage casing rather than the stomach lining, but his grandmother was determined to keep her version true to tradition.

"Make yourself at home! I'll be along in a tick!"

Garrett smiled as he looked over old photographs on the mantle above the fireplace, which had a small fire burning. It showed half of his family at various points in their lives, as well as several black and white prints of his grandparents during the war. In one, his grandfather was dressed in a crisp, new RAF uniform, clearly taken before he had seen any action. He was much younger than Garrett was now, and smiling broadly, he looked like a shiny new tuppence. His grandmother, in a separate photo, was garbed in the rather drab two-piece outfit of the MTC, the Mechanized Transport Corps. He remembered being told that both images had been taken within a week of one another, and just two months before his grandparents met, the year before his mother was born. They both looked handsome and happy.

He heard a noise, and then a gasp, behind him.

He turned, smiling. "Grandmom."

"My goodness!" She rushed into the sitting room, nearly tripping on the threshold of the kitchen. "Sean! Oh, my goodness!" she said again with the same high-pitched enthusiasm, as she hugged him.

She was as slight as ever, but older than he imagined she would look even one year later. He had known then that the destruction of King's Cross would take its toll on each of them in its own way. Yet she looked spry for someone approaching ninety.

"You look great. The house looks great," was all he said.

She had teared up, but was still beaming. "Let's have a look at you—" She stepped back and exaggerated giving him the once-over. "Hmmm, rather dashing. Like Errol Flynn, I should think."

"No one knows who he is anymore."

"Well, they should!" she replied. "You're just in time. Can you guess what I'm preparing for dinner?"

"The whole of the glen can smell it," Garrett joked. "And if there are any Campbells still around, they would steer well clear of the cottage."

She assumed an expression of mock offense. "Such cheek! I thought I raised your mother better."

"You did. That was granddad talking." Garrett grimaced, thinking he should not have said it, but his grandmother only smiled.

"How right you are," she finally said with a laugh, and hugged him tightly again. "Shame on you for not letting me know you were coming over. I do have a room free, my dear, so you're in luck."

"I wish I could stay," he was quick to reply. "I've got to be back in Edinburgh early tomorrow."

She eyed him for a moment. "Well, I hope you have enough time to sit down over a cup. Cream, no sugar?"

"Cream, no sugar."

She disappeared into the kitchen, and he turned his attention back to the mantel. Rows of photos from the last sixty years covered the timbered slab. He watched his family age quickly over a span of several feet. Next to the last photo taken of them together was a picture of his grandfather holding a cane, dated a year before the bombing. Madeleine was standing beside him, and looked like she always did, vibrant, and stunningly attractive.

He heard his grandmother reenter the room. "I see you were looking at the photo we took at Harvard."

"Maddie looks like Maddie," Garrett responded. "Always smiling. Always beautiful. That was graduation?"

"It was. Finished top of her medical class, if you remember."

Garrett didn't answer, and only stared at the photo. He heard his grandmother say something to him.

"I'm sorry?" he asked.

"Have you been to see her?" she repeated.

He shook his head. "Not since in the months after King's Cross. I've stayed in contact with the hospital. Her doctors tell me her condition hasn't changed."

"So they say. I take the train down once a month, and *I say* I will live long enough to sit and chat with her again."

Garrett decided not to dash any hope his grandmother clung to, for his conversations with the chief surgeon at the neuro-rehabilitation unit at the National Hospital for Neurology and Neurosurgery in London were of a markedly different tone. "I can't see Maddie again in that condition. I want to remember her the way she was."

"We all long for better times, Sean. Ask survivors of the war generation, or anyone who lived through the Great Depression. If I could erase the last year and stop your grandfather from getting on that train, I would, and whatever happened because of it be damned."

Garrett shook his head. "Well, I can't reconcile what happened. I can't move past it. That's as simple as it gets for me. He was my granddad, and she was my sister."

"She still is your sister, Sean, and your grandfather will always be there for you in memory. Like your mum, and your da."

He nodded.

"Can I ask you something?"

"Of course."

"Why are you in the U.K.?"

Garrett stared for several moments out of the bay window that overlooked the loch. "Redemption."

"For whom, my dear?" she asked.

He eyed her for a moment, but did not speak.

She smiled at him. "Let me tell you something you already know. If it is reconciliation, or redemption, you seek, you won't find it in Scotland, or North Carolina. Or anywhere else that you can physically set foot, for that matter."

"I know."

"*Und wenn du lange in einen Abgrund blickst—*" she trailed off.

"The abyss stares back at you," Garrett finished the famous quote by Nietzsche. "Are you testing my German, or my soul?"

"Just remember, my dear, we are nothing more than what we see our world to be. If that be emptiness, or hopelessness—"

"I know."

"So you keep saying."

Garrett nodded.

"Then you know where to find it."

They heard the scrape of tires on the parking pad. "That would be my lodgers for the night. Why don't you go for a walk around the loch, or take my car wherever you'd like. Come back when you're ready, and we'll have that chat, no matter how late."

As he turned to leave, she reached out and touched his arm. "Nietzsche had enough demons to fill two abysses. Do be a good boy and remember what he said of monsters and men. Run along now."

Garrett exited through the kitchen door. He slipped around back and circled the wooded side of the cottage, avoiding the guests chattering away excitedly as they unpacked their hired car. They sounded American, and he was suddenly envious of them. Jealous of their time together, jealous of their life. Tolstoy was right, happy families are all the same. His had been ripped apart by a reckless driver and a bomb.

Garrett continued around the drive and turned back through the woods, sidestepping his way down a steep embankment to where a small rocky outcropping crested the loch shoreline. It was early evening, and the temperature had dropped to near freezing. The wind raked the surf, and whitecaps formed on the surface water out from the protection of the small cove. It had begun to rain, and he found shelter under a circle of birch trees. More boats had anchored off a small island in the natural harbor, hoping for sanctuary from the rising water and rough winds, which matched the rain in ferocity.

Through the driving storm, Garrett could see the bridge, and the south end of the *Caolas Mhic Phàdraig* narrows. He could see his father walking along the opposite bank, holding his hand, and telling him stories of Highland lore. He saw his sister, four years old and freckled, with her blond hair pulled back in the ponytail she always stubbornly insisted upon, skipping beside him. His mother was walking behind them and between his grandparents, arms looped together and laughing about something.

He watched each of them falter and fade as thunder cracked above. Garrett sat back on the hillside heather, and suddenly broke down. The fierce wind drowned out his sobs, and the salt water blowing off the loch mixed with the tears. He hadn't cried once, for any of them, in the hopes that to ignore the pain that crashed against him in waves would render it inert. One after the other they had fallen, like a shelf of wet sand giving way to its own weight at the overhang of a sea dune. And he was left standing, alone on the precipice, waiting his turn.

Garrett saw himself struggling in the surf beyond the channel, bitter and paralyzed. Drowning, for years.

He strained to hear the storm, but all sound had died off and the water had dried up. Garrett searched the chasm left in its wake and saw the battered front fender of a shapeless vehicle, and the remnants of a shattered train. Between them was a man fighting desperately to save his own life. Pieces of everything he had become were scattered across an abyss that had stolen everything from him.

Death I am, it echoed, vacant and indifferent.

Destroyer of worlds.

Garrett opened his eyes. He felt the extension grip of the Sig Sauer digging into his back. His clothes were soaked, and lightning had begun to flash across the inlet. He stood, and could see the glow of his grandmother's cottage parsed between the copse of thin hardwoods, themselves illuminated in two-second bursts.

Mohammad Ahmad was dead, and with him, the only chance to find out who was behind what happened to his grandfather and sister. Garrett turned his back to the loch, and the storm, and began to walk calmly through the wood in the direction of the house, toward Edinburgh, and home.

CHAPTER
THIRTY-SEVEN

Scotland Yard
London

Roger Holland watched a slip of boats moored at Westminster Pier bob in the waves made from a hop-on, hop-off river cruise on tour down the Thames. He had just finished dinner, having abandoned his latest attempt at unpacking file cartons at the new office in the Curtis Green Building. The Central London venue had housed Scotland Yard a half-century earlier, until the Met outgrew the space and relocated to Victoria Street. Now, a billion pounds in government cuts had forced the iconic police force back to the municipal structure on the embankment overlooking the river. The recent downsizing had also necessitated Holland's move to superintendent quicker than he expected. In less than one week, he had improved both his position, and view.

He had just launched back into the job at hand when he heard a knock on his door. "Come."

Sam Anderton breezed into the office, nearly tripping over a stack of sealed containers. "Still boxed in I see," she joked.

"Thirty years ago there would have been a pretty, young secretary to bring me coffee and organize everything."

"Thirty years ago that comment would have been considered appropriate." Anderton gave Holland a sideways glance.

"I only meant that your lot have always been better at things like that," Holland replied, and then added, "at most things, actually."

"Do you need some assistance?"

Holland laughed. "With this office, or the Ahmad case?"

"Perhaps I can help with one of those." Anderton held up a large envelope.

"You found something."

"That depends on what we are looking for."

Holland took the file and walked it back to his desk, which had been pushed against the window. The only thing on it, other than a dried stain from spilled coffee, was a handful of documents taken from Ahmad's office, and several letters from a flat the professor kept in Notting Hill. Typically, the majority of victims Holland investigated left something behind that appeared incriminating on the surface, but which was almost always dismissed as circumstantial under deeper scrutiny. With Ahmad, there was nothing out of the ordinary, at all, and nothing usually meant something to hide.

Holland emptied the contents of the A4 envelope onto his desk, which included the key Anderton had found in Ahmad's shoe, and a small spiral bound notebook, which was filled with dates and amounts.

"Ahmad kept a safety deposit box at HSBC."

"Is that so." Holland hadn't failed to notice that his sergeant was clearly pleased with herself. She was an exceptional investigator, and as superintendent, he would miss working with her on a regular basis. "Wasn't that service phased out at most institutions?"

"Most banks discontinued safety deposit boxes several years ago. HSBC stopped their service just this spring, and gave customers sixty days to clear out the contents."

"And this ledger?"

Anderton said nothing, but turned to shut the door.

"Uh-oh—" Holland said, as Anderton turned back to face him and crossed her arms. "Let's hear it," he said, crossing his own.

"It came from an assistant manager at the HSBC in Cambridge."

"Ahmad kept a safety box there?"

Anderton shook her head. "His was actually at the branch on Queen Victoria Street, in London. I found a receipt hidden among a collection of old papers in his flat, which led me to a box he rented out eight years ago."

"And?" he asked, looking over the contents of the ledger.

"And I couldn't make any headway with the two higher-ups who did little but deflect my questions. I was told the inquiry needed to be official, and even then, there was the suggestion it wouldn't get far. Privacy issues and client confidentiality, they said."

"I'm surprised they bothered at all. It wasn't too long ago that HSBC were caught up in a tax evasion and money laundering scandal. Very public and very bad for business. They have been closing branches and rebranding ever since, and will tread carefully as a result."

"The same can't be said for some of their smaller offices." Anderton gestured toward the book. "On a hunch, I visited the branch nearest Ahmad's flat in Cambridge. I had no sooner mentioned him to an assistant manager, a very old, very sweet lady, when she offered her condolences and brought me that ledger. I think she assumed I was a family friend. She said she had known the professor for thirty years, and when Ahmad hadn't emptied his box in the allotted time at Queen Victoria Street, someone over there sent the contents to his local branch as a courtesy."

"Let me guess, when she brought you the book, you hadn't officially identified yourself."

Anderton shook her head. "And I didn't afterward, either."

"Well, sergeant," Holland replied as he sat down in his chair. "That was either very stupid, or very clever."

"To be determined by?"

"Where this goes, and who finds out."

Anderton frowned, but Holland held up his hand. "We'll deal with that at the appropriate time. As for the ledger, what do you make of it?"

"Lots of money going somewhere. Deposits, I assume, but nothing to distinguish what they might pertain to."

"Which begs the question—"

"Why Ahmad kept it in a safety deposit box."

Holland nodded.

"And Healey? How much has the Security Service cut us out of the investigation?"

"To the extent that I'm getting little more than scraps from MI5's table. Just enough to maintain the appearance of a joint effort."

"So your assumption was correct," Anderton replied. "What is going on?"

"I don't know. I am usually kept in Healey's loop, primarily because he just can't help himself. The man relishes providing me details if for no other reason than to show how clever he is." Holland stood and walked over to the window. "But with the Ahmad case, he's given me the shove off."

"Sounds like you're officially off the case"

"I am officially in this office, earlier than expected, which might as well be the same thing." Holland moved back to his desk, and placed the ledger beside a stack of files he had been organizing earlier. "You're being reassigned to Billy Barclay, by the way. Until then, I need you to keep on the paper trail from the bank. Quietly, mind you. You will report only to me."

"There is something else, sir. Ahmad's last call was to his housemaid. She said he rang at just after 7:00 p.m. to remind her he would be in London for supper. Apparently, someone knocked on the office door during the call. She said she heard Ahmad bid the person entry, and then say, '*you're late, I presume.*'"

"What do you make of it?"

"Ahmad had a dinner reservation for 8:30 p.m. at Simpsons, in London. His satchel was packed and he had already wrapped his scarf, which means he was on the way out. And what did his housemaid overhear? 'You're late, I presume.' *I presume.* Ahmad wasn't certain if the person at his door, whom he didn't know or recognize, was the one with whom he was to meet. I think it was the assassin who set the meeting, for after hours, and was then intentionally late, to ensure the professor would be alone at the end of the workday. Once Ahmad realized he was in danger, he threw his shoe in self-defense, which shattered the window. The unexpected move, and attention, hurried the killer into action before he intended, which may also explain why he was caught on camera exiting the Lodge."

"Very good, sergeant."

"Something still doesn't add up."

"No, it doesn't." Holland handed Anderton back the notebook. "Which means you have your work cut out for you."

"A term I've never understood."

"It originated with the business of tailoring in the nineteenth century. The easiest step was cutting the cloth. Putting the garment together afterward was the difficult part."

"Meaning?"

"Meaning," Holland replied, "I think Ahmad reaped what he sowed. Find out what he was into that got him killed."

CHAPTER
THIRTY-EIGHT

London

The patio of Da Mario was overbooked, and the small table at which Nasir Hajjar sat had been pushed uncomfortably close to a wrought iron window box. The Italian trattoria in South Kensington, the reputed favorite of Princess Diana, drew a steady stream of tourists eager to see her name etched in memoriam in the building's entryway, and order her preferred dish from the menu. When he was shown his seat on the crowded terrace, Hajjar had not complained—it provided a direct line of sight to the Gloucester Arms across the street, the pub where he had prevented an attempt on bin Halabi's life when they were both students at university.

The moment he received the cryptic message a day earlier he knew something was wrong, and Hajjar was apprehensive about sitting over his high-end whiskey much longer. He kept his eye firmly fixed on the pub, and decided that if he did not see the prince in the next fifteen minutes, he would leave, and wait for bin Halabi to contact him again. Better to beg for forgiveness, Hajjar reasoned.

At that moment, the seasoned intelligence operative was unaware that he had more to worry about than a Saudi prince, or Scotland Yard. He had allowed himself to become too distracted by his own affairs in England, and had uncharacteristically failed to surveil his surroundings in appropriate intervals. If he had, Hajjar would have tagged the well-dressed man who exited a British Telecom phone booth across the street as a potential threat, and monitored his movements as he crossed through traffic and advanced toward the restaurant.

By the time Hajjar began to rescan the intersection, the man had circled behind a lorry parked the wrong way in front of the residential building beside Da Mario. He was middle-aged and Middle Eastern, and outfitted impeccably from Savile Row, though he no longer sported the red scarf he had worn at his meet with David Laurent at the Round Pond in Hyde Park. His movements were slow but deliberate, and he casually adjusted his grip on the Gen4 Glock 27 .40 caliber in his front right pocket as he neared the patio. He gave a gentlemanly nod to two female students who passed by, and was attractive enough for one of the schoolgirls to giggle and smile back.

Hajjar's position near one of two large columns on the restaurant's facade obstructed his view of the man's final approach, until he stepped from behind the pillar nearest the sidewalk. Hajjar suddenly noticed him, standing squarely five feet away, and smiling.

"Haji!" the man said, enthusiastically.

Hajjar was startled, though he did not show it. He quietly cursed his careless slip in surveillance, and said nothing as he flipped the safety off of his Kimber Pro Carry .45 caliber pistol, which lay concealed in his lap beneath a napkin.

The man continued to smile. "It has been a long time, my friend."

Hajjar remained silent, but his attention pinged rapidly around the street corner and intersection, seeking anyone else out of place.

"Twenty-three years to be exact," the man added.

This got Hajjar's attention, though he only nodded. He was stuck in no man's land, a place he rarely found himself, and knew he had only a few moments to determine his next course of action. Prudence demanded he assume that the man represented the prince, but warning lights were still flashing red. "Yes, indeed," Hajjar finally answered.

"There is never a better time to catch up than the present. I have booked us a table at the Tandoori," the man gestured to an Indian restaurant across the street. "I hope you will join me."

The stranger kept his hand in his pocket, though he continued to smile. Hajjar could shoot him, and take his chances getting out of England on his own, or, he could gamble. "What news of our mutual friend's favorite football club?" Hajjar finally asked, choosing the latter.

The man mulled the query for a moment. "Though he still proudly flies the red and yellow of Galatasaray F.C., no doubt he secretly supports Sheffield United."

Hajjar suppressed a smile of his own, for though bin Halabi owned shares in the Turkish football club, the prince's cousin had recently purchased a half-stake in the English League One football team, a move that bin Halabi had privately mocked as a bad business decision.

The man pulled two cigarettes out of his pocket and offered one to Hajjar, an old espionage signal that he had something important to discuss.

"*Shukran*," Hajjar said, taking one and leaving the other, the sign he accepted his invite.

"You are most welcome."

Hajjar settled his bill and exited the patio, allowing the man to take the lead across Gloucester Road. They entered the Indian restaurant, and were shown to a small table near the back bar.

Hajjar was about to speak when the man held up his hand, and pulled a small device from his pocket. It was roughly the size of a mobile phone, and the man switched it on as he placed it on the table. He waited six seconds and nodded.

"Amazing little machine," he said as he sat down. "It jams GPS signals within a hundred-meter radius, and emits enough white noise to prevent conversations from being recorded in the immediate area."

"It's useless where the NSA or GCHQ are concerned." Hajjar gestured at the device." They're light years ahead of that."

"The prince has bigger worries," the man smiled. "Galatasaray is going bankrupt."

"He is well aware."

"And do you think he will up his ante, or offload his position?"

"The prince has not yet made a decision."

Hajjar decided he did not have time to engage in any kind of informal chitchat, but the man sensed this and again held up his hand. "I recommend the *Raitha*, and *Keema Nan*, to start."

"I'm not hungry, but I am curious as to who you are, and why the prince is not here."

A waiter appeared, and the man placed an order for both of them. "No doubt the prince has referenced me on occasion, and if so, then you know why he sent me in his stead."

Hajjar had speculated that the man, named Danesh, was indeed the same proxy who bin Halabi had long kept confidential. He had never been comfortable with the arrangement, chiefly because he had never been able to vet the man. The impromptu meeting did nothing to assuage Hajjar's suspicion. "He has told me very little about who you are, or what you do for him."

"And I'm sorry there is no time for an extended backstory, but I can assure you that I, like you, solve logistical issues that arise in England for EuroPen."

Hajjar said nothing, knowing that it was better to let someone talk themselves into a corner, than give them any subtle clues of what, or what not, to say.

"And, at the moment, there exists a considerable threat to our entire operation here."

"In what form?" Hajjar asked, taking note of the man's use of "our" to describe EuroPen's business.

The man removed a photo from his vest pocket and pushed it across the table. It showed a man near to Hajjar's age, with hazel eyes and deep-toned skin. He did not look traditionally Middle Eastern, but could pass for any number of nationalities.

"Who is he?"

"The man who assassinated Mohammad Ahmad. The same man who left alive a witness to the killing. The name he is using in England is David Laurent, and his arrest by either the Americans or the British has the potential to knock down the lead domino in a chain that can lead back to us."

Hajjar had chosen not to delve into the possibility of the prince's hand in Ahmad's assassination when they discussed it at Heathrow Airport. He decided he would leave it to bin Halabi, and not some surreptitious point man, to involve Hajjar after the fact. "Who is the witness?"

"We aren't privy to that, at the moment. We do know he is in Edinburgh, and that both the CIA and British Intelligence are in a race to find him."

"A race against the clock, or one another?"

"Unknown, but we have reason to believe that Langley has several teams in the U.K. whose presence has not been made known to the British. If they are indeed working independent of one another to find either Laurent, or this witness, then we are in a race ourselves."

"And how have you come by this information?" Hajjar inquired.

"You have contacts in British Intelligence, as do I. You would like to conclude your business in England, so do I. I wish to find the man who has the ability to compromise the prince's financial well-being, and by extension, mine, and I assume you do as well."

"The prince will be fine," Hajjar replied. "That, I can assure you."

"Perhaps, but the same cannot be said for EuroPen's future, or of our respective ability to retire as wealthy men sooner than not."

Hajjar acknowledged to himself that if the prince became publicly embroiled in Ahmad's assassination, there would be few repercussions in England, and a slap on the wrist back home. But EuroPenninsula would be finished in the U.K., and with it, the six-figure bonus Hajjar was set to earn from the Liverpool deal. "Where is the prince now?"

"In Wales. He has moved the Gulfstream to Cardiff International. We have very little time to keep this mess from getting messier." He pointed to the photo. "Laurent is in Edinburgh, but will not remain there long. My contact in London will keep me informed of his position, and I will relay it to you. We will take care of the witness from King's College, and you will eliminate Laurent. After we tie off these loose ends, we will both accompany the prince out of the U.K. and back to the Kingdom."

"You are Saudi, then?"

"For the time being," the man smiled.

"And who is your man inside British Intelligence?"

"Someone well-positioned to supply me with real-time information."

Hajjar stared intently at his forced partner by proxy, thinking about his own incentive to en-sure the deal in Liverpool was signed and sealed. "Alright," he finally said. "But I travel alone, and you will make contact with me only once. After I find this man, I will kill him and make my own way to Wales."

"Of course." The man handed Hajjar a slip of paper. "Memorize this, and we will talk after you arrive in Edinburgh."

Hajjar wrote his own mobile number on a bar napkin and held it up. After several seconds, the man nodded, and Hajjar submerged the scrap in his cup of water.

"My name, as you are most certainly aware, is Danesh," the man said, and then added, "*Bittawfeeq.*"

"From your lips to Allah's ear," Hajjar said as he turned to leave. "But I won't need luck."

CHAPTER THIRTY-NINE

Biel, Switzerland

The courtyard of Café de la Tour was unusually crowded for a Tuesday afternoon. Charles Walsingham bypassed his preferred table near the outside gate for one beneath a covered porch at the back of the terrace. The popular restaurant was located in the heart of Switzerland's watchmaking district, in Biel, or Bienne, depending on whom was asked, as the bilingual city was positioned directly along the alpine country's French and German language border.

Walsingham, Sir Charles since 1994, had enjoyed living as an ex-pat in the picturesque Three

Lakes Region for nearly a decade. The retired British financier relished the opportunity to regularly practice his linguistic skills, and from his home on Lake Biel, at the foot of the Jura mountain range, Walsingham could see the entire world.

At least the only one that still interested him at his age.

He approached his friend and playing partner, Heinrich Sommer. "*Grüezi*, old chap." Walsingham greeted him in the typical Swiss hello, and pulled out an empty chair to sit down.

Sommer glanced up from his reading. "The crowd has forced us to the French side of the café today, so I do not understand you." He closed his book and placed it on the table. "You are late, as usual. For someone who loves expensive watches so much, one would imagine you could manage a timely appearance for our morning game at least once before we both die of old age."

"Allow me to apologize."

"Do I always not?"

"This time, I have a good reason."

"But, of course, and I will add it to the others you have offered to pardon your chronic tardiness."

"I have been trekking the *Chemin des Crêtes*," Walsingham said, referring to the Jura Ridgeway, the long-range hiking trail that ran from near Zurich to the outskirts of Geneva. "From Obergrenchenberg to Chasseral, and I have returned just this morning."

"Hiking the Höhenweg? At your age?" Sommer mocked in friendly jest. "I would recommend you stick to *loto*, and gondolas."

"Admittedly, I cheated, and only walked the first and last bits, but it was refreshing." Walsingham moved his queen pawn forward. "You should join me on one of my trips. It would do you, and your chess game, some good."

Sommer shook his head as he pushed a pawn. "The only thing that would do me any good is to quit playing you altogether. Then I can live out the remainder of my time, *on time*, and in peace."

"Something you Swiss are quite good at."

"Mock us all you want, but you should know that next year marks two full centuries since the last time we Swiss were officially at war."

"And you must remember what Harry Lime said about that." Walsingham referenced Orson Welles' character from the film, *The Third Man*, as he moved his king's knight. "Through three decades of Borgia terror and bloodshed, the Italians produced Da Vinci, Michelangelo, and the Renaissance. After five hundred years of peace and prosperity, Switzerland gave the world the cuckoo clock."

Sommer shook his head as he played his king's knight. "I do not know why I bother having anything to do with you."

"What else would you do?" Walsingham laughed, as he took king's pawn.

"I am cursed. This is the problem. I have no other alternative."

"You believe in free will, don't you? After all, as the saying goes, what other choice do we have?"

"I can resign, and save us both thirty minutes of the little time we have left."

"Before you do, catch me up on what's been happening around our little hamlet."

"Since you have been out wandering the wilderness, you have missed the big news, even for a remote place such as this." Sommer slid a copy of the local newspaper he had been reading across the table. "Your old stomping ground, I believe."

On page three of the weekend edition of the *Bieler Tagblatt,* Walsingham read the headline, "*Cambridger Wissenschaftler Ermordet,*" with a photo of Mohammad Ahmad accompanying it.

Cambridge Academic Murdered.

Walsingham shot up from his chair, startling several tables around them. He tipped his king over, and without a word to Sommer, who stared at him in shock, hurriedly left the café.

PART II

CHAPTER FORTY

Edinburgh

Sean Garrett watched cargo ships navigate the River Clyde, once the superhighway of the British Empire, as his train departed Dumbarton Central Station. He was one stop from Glasgow Queen Street and twelve hours from his meet with Deacon. The brick façade of the depot darkened the window enough for Garrett to better assess his reflection, one noticeably different than what he had become accustomed to over the past several years.

When he returned to his grandmother's cottage the evening before, he had taken scissors and trimmed his hair shorter. With the electric razor in the bathroom cabinet, which his grandfather had apparently kept since the Berlin Wall went up, he shaved himself clean. And, as he wondered whether he would see his grandmother again, Garrett accepted her offer to the spare room, and they had wound down most of the night and early morning catching up.

To avoid returning along the same Citylink bus route he had taken into the Highlands, he also agreed to let his grandmother drive him into Perthshire County in time to make the first train south. Before departing, Garrett purchased a return ticket he would not need, and booked two nights at a Highland hotel he would not use. He had also wedged the disposable phone Deacon had given him between two train seats, and for the foreseeable future, it would ride the Western Highland Line back and forth from Glasgow.

Deacon had rung just after midnight and set the meeting for 8:00 p.m. the next day, at the National Monument, the Acropolis-styled memorial dedicated to Scots killed in the Napoleonic Wars. The large structure dominated Calton Hill, an elevated open space east of Edinburgh's city center, which offered a panorama of some of the area's most notable features. Although a popular draw for tourists and townspeople, the hill was typically quiet in the evening, and would serve as a good location for a quick exchange. Considering his two prior encounters with the enigmatic contact, Garrett was certain the third would be no less brusque, or brief.

He changed trains and quickly scanned the crowded coach. The first leg of his return trip had given Garrett time to assess his situation, and he still had not decided whether one assassin who had seen his face posed more of a threat than a faceless security service that might know his identity. Regardless, what had become evident to Garrett over the last week was that he had slowed a step, and needed to quickly rehone skills that had once been razor sharp. What happened at King's College was unavoidable, though clearly someone was running an operation parallel to his own. Whether the timing was a coincidence was something he would deal with later.

But to allow the man who called himself Deacon to so easily gain the advantage in the pouring rain in some dank Edinburgh close was unacceptable. That kind of momentary lapse of attention could not happen again if Garrett was to have any hope of making it home. It was irrelevant that the man was veteran CIA—if the lads from the old unit knew, he would never hear the end of it.

His train eased into Haymarket. Garrett exited the station and found a small room at a cheap accommodation near the Water of Leith. He paid for three nights in advance, and decided to remain at the hotel until late-morning, after which he would make his way to Waverley Station, and bide the remainder of his time in the role of a long-distance traveler awaiting a connecting leg.

However the coming days played out, Garrett realized his grandmother was right, and that his redemption had never been tied to Ahmad. He would soon be given the credentials to get out of the U.K., and the chance to put what had happened in England, both fifteen months earlier, and several days ago, behind him. He knew his fate until then, and his absolution thereafter, was in his own hands.

CHAPTER FORTY-ONE

Waverley Train Station
Edinburgh

A disabled lorry on Waverley Bridge brought traffic to a standstill at an intersection that was congested even when everything ran smoothly. Angry motorists leaned on their horns, as if the sound would encourage the towing service on-site to hurry it along. David Laurent stood near-by, outside the entrance of a Chinese buffet, and took intermittent pulls on a Camel Blue. He did not smoke, but in his experience, one could loiter almost anywhere and become nearly invisible if holding a cigarette.

Since his arrival in Edinburgh, tasked with killing the man who had witnessed the assassination of Mohammad Ahmad, Laurent had more or less been at the mercy of the mobile given to him by his contact at Kensington, a man called Danesh. He was to wait for confirmation of his target's re-acquired GPS position, and while the information would facilitate the assignment and shorten his time in Scotland, Laurent knew it also made him vulnerable to exposure. In the meantime, the assassin decided to rely on his own skill and experience to locate the witness.

To do so required Laurent to think like his target, which meant establishing a baseline for how the man would act, and react. The FBI had developed the science of profiling as it pertained to criminal conduct, but Laurent had learned over a long career that the everyday behavior of the average person was also predictive, and more or less followed the same pattern. Hence the notion of *average*.

Foremost, Laurent knew his witness was an amateur, for anyone who allowed himself to be caught on camera and his cell phone to be tracked was not a professional. In addition, the man had not gone directly to the authorities, and had instead decided to run. In Laurent's experience, this type of behavior was not uncommon, as governed by the *10-80-10 Principle*. In almost every type of stressful situation or disaster scenario studied in its aftermath, a small percentage of those involved, the positive ten percent, reacted quickly, and in a manner that better guaranteed their survival. The negative ten percent panicked, with some literally sitting on the ground and screaming. But what did the middle eighty percent do? Wait to be led. *Eighty percent.*

Laurent knew that his witness was part of this group. The man had fled, traveled to Scotland, uncertain of what to do, and was in all likelihood planning to rendezvous with someone he hoped would assist with a best course of action. His last position had been Waverley. Laurent gambled that if the man was still in Edinburgh, he would stay close to the station. All Laurent had to do was remain vigilant. If he was lucky, his witness, in choosing to remain put, would essentially come to him.

The assassin took another pull on his cigarette, exhaled, and waited.

CHAPTER FORTY-TWO

Princes Street Gardens
Edinburgh

A group of buskers playing near the statue of David Livingstone kept the east entrance of Princes Street Gardens crowded, and loud. Tre Ward sat on the ground with his head between his knees and his back against an iron rail fence near Waverley Bridge. He was dressed in an old pair of jeans and a tattered brown jumper with the hood pulled over his head. Several empty liquor bottles were scattered at his feet, and the small cup beside him held several pounds in change, collected over the four hours he had occupied the spot near the Scott Monument.

The two operators had arrived in Edinburgh a day earlier, Ward on an East Coast train and Bishop via a National Express bus. Both men had been instructed to steer clear of CIA safe houses in the area, knowing they might be monitored by MI5, and instead had checked into separate hotels near Old Town.

"You owe me dinner with that money," Brian Bishop relayed over the small receiver in Ward's right ear.

Ward lifted his head and scanned the crowd near the monument. "I can't watch you put down that *bag nasty* anymore, buddy," he responded, using military slang to describe the fast food his partner had eaten for most of their meals since arriving in the U.K.

Bishop monitored the gardens from across the street, near an entrance of Waverley Mall. "Best chow anywhere, bro. Chicken nuggets are God's gift to mankind."

"More like chicken pits and bits," Ward answered.

"Don't knock before you try. You should live a little."

"I avoid that crap so I can do just that. But I'll speak at your wake."

"It will be standing room only," Bishop joked. "Doing alright?" The temperature had dropped steadily as the afternoon wore on, and Ward had not moved since lunch.

"My stomach hurts."

"You had a salad, for Christ's sake."

"A term loosely applied. It was green."

"Still no sign of our man, *I presume.*"

Ward shook his head. "I wondered if I would be forced to suffer that allusion at some point," he said, referring to arguably the most famous greeting in history. "I'm impressed you even know who David Livingstone is."

"West Coast education, baby." Bishop refocused his attention on the park entrance opposite of Ward's position. "Intel says *Acolyte's* mobile is still pinging from Waverley, but two teams with eyes all over this place have come up with exactly *nada*. Five to one this guy is long gone."

"We'll give it thirty more minutes, and rotate. And I'll take those odds, at five pounds."

"Roger that, on both counts."

John Campion stepped away from the monument and feigned a phone conversation as he eyed the homeless drunk with his head down. *But with his eyes up.*

He walked slowly toward Ward, keeping up the pretense of a call. "No mate, I'm by the monument, not the mall," he said loudly, as he moved to within a few feet of the operator, who sat unflinching. "You and your buddy across the street might as well wear a bloody sign," Campion said in a low voice.

Ward said nothing.

"Meet me in Whighams, off Charlotte Square, in two hours. Come alone."

The operator nodded.

"And change your clothes, for fuck's sake," Campion added, as he moved away from Ward and back toward Waverley Street.

CHAPTER FORTY-THREE

London

Seven Park Place, the renowned French restaurant at the St. James's Hotel, was standing room only. The crowd waiting to be seated was surprisingly patient for a late Friday lunch, as patrons already at tables certainly seemed in no hurry to give them up. Samantha Anderton waved as Dominic Adair crossed Park Place. He was still as handsome as he had been at university, she acknowledged, and Anderton was surprised that one drunken night together during their second year had blossomed into a close friendship.

"Hello, luv." Adair kissed her cheek, and allowed the ensuing hug to linger a few extra seconds. "My God, Sam, you are still gorgeous."

"And you are still relatively charming, though less subtle than I remember."

"I'm afraid it goes with the new territory."

"Working for a poncy bank?" she smiled.

"Age."

Adair whispered something to the hostess, and despite the crowd, they were immediately seen to a quiet table near the back of the restaurant.

"Wasn't this place awarded a Michelin star?"

Adair nodded as he took a sip of sparkling water. "You won't find a better lunch in London."

"The décor reminds me of the inside of a cheap jewelry box, truth be told."

Adair laughed. "I thought we worked on your habit of being so blunt back in school."

"It goes with *my* new territory."

"I should expect so, though I guarantee you've got better stories from Scotland Yard than I do the bank."

"You've no idea."

"Care to indulge?" Adair smiled. "You know how well I keep a secret."

"And you know I can't divulge the details of any ongoing investigation," Anderton replied in an exaggerated official tone.

"Fair enough. Care to divulge the details of any ongoing relationships?"

She gave him a sideways glance. "No comment at this time."

The two caught up while dining on tuna loin and lamb. After the main course, they ordered two coffees and one dessert between them, and Anderton insisted on picking up the check, over Adair's protestations.

"Thanks, Sam," he finally submitted. "I owe you."

"Good, then you can pay me back right away."

"Well, I've only got an hour, and the hotel is quite expensive, but I'll be happy to get us a room," he replied, only half-joking.

"Then you should have insisted on a second glass of wine," Anderton winked.

"Now you say. I'm gutted."

"I actually need your help with something I'm working on, if that makes up for it."

"Not even close, but if it will help you crack a case, count me in."

"Is it possible to match a safety deposit key to a specific bank?"

"Do you have it?"

Anderton pulled Ahmad's key from her pocket.

Adair flipped it over several times. "Well, I can tell you that it's not for a bank box."

Anderton was surprised. "Are you certain?"

"It doesn't bear the appropriate markings, which would consist of an identifying number, typically three or four digits, that can be matched to a sister key at the branch. It would also be stamped with the name and location of the company that cut the key. This looks similar, but I'm guessing it fits some sort of lock box, or safe."

"At a bank?"

Adair shook his head. "A hotel safe, maybe, or station locker, if there are any still around."

"Well, shit." Anderton's mobile began to ring. "I've got to take this." She stood and kissed Adair on the cheek. "Thanks, Dom, let's do this again soon."

"Absolutely, and next time, I'll bring the key." He gestured toward the hotel side of the building, and she blew him a kiss before pushing through the crowded lobby, and out the door.

"Anderton."

"It's Holland." He sounded irritated. "MI5 want everything we've got."

"How soon?" Anderton waved a taxi.

"I can put Healey off until tomorrow morning, by which time you'll officially be off the case and reassigned to Barclay," he replied.

"Understood."

CHAPTER FORTY-FOUR

Secret Intelligence Service
London

The path between his desk and office window was well worn, and the location where Montjoy sat had become his go-to spot when stuck on a problem. Over the last twelve months, it was the place he seemed to find himself most often.

His drink, only the second, rested atop a colony of concentric rings dried into a side table that had been gifted by his mother, and whose only purpose was to support his scotches. Montjoy needed a clear head, and so he had veered away from his customary string of afternoon whiskeys. Gavin

Abbot pushed into his office just as Montjoy had begun to second-guess that decision.

"I've got it."

As Montjoy had tasked him with several jobs, he sat expressionless, waiting for Abbot to clarify.

"Firstly, I brought your favorite." Abbot placed a small bag on Montjoy's desk. "You remember you asked me to find anything that stood out surrounding the period of your being removed as Ahmad's handler."

Montjoy nodded. In late 2010, he had abruptly been pulled from *Dalmatia*, the program he created that oversaw all intelligence provided through Mohammad Ahmad. Berwyn Rees had been assigned as the new case controller, and Montjoy assumed at the time that William Lindsay had initiated the move. In the years since, however, he had begun to suspect that it was his Welsh counterpart, with heady aspirations beyond head of section, who had instigated the takeover and convinced the deputy chief to sign off on it.

Montjoy opened the bag and pulled out a sandwich rolled in silver foil, as Abbot looked over something he had written on a piece of paper. "I reviewed all files that were accessed leading up to when *Dalmatia* was moved from this office. There is nothing beyond March 2011, when all new intelligence was housed elsewhere."

"Rees would have wanted full operational control. I would have done the same thing."

"Granted, but new information pertaining to *Dalmatia* continued to be shelved at the original file location as late as mid-February of that year. One in particular includes a reference, with no other details, to an asset called *Albatross*."

"I don't recall it offhand. Each asset file is labeled by its cryptonym, and a three-digit reference to a secondary location where all gathered intelligence is kept. The most sensitive files can only be accessed with *Developed Vetting* clearance. That is why the files you have are in a blue or white sleeve." He motioned at several folders Abbot carried under his arm.

"The file I am referencing was gold."

"That's not possible," Montjoy replied, as he bit down into a black pudding sandwich. "Quite good, by the way, ta."

"You are most welcome." Abbot pulled a yellow-colored file from beneath the others, and held it up. "Twice, I might add."

Montjoy wiped his mouth and sat back in his chair. "You're not cleared for that," he said, tongue in cheek, considering that Abbot held in his hand a file that he should not have had access to.

"From its contents, I can see why."

Montjoy gestured, and Abbot passed him the folder. Inside was a single sheet, a letter dated 1966. Montjoy quickly scanned its contents, which involved a name that he, and anyone paying attention over the last fifty years, would immediately recognize. The accusation leveled at Sir Charles Walsingham was damning both in its subject and scope. Montjoy flipped the page over, which was blank. "The letter doesn't finish with this page, were there any additional?"

"Not that I found."

He flipped it back over and read the partial letter a second time.

Abbot gave him a moment before noting, "someone either confused file colors, or cocked-up royally."

"Both, perhaps," Montjoy replied.

"What are you going to do?"

"Tread carefully, considering who, and what, appears to be involved."

"What do you want me to do?" Abbot asked, knowing the answer.

"Bash on."

"Right away."

"Gavin," Montjoy called after him. "Well done."

"Thank you, sir."

CHAPTER FORTY-FIVE

Whighams Wine Cellars
Edinburgh

Whighams was standing room only, but John Campion sat alone in a dimly lit alcove that had served as a storage cellar in the nineteenth century. He had first patronized the popular wine bar when it opened thirty years earlier, and the current front of house manager did not hesitate when Campion slipped him several hundred quid, and requested the space be his for the next hour. It was not his money he was spending, so squander it he would.

When the SOG operator from Princes Street Gardens showed, he would want the meeting to be over as quickly as it began. And Campion would not disappoint. He had been tasked to arrange the acquisition of a man who found himself on the wrong end of an assignment gone bad. A man who would not be able to sidestep the trap in which he now more than willingly walked. Desperation dulled the senses. This maxim had been proven to Campion more than once over an embattled career.

It had nearly gotten him killed during a high-risk assignment in Caracas just six months out of Camp Peary, the CIA's training camp for new recruits. It was Campion's first time in South America, and it ended with him sweating out a failed operation in the basement of a two-bit bar on the outskirts of the Venezuelan capital. It had not been his fault, but that mattered little for the lone agent waiting to be extracted under blown cover from a Cold War hornet's nest. The small room he found himself trapped on that long night in November, courtesy of a twice-turned CIA informant who was also coordinating with a KGB hit squad en route, was not unlike the one in which he now waited. Had the untested operative not snapped from a near paralytic state in time to shoot his way through the SEBIN team tasked with handing him over to the Soviets, the only thing left of Campion would be a star etched into a marble wall in the lobby at Langley, an anonymous tribute to CIA employees who died in the line of service.

But at least then he could have avoided the lie.

Though there was little risk for Campion in the trendy restaurant that night, no longer did he intend to extricate himself cleanly from dangerous situations. His only aim now was to take as many with him as he could. He sipped a third Glenfiddich, and gripped the Glock under a napkin in his lap.

Tre Ward slipped fluidly into the confined space, and sat down. He was dressed smartly in dark jeans and a black jumper, and kept one hand in his jacket pocket. "Not the best place for a meeting," the operator said flatly, as he glanced at Campion while keeping his surveillance on the doorway.

"That depends on how good you are," Campion answered sarcastically, calling attention to the ease at which he had singled out the SOG team earlier in the gardens.

Ward said nothing. He was here for intel, not some inter-agency pissing contest. What he wanted to do was warn the man against compromising him and his partner a second time with a stunt like he had pulled that afternoon.

Campion lifted a dark brown envelope from the seat beside him and flipped it across the table.

"Is *Halfback* still running the op?" Ward asked as he pulled the folder into his jacket without checking the contents.

Campion ignored the question. "Target arrived in Edinburgh this morning. Delivery will be this evening. Note the change in the primary hand-off and secondary exfil location." He finished his scotch and added, "I'm leaving now."

Ward said nothing as Campion pushed himself from the table. As he eyed the burned-out agent, Ward assured himself that he would not end up like the man struggling to stand and leave, who-ever he was.

Campion smiled as he registered the slight microexpression of disdain from the young operator. "Give it time," he said, as if reading Ward's mind, before exiting the alcove.

CHAPTER FORTY-SIX

Edinburgh

Nasir Hajjar finished his latte and the latest copy of *The Guardian*, which had been left on a table overlooking Edinburgh Castle in the upstairs section of the Starbucks on Princes Street. It was almost dinner, and he did not need to consider where to eat. An Italian restaurant on Hannover Street had long been his favorite in the city, and he smiled at the irony. The last time he was in the Scottish capital, it was to kill someone, which Hajjar had done following a nice Fillet Rossini.

His target then had been a restoration expert whom bin Halabi had entrusted with several original maps of Persia. They were four-hundred-year-old family heirlooms, and the prince wanted a tinge of color added to where the Gulf of Oman met the coastline of modern-day Iran. The man had butchered the job, spilling a tin of blue oil on the center of one of the best pieces in the collection. He had apologized profusely, refused payment, and promised to complete the remainder of the maps for free. The prince graciously forgave him, and even paid for what had already been finished, though he ultimately commissioned an expert in Berlin to complete the work. Hajjar was less charitable, having recommended the bookshop owner to bin Halabi. He bludgeoned the man on an overcast afternoon in Glasgow, and dumped his body in the River Clyde.

While the new assignment would prove more difficult than killing some hapless bibliophilic, Hajjar was confident that by that time next week, he would be sitting comfortably on the balcony of his luxury flat in Dubai. Until then, he was to wait for a phone call from the prince's proxy, a man named Danesh, who would provide him the details of where he could find and kill David Laurent.

Hajjar looked at a photo of the assassin, a man close to his age, and, he guessed, of similar skill and expertise. But no matter how good David Laurent might be, it was Hajjar's own experience that the element of surprise tended to trump almost everything else when it came to killing.

Hajjar had booked a room at the Witchery by the Castle, one of the most expensive hotels in the city. The Gothic bed and breakfast, which boasted only a handful of rooms, was rumored to be haunted by those burned as witches near the site five hundred years earlier.

Hajjar checked the time on one of three disposable mobiles he carried. He had decided earlier that he would remain in Edinburgh for two days only. If Danesh provided Laurent's itinerary and location in that time, Hajjar would complete the assignment as ordered by bin Halabi. Anything more, and he knew he was being put at too great a risk, one that he was unwilling to chance for anyone, even a Saudi prince who wanted someone else to clean up a mess he had created. If need be, Hajjar would get himself out of England, and determine his best course of action from the safety of the U.A.E.

Until then, a nice steak awaited him.

CHAPTER FORTY-SEVEN

Waverley Train Station
Edinburgh

G arrett climbed the steps to an overpass that spanned the length of Waverley Station. The bridge was covered with travelers hurrying to catch trains leaving from backside platforms, and he stood against a center guardrail to let the steady stream pass. Since jumping a quick leg from Haymarket, Garrett had used the massive depot as cover until his meet with Deacon later that evening. Over the course of the day, he had finished off every English language newspaper in the main hall, along with three cups of coffee.

The crowds came in waves, and Garrett used the surge to rotate his position between interior and exterior points of the station. The latest Flying Scotsman from London had just pulled in, and he mixed with a group who hurried to the access road behind Waverley, where coaches waited and taxis queued in long, but rapidly interchanging lines. He descended a set of stairs to ground level, and scanned both sides of the street as he moved between two lines of travelers awaiting pickup.

Garrett spied an orange and gray blaze work jacket that had been hung on the handle of a storage door. He nicked it as he neared a roped-off work zone, and stuffed his hands into the pockets of the dusty coat, slowing his pace and assuming the guise of a worker on break.

Across the road, a luggage cart overturned. Two men gestured angrily at one another, and Garrett glanced up as the argument became more agitated. The crowd around the altercation cleared as it escalated, but he ignored the scuffle and turned his attention back to the meet with Deacon. If the man delivered as promised, Garrett would soon be back in the States.

Garrett checked his watch, and decided it was time to slowly make his way to the rendezvous. He returned back to the main ticket hall, ordered another coffee from Costa, and exited the station.

CHAPTER FORTY-EIGHT

Laurent was set to alternate his position between the access road and overpass, when he saw him. Walking slowly down the lane. Easily dismissed, if he wasn't moving too alertly among a group of distracted tourists. A man too young to belong to the group he shadowed, pensioners preparing to board a tourist coach. A station worker whose coat was too small for his frame.

It had happened by chance, Laurent could admit that. The assassin had mixed with a group of travelers who had, up until the moment the argument broke out, peaceably queued for rides. He was standing back from the crowd and hidden by a rack of luggage trolleys when two men attempting to hire the same taxi began to exchange words, then shout, then shove one another. The crowd around the altercation cleared faster than Laurent could retreat from the hole that opened, exposing him to the man across the street, whose attention was momentarily drawn by the disturbance. The second time in a week the world slowed to a stop, and Laurent locked eyes with the witness from King's College.

His hair was shorter and he was clean-shaven, but his face was etched into Laurent's memory. The assassin quickly stepped behind a luggage stack and watched as the man, who seemed unfazed by the fight, slowly turned and walked back toward the stairs that led to the access bridge.

Laurent mirrored his movement from the other side of the street, and climbed a parallel set of stairs as the two of them made their way back over the walk and into the main booking hall. The assassin moved fluidly through the crowd and pretended to buy a ticket from a self-serve kiosk, as his target purchased a coffee and exited the station. Laurent followed him into Waverley Mall, and kept a manageable distance as he turned up Princes Street. He marked the time at 6:00 p.m. By nightfall, his target would be dead, and Laurent would be home free.

CHAPTER FORTY-NINE

London

The entrance to Green Park Station had been cordoned off, and a group of Irishmen stood by the gate yelling loudly, and in vain, at a guard stationed to keep people out. Berwyn Rees lit a cigarette and watched the scene from a small grove of trees in the park across the road, a stone's throw from the upscale London club on St. James's Street. He had not smoked in five years, yet here he was, taking nervous pulls on a Chesterfield. Waiting for Leighton Thackeray. *Again.* The MP had been livid when Rees requested a follow-up meeting, not twenty-four hours after Thackeray had essentially ordered that under no circumstances were they to cross paths until the circus surrounding Ahmad's death had died down. Until he heard what Rees had in mind.

Thackeray was dining at White's, London's oldest and most prestigious club, no doubt sitting down to an early dinner over roasted grouse, and situated near the likes of Prince Charles. Rees envisioned that after being made deputy chief of MI6, he would be invited to join, and thus attain one of only two things that nineteenth-century prime minister Benjamin Disraeli claimed an Englishman could not command on his own, other than a Knighthood. A membership to White's would catapult Rees into the upper echelon of English society, and place him on equal footing with men like Thackeray.

Rees had spent the better part of a week seeking a way out of the potentially career-ending mess he found himself. Thackeray had made it abundantly clear that it was on him to scrub their connections from the one man, a dead Cambridge scholar, whose untimely murder could pull their little fiefdom down around them. It was an unfair demand, but Rees well knew that a more accurate definition of accountability was that shite always flowed downhill. Where everyone involved with Ahmad was concerned, only he and Montjoy sat in the valley. It was simply a matter of getting out of the path quicker.

The solution, bloody brilliant as it was, had come to Rees a day earlier. He would use Montjoy's own *Dalmatia* files against him. When Rees convinced Lindsay to turn the program over to him five years earlier, he had argued that a change of handler might be good from an operational standpoint, as asset and intelligence acquisition had begun to lag. Lindsay had ultimately acquiesced, with hesitation, but also with the stipulation that Montjoy would retain access to all files he had controlled to that point.

Rees had chalked the caveat up to residual loyalty to Montjoy's grandfather, Sir *bloody* Nigel, king of Cold War exploits and Lindsay's best mate from back in the day. The duo had supposedly been responsible for a spate of legendary intelligence coups in East Germany during the Cold War. Urban legends were more like it, Rees was certain, overblown tales cooked up to keep Lindsay relevant this late in his career. Clearly the man's fidelity had clouded his judgment, and there was little Rees could do but begrudgingly accept the condition.

"I didn't realize you smoked," Thackeray interrupted Rees' train of thought, and caught him off guard. "Good, you can lend me a fag and a light."

"Good evening, sir." Rees handed over a cigarette and struck a match. "How was your dinner?"

"The filet was bloody good," the lanky MP quipped as he took a long drag, and made only a half-hearted attempt to exhale away from Rees.

Rees waved the smoke away and tried his best to laugh in earnest at the well-worn joke.

"Philby and his lot were turned by the Russians in that very bar," Thackeray said, nodding in the direction of White's. He was referring to the Cambridge Five, a ring of spies recruited during their years at university, who later went on to the highest levels of British Intelligence, all the while turning England's most guarded secrets over to the Soviets.

"*The one that has been open for two-hundred years*," Rees replied, quoting a famous line and hoping Thackeray would register his intimate knowledge of, and interest in, the club. He wondered if the MP was aware that it had been originally founded as a hot chocolate shop by an Italian.

Thackeray ignored the comment. "I met with Walsingham."

Rees was speechless. "Here? In England?"

"Well I didn't bloody well jet off to Switzerland, did I? I've just had dinner with him, and he's less than pleased with what has happened."

No shite. Rees hoped his reaction did not betray what he was thinking. The legendary financier was putting himself, and them, in a risky spot, considering what Ahmad had threatened.

"Did you reassure him that everything is under control?"

"Is it?"

Rees hesitated. "Yes," he finally replied. All three of the men were linked, and the situation was guaranteed to implode if he couldn't contain the potential fallout connected to the professor's death.

"You will need to broker a better poker face if you're to survive in there." Thackeray thumbed in the direction behind him.

Rees immediately livened up at the implication that Thackeray might vouch as one of the thirty-five signatories needed for consideration for membership at White's. His spirits lifted, Rees asserted, "I will take care of my end. I'll leave it to you to manage Sir Charles."

"Walsingham was foolish to come back to England. I will convince him that it is in his best interest, and ours, to go somewhere he won't be so quickly extradited, should you fail."

"I won't."

"Of course not." Thackeray took a final drag and flicked his cigarette. He pulled a large envelope from his coat and handed it to Rees. "As requested."

"Thank you, sir."

"This is a risky gambit, Rees. Don't bullocks it up."

"No, sir." Rees assured Thackeray, who had already begun to head back in the direction of St. James's Street.

CHAPTER FIFTY

Edinburgh

"Anything?" Bishop asked, adjusting his position near a covered bus shelter on Princes Street. The rain had stopped, but the sky remained overcast and threatened more before nightfall.

Tre Ward checked the time, and several exits of the building. "Negative."

Bishop studied the photo they had been given earlier by John Campion. It was of a man who was middle-aged and Middle Eastern, their new target. "Our boy has changed his look," he joked. "And what do we do if we spot *Acolyte*?" Bishop referenced the codename given to Sean Garrett. "To wit, what the fuck is going on?"

"*Acolyte* is not our problem right now. All clear with the new parameters?" Ward referred to the change in exit points, which moved the handoff to the Scottish port town of Queensferry, and Bishop's exfil through Rotterdam.

"Oh, yes, I love Dutch women."

"Yesterday, it was French."

"A man must be balanced."

"That's how I've always thought of you. A true renaissance man, very well-rounded."

"I couldn't agree more. I love all well-rounded women equally. You should try it some time."

"I'm a go home and go to bed type of guy, until I meet the right one."

"Try going to bed and then home, and you'll be a much happier *hombre.*"

"Heads up. Target is in the open and on the move," Ward said, as he caught movement near a side exit. "Confirm."

"Indeed he is." Bishop moved behind a group of commuters queued for the bus.

"Intel says *Blackbird* will head toward Leith."

"He's turned left. That's a good start." Bishop began moving slowly along Princes Street, shadowing Nasir Hajjar as he walked. "I'm with him."

"I'm switching to position two."

"Roger that."

Ward left his vantage point near a small kiosk selling coffee. "Team one," he voiced into a throat mic concealed beneath a zipped-up jumper, "rotate your surveillance at the next roundabout." He heard an affirmative as he began walking along St. Andrew Square. If the op went smoothly, Hajjar would be bound and blindfolded, and on a boat heading to Norway in less than one hour.

CHAPTER FIFTY-ONE

Edinburgh

Laurent circled the roundabout where London, St. Bellevue, and Broughton Streets intersected. His target had made his way slowly from Waverley Station, and though the crowd on the outskirts of the city had begun to thin out, the avenue was sufficiently populated with pubs and shops that the assassin could disguise his pursuit by pretending to peruse menu placards and window adverts.

Laurent was familiar with Edinburgh's layout well enough to know that if they continued in their current direction, he and his target would pass a massive block of parks and gardens along

Inverleith Row. Laurent had planned to shadow the man until dark, but if his witness ended up in a public place, or was en route to meet someone, Laurent would be forced to wait another day, or worse, lose the chance altogether. The assassin decided that if the opportunity presented itself, he would intercept and kill the man sooner than later.

Regardless, he knew his victim would put up little or no fight. It was Laurent's experience that few people resisted when under threat of harm, particularly if it was coupled with the assurance of safe passage upon cooperation. And, after Laurent guaranteed his witness that he only wanted information, it would be accepted at face value, because this is what the man wanted to believe. It came down to the simple human construct of *resolve*. The man would not believe that Laurent would kill him because he himself, like the vast majority of people the world over, lacked the ability, the resolve, to take the life of another human being.

The simple reason, Laurent had learned over a lifetime of killing, was because the ordinary subconscious had signed on to the social pact that viewed violent behavior as abhorrent. The average person had difficulty with even minor representations of real violence, so to watch someone accidently snap their ulna would cause most observers to recoil in horror. Amplify the physical, emotional, and psychological effect of an arm dangling at an irregular angle, to the level of murder, and the concept becomes unmanageable. A protruding bone paled in comparison to neural tissue and solid brain matter exiting the skull, which would cause even the most desensitized person to go into varying stages of hysteria, denial, and shock.

This is where most people ended, and men like Laurent began.

Even more incomprehensible to Laurent, was the behavior of the average person when confronted with the reality that everything was *not* going to be okay. In addition to his own experiences, the assassin was familiar with case studies of murder victims who, even in the face of their own death, could manage to inflict only superficial and non-threatening injuries to their attacker. Most people simply could not bring themselves to act in the savage manner requisite to save their own lives. This is why the witness from King's College would do exactly what Laurent demanded of him, because of the optimism that all would end well, particularly in a place surrounded by nice houses and neighborhood parks, and where children ate ice cream and played on the weekend.

Laurent watched his target pause momentarily at an intersection, before turning down Inverleith Row. He could not have asked for a better turn of events. The Botanical Gardens, and the park, were only blocks away. The assassin picked his pace up slightly, and kept an eye on where to best intercept the man.

CHAPTER FIFTY-TWO

Edinburgh

Hajjar quickened his pace. The phone call he had received from Danesh an hour earlier informed him that David Laurent would meet him at King George V Park, near Inverleith, at 7:00 p.m. Hajjar was to rendezvous under the guise of providing Laurent with the location of the witness from King's College, as well as to give the assassin new credentials to leave England. Hajjar knew the pretense would allow him an easy kill, but the situation did not afford as much time as he would typically want to canvas a location in advance of his target, and establish a position that would give him the advantage. Nonetheless, Hajjar was confident that, by midnight, Laurent would be dead, and he would be on his way to Cardiff.

By his best calculations, Hajjar had killed just shy of seventy people, most of them men and all of them unlucky enough to have ended up on his radar. He had long erased, from whatever conscience some dime store psychologist might argue he still possessed, the memory of the score of women and children he had also murdered. Some of them had been collateral damage, innocent bystanders in the wrong place at the wrong time. For others, it had come down to simple misfortune, no different than catching a cold. Viruses spread freely around, attaching themselves to everyday surfaces and lying in wait for some unwitting victim to initiate contact. Bad luck was the same. In this case, it had been picked up, deservedly or not, by an assassin who should have known better, and been able to avoid it. But as bin Halabi would have had Hajjar repeat, *deserve has nothing to with it.*

Hajjar neared the junction at Calton Hill and began to slowly circle the roundabout, back in the direction he had come. He took photos and pretended to study a map, exhibiting the behavior of a tourist enjoying himself, all the while keeping a watchful eye on his surroundings. The maneuver was not unlike that used by submarines, known as *clearing the baffles.* Subs were typically the hunters, like Nazi U-boat wolf packs in the North Atlantic during World War II. However, because early sonar arrays were mounted on the bow of a vessel to avoid intercepting the mechanical footprint of its own noise, captains were left vulnerable to what lay behind them. Enemy subs could move in tow and follow their target without detection. To counter this threat, skippers would swing their vessels in a three-hundred-and-sixty-degree arc. If done without warning, the sudden move would expose a predator in their wake.

Professionals like Hajjar used the same technique on the street. It was highly effective, and only seasoned operatives, or highly trained teams, could avoid detection. Hajjar had nearly completed his turn, when he saw him. A man who had gone unnoticed during the first double back, but when Hajjar changed his pace this time, his pursuer checked his own. The hesitation was almost undetectable, but it was enough for someone of Hajjar's experience to spot it.

He had seen the man before, standing across Princes Street and dressed like a tourist waiting for a bus. There had been no reason to mark him as a potential threat at the time, but Hajjar's life depended on being aware, and remembering, when need be, everything around him. He recognized the man from earlier, and his reaction on the roundabout betrayed him as something other than just another tourist who happened to be on the same sightseeing route as Hajjar.

He was in pursuit, and Hajjar needed to determine whether the man was alone.

CHAPTER FIFTY-THREE

King's College, Cambridge

S am Anderton stood behind Mohammad Ahmad's desk. Much of the room had been boxed up and taken away, with the exception of the larger furniture, and the professor's extensive book collection, which was still neatly arranged on wall-to-wall shelves. After hanging up with Holland, she had jumped on the M1 and made the sixty-mile drive to the university in the hopes that something from the scene of the assassination would answer what the ledger and key by themselves had not. For the better part of an hour, the office had told her nothing.

In eighteen hours, Anderton and Holland would meet with Healey to discuss their progress on the case. Which would amount to little more than Scotland Yard handing over what they had un-covered, effectively rendering them subservient to the Security Service's own investigation. Holland would protest, and Healey would remind him that the 1996 Security Service Act mandates MI5 coor-dinate on cases of this nature. If Holland persisted, Healey might stoop low enough to argue that since a former officer at the Met had been suspected of being an al-Qaeda sleeper agent, MI5 needed to be absolutely certain that nothing would be compro-mised from the inside. Holland could counter with accusations that MI5 incompetence failed to pre-vent the bombings at Bishopsgate and Docklands years earlier, but the point would be moot. In the end, the Security Service would take over.

And if that happened, it was highly probable that anything Ahmad may have been involved with would be buried for reasons of national security, whether that was actually the case.

It was at the moment that Anderton had re-signed Cambridge as a lost cause and decided to give the professor's flat in London one last try, when she saw it. One book which stood out among hundreds of others. What drew the sergeant's at-tention to that one particular volume was its bind-ing, which stuck out slightly more than the rest of the row pushed flush against the wall. Anderton walked to the shelf and examined the book. It was the only one out of place, and she guessed that the edge must have caught on an adjacent flap the last time the volume had been read and reshelved.

The manuscript, published in 1972, was a hardback monograph written by Ahmad. Anderton quickly flipped through the pages, but saw nothing out of the ordinary. She was about to put it back, when she remembered a trick spy-catchers used during the Cold War to find pages that might have been used as code ciphers. She placed the book on its spine and released the sides. The reasoning was that the book would open naturally to the section frequented most, where a natural crease had been created.

The volume fell open to its middle, to a page with two illustrations. Along the inside ridge, near the fold, were several lines in faded black ink, written so small that Anderton almost missed them. She strained to read the text, but could make nothing of the part penned in Arabic. An address, and several numbers that accompanied it, however, were written in English. It was a location in the town of Ely, a thirty-minute drive north of Cambridge.

Anderton was set to dismiss the find as insignificant, when she noticed something she thought she recognized. She quickly produced the key from

Ahmad's shoe and pressed it against the binding. The string of numbers etched into the book matched perfectly.

She drove fast, and made the half-hour trip up the A-10 in just over twenty minutes. After several U-turns, Anderton drove down a narrow access road, and stopped short of the parking lot of a self-storage company. The business looked more like some sort of compound, with large, elongated shipping containers arranged side-by-side in rows. The entire facility was enclosed by high wire fencing, with motion-activated floodlights mounted around the perimeter and on high poles at each corner of the facility.

The sergeant switched off her car and sat in darkness for several minutes. She had already obtained evidence illegally, and knew that if she got caught breaking and entering into a locked, private, firm after hours, what had happened at the HSBC branch in Cambridge would be the least of her worries. Holland's support would go no further than the bank, and she would lose her job, or worse.

It took only a moment to determine her course of action. She backed up onto the soft shoulder of the access road and made sure her vehicle was out of range of any CCTV cameras. Anderton decided to leave her baton behind as she quietly exited the car, and skirted a shrub line to one section of the fence that bordered a small wooded area.

From a dead start, she leapt halfway up the barricade and quickly pulled herself to the top, which was twisted and sharp. Anderton grabbed a support pole and swung over, cutting her wrist in the process. In one, athletic motion, she dropped the full ten feet to the ground on the other side and sprinted to the nearest container. There was a large "10" painted on its exterior, and she pulled Ahmad's key from her pocket, verifying the number "32," which had been written with a permanent marker.

She could make out a "21" stamped on the last container on the next row over, across an internal lane cut wide enough for lorry access. She counted down the line, ten deep, and noticed that cameras had been positioned at each end of each column. Anderton knew that if they were being monitored, she would have little time to get out if she was seen, and security dispatched. She darted down the gravel path, quickly scanning each container as she ran. The one she was looking for was last in the line, and the sergeant stayed flush against the side of the massive canister as she moved to its front door.

On it was a combination padlock, and it only took two tries using the six-digit number written on the key before the bolt clicked free. Anderton pulled down the locking bar, and twisted it just enough to open the large doors and squeeze through. The air inside was dry, but stale, and she flipped on her flashlight. The box was around ten by twenty feet, and looked empty. As she walked slowly to the back of the container, her footsteps echoed off the metal walls, and sounded like someone beating a kettledrum. Anderton had just pulled off her shoes when she thought she heard voices outside, and stopped dead as a measure of panic welled up. She suppressed the instinct to bolt, and strained to pick up additional sounds.

She heard nothing, and had just committed herself to spending only a few more seconds in the storage unit, when her beam illuminated a small mound of books. The pile, consisting of novels, many of them appearing to be American Westerns, had been shoved into a back corner, creating a half-pyramid. Anderton bent down and began to rummage through the haphazard collection of paperbacks. She saw nothing out of the ordinary, but the top half of the heap suddenly came spilling down as she pulled several rows from the bottom, exposing a neatly ordered stack of large, hardbound volumes.

She pushed these aside, and beneath an oversized copy of an Arabic to English dictionary, was a safe. The small vault was barely the size of an A4 sheet of paper, and only about six inches deep. It was old, sturdy for its size, and had faded script she could not read written across one side. Anderton took a breath, slid the key into the lock, and waited a moment before turning it. The catch released with a click, and the lid popped open.

Inside was a small, brown, leather-bound attaché case. Anderton carefully removed it and pulled the top flap back, revealing two ledgers, and three sheets of vellum. Written on the fine parchment paper was what appeared to be a letter, penned to Mohammad Ahmad from a man named Roland. The deliberate, and rather ornate calligraphy, was in English, though this was accompanied by notes scribbled in Arabic in different colored ink along the margins. She knew she could not linger long enough to read the contents in full, but scanned the script closely enough to recognize one name, Charles Walsingham. As Anderton was set to refold the letter and leave, she caught a glimpse of the date, May 10th, 1966, and a Nazi swastika emblazoned beneath it.

CHAPTER FIFTY-FOUR

Secret Intelligence Service
London

Montjoy sat in the leather seat opposite his desk. During an impasse in his work an hour earlier, he had put the question to himself as to whether he had actually ever used the chair even once in the six years it had been in his office, and decided that he had not. But as papers had piled up to the point that Montjoy could no longer see over them, nor make heads or tails of anything, there he sat.

Other stacks, almost two hundred in total, covered nearly the entire office floor. Over half carried a large X, a scarlet mark of sorts, demarcating them officially as a *bloody waste of time.* Another group, strewn beside the discarded lot, was highlighted in yellow. A final set, substantially smaller, contained single lines of numbers circled in red ink.

Gavin Abbot entered Montjoy's office without waiting for a summons, a habit he had acquired over the last few days of ferrying back and forth between the office, records, and a small conference room set up for his use. He was reading over his own set of documents as he barreled through a tower of A4s in the middle of the room, scattering them in different directions.

"Sorry, sir," Abbot said, surveying the bigger mess he had made. "I hope those weren't important."

"Not if they have Xs on them," Montjoy said without looking up. "But if they are marked red, you're sacked."

Abbot began to look frantically at his feet.

"I'm taking the piss, mate. You need to get more sleep. What have you got?"

It took Abbot a few seconds to gather his thoughts. "I've isolated a series of mobile numbers flagged as suspicious by GCHQ for one week on either side of January 20, 2014, specifically, any that pinged off two specific towers near St. Patrick's Cemetery, in Waltham Forest."

Montjoy knew the date, and the reference, well, as did anyone who was part of the painstaking effort to piece together the movements of Mohammad Basha prior to the King's Cross bombing. It had been determined that Basha had made contact with someone, likely his handler, in northeast London two weeks before the bombing.

"And?" Montjoy asked.

"And, have all of these numbers been tracked down?"

"Of course, and all are dead ends."

Abbot looked puzzled. "Then what are we looking for?"

Montjoy didn't immediately respond. He had waffled over the past week whether to bring Abbot fully into the loop. "Shut the door," he finally said. Abbot turned and obliged. Montjoy pointed to a stack of papers on his desk. "I am looking for anomalies, specifically from mobile numbers taken off surveillance of the Leeds' cell responsible for the King's Cross bombing, and all communication to and from Mohammad Ahmad during the same period."

Abbot was taken aback. "I don't remember talk of any connection between Ahmad and the bombing."

"There was no official inquiry because the potential link wasn't on anyone's radar."

"But it's on ours? Where does this come from?"

Montjoy could see a measure of panic welling up in his subordinate, as he played out a variety of scenarios, none of them good, which involved his being drummed out of SIS, or worse. Trading football tickets for a few files was one thing.

"How long have you suspected there might be a connection between the professor and King's Cross?" Abbot questioned.

"Not really a suspicion, but more a desire to chase down any leads which might help us." Montjoy continued to be evasive.

"With the bombing, or Ahmad? Shouldn't we focus on the search for his assassin?"

"We have access to intelligence that might give us better insight into the bombing, which in turn could lead us to Ahmad's killer."

"So you believe there is a definite link?" Abbot pressed, and Montjoy could see that he wasn't willing to blindly buy into his boss' explanation. "I wish you had been more forthcoming about all this cat and mouse. This is my neck out, you know."

"Mine is much further on the block, mind you." Montjoy poured himself a drink and raised the bottle in Abbot's direction. "If you have reservations, I can move you out of the office until I wrap this up. No hard feelings, and you'll be protected from the powers that *might* be, in the aftermath."

Abbot stood still and said nothing, and Montjoy could see him weighing his options. He knew he only needed to give the word, and Montjoy would cut him loose, free and clear.

"And how is the letter connected to all of this?" Abbot finally responded after a long moment, nodding to the second glass that Montjoy had pulled from the bar behind his desk.

Montjoy smiled as he poured Abbot a drink. "Likely, not at all."

"Then where do we start?"

"With these LUDs."

"We are looking for patterns, I assume." Abbot bent down and began to organize the papers strewn in front of Montjoy's desk.

"The opposite. Short calls from numbers that show up only once or twice."

"Wouldn't it be easier if we scanned these into the system and let the computers do the work?"

Montjoy thought of Rees. "It would, but I thought we'd keep this old school."

Abbot nodded. "Alright, where do I start?"

"'Compare both sets of intelligence, and concentrate only on numbers circled in red, from this pile here."

"Yes, sir," Abbot replied, taking the stack from Montjoy.

"I'm off to dinner." Montjoy tipped his hat as he donned it. "Find me a needle."

CHAPTER FIFTY-FIVE

Holyrood Palace
Edinburgh

Hajjar did not panic. He had been in this position before, and regardless of the level of experience of his pursuer, the man had forfeited the element of surprise, which meant he had lost everything.

Hajjar realized that he would need to deviate from his original plan, unsure of whether the man in pursuit was aware of his directive to kill Laurent, or was possibly in league with the assassin. He had to assume that either might be the case, and that Laurent was waiting at the park, not to meet for information and credentials, but in fact to kill Hajjar. The first thing Hajjar needed to do was determine whether the man was alone.

He immediately turned back along Royal Terrace Road. It bordered Calton Hill, which was less than a mile from Holyrood Park, the massive Highland-esque preserve on the outskirts of Edinburgh that was filled with lochs, gorges, and cliffs, including Arthur's Seat. It was getting dark, and if Hajjar needed to, he could lose the man in the Salisbury Crags and make his way back to the city center. From there, he would carjack an unsuspecting motorist, kill them, and drive into northern England. From Newcastle, he could arrange his own escape out of the U.K.

Brian Bishop watched as Hajjar left Leith Walk. "Shit. *Blackbird* has changed course."

"Did he make you?" Ward asked, from his position off Queen's Road.

"I don't think so."

"Can you tell where he's heading?" Ward jogged back along Broughton Street, near the roundabout intersection of Picardy Place.

"Unknown. Ali Baba has bypassed Regent Gardens and moved onto Abbeyhill."

"He's heading toward the palace. Stay with him, and watch yourself."

"Damn right I will."

Hajjar did not want to raise any suspicion that he was aware of the pursuit, so he slowed his pace and casually redirected his route toward Holyrood. He passed in front of the palace and mixed with tourists posing for selfies and gawking for a look of any member of the Royal Family who might be in residence. He had reached the roundabout in front of the entry gates, when Hajjar spied a woman who couldn't check her surveillance quickly enough.

Part of a team.

Hajjar knew now that he needed to get to the relative safety of the park, and lose his pursuit. He adjusted the Glock tucked into his waistband, and pretended to take photos. The man who had followed him from Princes Street had stopped on the far side of the palace perimeter and also took photos, while the woman consulted a map. Hajjar smiled, and began to make his way toward Holyrood Park.

CHAPTER FIFTY-SIX

L aurent maintained a safe distance behind his target as the pair approached a crossroad near the Water of Leith. He had kept an eye out for an acceptable location to intercept the man before dark, and as they approached an entrance to the Royal Botanical Gardens, Laurent immediately recognized that the massive, densely forested area was the perfect place to dispose of a body. He estimated how much time he would need to close the distance in order to get the man off the main road as quickly and quietly as possible, and decided to use the next intersection to make his move. He had just accelerated his pace, when his target suddenly turned off Inverleith Row and onto a walkway that bordered a large cemetery.

Even better, Laurent thought to himself.

The assassin switched to a parallel path that cut through a series of linked playing fields, and the two men moved almost in tandem as the witness neared a massive graveyard. Laurent was now astride his target, hidden behind a row of trees, and checked his pace as the man continued along a gravel road that connected to the interior of the cemetery.

Laurent decided it was time. He cleared the hedgerow that had disguised his pursuit, and moved closer to the man, cutting behind a row of gravestones. The witness continued straight, which allowed Laurent to flank his position and move around and in front of him.

The assassin came to a row of tall grave markers covered with ivy and surrounded by trees and weeds. He placed himself between two, ornately decorated granite memorials. One was slightly askew and adorned with a circular crucifix, the bottom half of which gave Laurent a concealed view of the man's approach.

It was an appropriate location to leave the witness, beneath his maker, Laurent thought. Someone to watch over the poor bastard from

King's College, a man in the wrong place at the wrong time. The assassin readied his HK 9mm.

Two silenced shots and he would be back at Waverley, through Glasgow, and Dublin, and then into France. From Paris to Brussels to Nice, and from there, the perfect place to vanish, the American Midwest.

Laurent lowered himself slightly, and glanced back at the path.

The man was gone.

CHAPTER FIFTY-SEVEN

Holyrood Park
Edinburgh

Hajjar crossed Queen's Drive and began moving up Radical Road, the main path into Holyrood Park. There were still a few people in the parking lot, and he knew that the team in pursuit would not risk approaching him until it was clear.

"He's entered Holyrood Park," Bishop relayed.

"I'm two hundred yards behind you. Let me know which direction he moves."

"He's heading straight in."

"Can you follow without giving your position away?"

"Can do."

"I'll be there in thirty seconds," Ward replied.

Hajjar quickened his pace. Most of the hill-walkers were on their way down, and he made sure that he was still being followed, before he suddenly moved off the path and began climbing the rocky outcropping that led to the Salisbury Crags.

"This fucker just jumped off-trail and is scaling the damn mountain," Bishop radioed to Ward.

Ward entered the parking lot and began up the main path. "He made you. Pull back, and let team one flank him."

Bishop slowed his approach along the road and ascended the sloping hill, keeping an eye out for Hajjar. "Negative. I can head higher and shadow him from the ridge above."

"Watch your six."

Bishop ran back along the road to a point fifty yards away, and quickly scampered up the small hill that accessed the rock line. There were a series of smaller dirt paths that stretched out in all directions, and the operator found the one he wanted. It ran along the ridge between two layers of rock outcroppings. Bishop crested the hill, but saw nothing.

His earpiece crackled. "Do you see him?"

"Negative. Shit. I'm heading back down and will try to come around behind him."

"Fall back to where I can see you, and I'll pick up the pursuit."

"Roger that," Bishop responded, as he passed a sign that warned of falling rocks. He had begun to retreat back down the graveled path when he registered movement to his right, and then a suppressed flash. The bullet hit him just below his right shoulder. It would have killed him, but Bishop had turned at the last moment, away from the man crouched between a natural rock wall and two trees.

"Fuck. I'm hit," Bishop called over his earpiece. "I'm down, repeat, I am down." His gun had been knocked out of his hand by the impact of the bullet, and Hajjar was on him before he could reach it.

"*Tisbah ala khair,*" Hajjar hissed, as he thrust a fixed blade into the man's neck near the ear, and pulled it across, severing the jugular and causing a ferocious stream of blood to spurt outward.

"*Good night,*" Ward heard in Arabic in his earpiece as he rushed up the hill beyond the main path. "Man down. Team two, move in." In less than ten seconds, Ward crested the hill and saw Bishop lying on his side. His right arm was slumped over his chest, and a growing pool of blood had formed beneath him. "Stay with me, Brian," Ward said as he clamped a hand down on Bishop's neck, while he surveilled his immediate surroundings. "I need someone on my position right now." Ward pulled gauze from a small pack and pushed it against the wound, as a member of team one rounded a large boulder on the path in front of him.

"I've got him, sir."

"Call in an immediate evac. I'm going after *Blackbird*." Ward began to sprint up the path, then stopped. He looked at the blood trail around Bishop, and then back down the way he had come. On a rock adjacent to their position, and leading down the slope that accessed the parking lot, was a partial bloody handprint.

"Team two, do you have eyes on the parking lot?"

"Affirmative."

"Do you see the target?"

"Negative."

Ward backtracked partway down the path, and then navigated the rocky slope. He moved quickly up a hill along the back end of the crag, and saw Hajjar running in the opposite direction. "Team one, I've got eyes on the target. He is heading toward the loch near the road. Do not let him get back across Queen's Drive."

Hajjar was moving up a hill across an open field, above a small loch. Ward scanned to ensure there were no hikers, but the operator gauged he was too far for a clean shot. He opened up into a full sprint and began to close the distance between them rapidly. He saw Hajjar look back, stop, and level his gun. Ward aimed his own weapon as he moved left and continued to close in.

Hajjar fired two shots, the second one coming close to Ward. He was fifty yards away when Hajjar turned and continued up the hill.

"He's heading toward the ruins. Move around to the backside, but don't engage him unless he comes at you. We need him alive."

Ward reached an outcropping of rocks just above St. Anthony's Ruins at the same moment Hajjar disappeared through the remnants of a stone archway of the disintegrated structure. Ward proceeded cautiously toward the chapel, his Sig Sauer at high ready. He circled the flat ground around the old church, and reached the chapel just as Hajjar stepped out from behind the arch-way, his gun raised.

"*As-Salamu Alaykum,*" he said sarcastically.

"There is only one way out of here, Hajjar."

"And I see you need an entire team to do it." Hajjar eyed two others who had moved into a position behind him. "How is your friend?" he taunted.

"He'll make it."

"Bullshit. I ripped his throat out. Put down your gun and I'll do the same to you." Hajjar lowered his gun slightly, off of Ward, and gestured for the operator to do the same. He knew he would not survive a shootout. His only chance was to get in close enough to take the man hostage. "What do you say? Professional against professional."

Ward responded by firing a bullet into Hajjar's lower leg, causing it to kick back violently and forcing him to drop his weapon as he screamed and fell to one knee. "*Neek Hallack!*" he hissed.

Ward walked over and kicked Hajjar's Glock away, as two members of team one moved in. "Wrap this asshole up and get him to the van, quickly."

He kneeled down beside Hajjar. "*There is no blame for the blind, or the lame, or the sick,*" Ward whispered, quoting the Koran, "but for you, we have something special."

"Fuck you," Hajjar said again, this time in English, and tried to spit on Ward.

The operator rose and stood over Hajjar. "Welcome to my House of War, *Haji*," he said.

Hajjar screamed and lashed out, but was subdued, his arms secured behind his back with flexicuffs. Ward had already begun to make his way to the parking lot. He could see several members from team two prepping a rapid medic evac for Bishop, and transport for Hajjar. He spoke into his mic as he approached their position, "Tell the boat crew to be ready to move. We'll be at the water with *Blackbird* in twenty minutes."

"Yes, sir."

He stopped at the stretcher where Bishop had been secured. A team member shook his head as Ward approached. "I know," was all Ward replied as he pulled back the sheet that covered his friend. "See you on the other side, bro."

CHAPTER FIFTY-EIGHT

Warriston Cemetery
Edinburgh

Laurent could not believe it. So little, in fact, that what had just occurred almost did not register. The assassin stood rigid in the position he had put so many others in over his career. He dared not move, and barely breathed. He knew exactly what the man behind him was feeling, what he was thinking. At this moment, it would be little more than waiting to see how Laurent would respond, and if that happened to be with even the small-est of movements, the man would likely depress a trigger set at only a few ounces of pressure. His assailant had shifted all responsibility for thinking from his brain to his hand, now concentrated in the distal phalanges of a single pointer finger. It was in charge, and Laurent was in command of it. In that respect, the assassin was in complete control of the situation.

Laurent had just begun to visualize the process that would get him out of this predicament, when the man spoke.

"I assume you are in Edinburgh because of me."

He had just given Laurent the smallest amount of room. "I might suppose the same about you."

Sean Garrett ignored the deflection. "Why are you here?"

More space to maneuver. The witness from King's College, as good as he might have been in outmaneuvering Laurent, was not there to kill him straightaway. Every moment that passed was another the assassin could turn in his favor. His concealed .380 could give him a way out, but he would need to put the man on his own heels in order to access it. "The International Film Festival, like everyone else," Laurent answered flippantly. In his experience, while sarcasm could agitate an aggressor, it was also the quickest way to dull someone's concentration. The assassin shifted his weight slightly, and mentally rehearsed the quick movement he would need to get to his secondary pistol.

Garrett stepped closer to the assassin from King's College. "I'm going to ask you one more question. If you insert any more clever answers into this conversation, I will insert a hollow point into the back of your head. It will literally blow through the front of your brain the one thought on which it is now focused, which is, how to divert my attention long enough to access your backup weapon. I'll leave it to you to decide if you want to end up face down and filtering short breaths through a puddle of your own blood and brain matter in the overrun ivy of some Lowland cemetery."

Laurent did not respond, and only nodded.

"I won't waste time asking who sent you to Cambridge, because you won't know. But, as you botched Ahmad's assassination about as much as a supposed professional possibly could, it means you were forced to abandon your original plan to leave England in order to meet with a proxy, who put you on to me. Who was it?"

"A Middle Eastern man, with an English accent. He's staying at the Hilton at Hyde Park," Laurent answered quickly and to the point, the .380 now the furthest thing from his mind.

"And what did he tell you about me?"

"He didn't know who you were, but he did have your photo, the one taken from a camera at King's College. He said he had a contact inside British Intelligence who was tracking your phone, which is how they knew you were in Scotland." Laurent, still angry about being caught off guard, then added sarcastically, "a professional wouldn't have been caught on CCTV, or allowed himself to be tracked all over this bloody island."

Garrett ignored the comment. "Is your contact with MI5 or MI6?"

"I don't know," Laurent answered, and then something dawned on him. This fellow was too calm, too collected. An absurd notion suddenly occurred to the world-class assassin, standing at the mercy of the man he had been sent to Edinburgh to kill. "You allowed your phone to be tracked to Scotland," he said, incredulously. "You saw me across the access road at Waverley, and let me follow you." Garrett remained silent, and Laurent grew more irate. Once more, he couldn't help himself. "You got lucky. The fight at the taxi queue drew your attention to me at the perfect time."

"The professional's facade begins to crumble," Garrett responded calmly. "You're referring to your position behind the luggage rack, which you had taken up twelve minutes earlier, after having left the coffee shop, and before that, the entrance near Waverley Mall?"

Laurent remained silent for several moments. He was in the one place he had never been in his career—confused, and with no idea of what to do. "How long had you been waiting for me at the station?"

"Seven hours. I rotated positions inside and out of Waverley since I arrived this morning. After I shut down my London mobile and cut the signal your people were tracking, I knew that if you had been sent after me, you would attempt to find me on your own. You were desperate, and it was only a matter of time before you gave your position away."

Laurent realized that not only had he made a mistake, he had been outmaneuvered by someone better. "Which was when?"

"An hour before I let you see me on the access road beneath the station. You were outside of W. H. Smith, in the main ticket hall, when you spied someone I assume you thought was me, and followed him. When you realized it wasn't, you moved back to the same spot, and continued the same routine. That was a mistake. You should have changed your pattern. After you crossed the access road, I moved closer and marked you as the man I stood opposite of outside Ahmad's office."

"And after I followed you?"

"Twice on Broughton Street, and just before I led you into the cemetery."

Laurent did not respond for several moments. "One more question?"

"One."

"Back at King's College. Why did you run? Why not finish it at Cambridge?"

Garrett measured his answer. "Because we are in England for the same reason. And that was two questions."

"Who are you?" Laurent asked, but immediately cringed at the stupidity of the question.

Garrett stepped closer to the assassin. "If you get close enough to me again to voice that question, you will find out."

Laurent remained silent, and did not move for what seemed an eternity. He thought he could hear the man breathing, and waited several moments before he dared turn his head slightly, expecting either to feel the butt of a weapon, or the impact of a bullet. Nothing. He heard two people speaking, somewhere in front of him. The assassin let out a breath and then turned fully around. The man was gone. Laurent listened as the voices drew closer, before he turned and disappeared into the tree line behind him.

CHAPTER FIFTY-NINE

Star Tavern
London

Montjoy sat alone in a corner of the upstairs dining room at the Star Tavern. It was his favorite spot for a lager and traditional haddock and chips, and as he waited for his dinner, he enjoyed the residual warmth from a small fireplace, which was ablaze even though it was not particularly cold outside.

As he watched tourist traffic on Belgrave Mews, Montjoy focused on what he and Abbot had been able to piece together. In his possession was a portion of a letter, dated May 1966. Montjoy smiled at the timing, as his great uncle had been an assistant manager at Everton F.C. when they defeated Sheffield Wednesday in the F.A. Cup final that same month and year. The victory was made even sweeter in that Sheffield was Berwyn Rees' favorite team, and they remained the only team in league history to lose a cup final in regulation, and with a full side, after being up by two goals. Rees had referenced the game years earlier, but after Montjoy replied with *Nil Satis Nisi Optimum*, Everton's motto that *Nothing but the best is good enough*, his counterpart had not mentioned it again.

The information detailed in the single page of what clearly belonged to a longer letter, had the potential to do considerable damage to Charles Walsingham. The knighted billionaire's influence was still palpable in the halls of power, even though the man had been retired and living in Switzerland for nearly a decade. The accusations leveled at the financier, that he was a war profiteer who had collaborated with the Nazis in Austria during the war, was damning enough. If made public, it would ruin Walsingham, and embarrass a parade of people in high places who had been closely connected to his empire from its early days.

What puzzled Montjoy, was how the letter found its way into his *Dalmatia* files. When Abbot first brought it to his attention, the head of section immediately suspected that there was more to Walsingham's past than was detailed in the incomplete correspondence. Moreover, he recognized that the letter had been planted, recently, which meant that someone at MI6 was involved and aware of the financier's disreputable past. Ultimately, Montjoy believed he knew which party was responsible, and who would ultimately need to be confronted when the time came.

He had nearly finished his meal, and decided that a second pint was in order, when Gavin Abbot surfaced at the doorway.

"Good evening, Gavin." Montjoy smiled. "Have a seat. Have a drink."

"I knew I would find you here." Abbot pulled out a chair and shook his head at the server. "You're lucky the Cold War is over, or the Soviets could have set their watches by your dining habits."

"It wouldn't have done them much good, considering that Stalin forgot to turn back his clocks in the fall of 1930, which put Russia off one hour for sixty years."

"I thought that was an urban legend."

"Perhaps, but I can tell you one that is not. You're sitting in the exact chair where Reynolds and Goody masterminded the Great Train Robbery."

"I'm aware of the Star's connection to the heist," Abbot replied tongue-in-cheek, "but I am impressed that you've managed to narrow it down to an exact seat."

"Well, close enough, at least. Rather exciting, don't you think?"

"Then perhaps you'll find what I have to tell you quite boring."

Montjoy paused as he was about to blow the foam off his pint. "You found something."

"I have."

Montjoy gave the room a once over, satisfied that the other two tables were sufficiently out of earshot. "Out with it."

Abbot drew several A4 sheets from his jacket and passed them to Montjoy, who pulled a pair of reading glasses from his pocket.

Abbot was surprised. "I've never seen you use those."

"Only for the good stuff," Montjoy joked. The pages contained a series of mobile numbers and dates arranged by location, time of call, and owner of the number. "Lay it out for me."

Abbot produced a second set of papers, and identified a grouping of numbers. "These are three, separate mobiles I've isolated, all seemingly unconnected."

Montjoy followed Abbot's progression on his page, intermittently switching between documents.

"One originates in the English system." Abbot pointed it out. "A phone that MI5 linked to Mohammad Basha. The second, was traced to a mosque at Finsbury Park."

"And the third?"

"Michigan, in a suburb of Detroit. Dearborn."

"Which boasts a considerable Muslim population."

"The Islamic capital of the U.S., some call it."

Montjoy said nothing for a moment, as he compared pages. "Go on."

"On January 20, 2014, two weeks before the King's Cross bombing, all three phones called the same number, within twenty minutes of one another. And it's a number that appears only *once* in the call history of each mobile."

The head of Near East Section considered the implications. The Leeds' cell, while not the most organized terrorist network British Intelligence had ever uncovered, was still professional enough to pull off the bombing at King's Cross. Montjoy knew they would have been more successful if not for a defective switch of one bomber, and the faulty commitment of another. The investigation of the bombing had uncovered the existence of an unknown middleman, but otherwise had only narrowed down broader connections. "And this number?" Montjoy asked.

"The number you're looking for. The one that links all three phones."

Montjoy glanced up.

"A mobile recovered from Mohammad Ahmad's flat in London," Abbot replied. "A connection that couldn't be made unless he was a suspect."

"I knew it," Montjoy muttered to himself.

"Which begs the question, sir," Abbot lowered his voice. "Why you suspected Ahmad was involved with King's Cross."

Montjoy put his glasses away, and took a sip of his lager. "I could tell you that it was something intuitive, born from three decades of experience, but you wouldn't believe that, now would you?"

Abbot shook his head, clearly dismayed.

"It's complicated, Gavin, and well above your paygrade. I know you'd like to hear a different explanation, and perhaps you've earned it. But unfortunately, mate, for King and Country will have to do."

Abbot sat silent for several moments, and then gestured to the server, pointing to Montjoy's beer. "So can we assume that the contact in Michigan is the architect of King's Cross?"

"Likely."

"Which leaves Ahmad as the middleman."

Montjoy nodded.

"What now? I assume we turn this over to MI5?"

"Not yet. There's someone I need to speak to first."

Abbot stood to leave. "Perhaps you'll explain what's going on when we're both at Wakefield, if they house us near one another," he only half-joked, referring to the prison for high-risk offenders in Yorkshire. The pint arrived, and Abbot pushed it across the table to Montjoy, who raised it in a toast.

"*We too alone will sing,*" Montjoy responded, quoting *King Lear,* knowing Abbot couldn't resist.

Abbot turned back, and answered, "*Who loses and who wins; who's in, who's out—*"

"We'll know soon enough," Montjoy replied.

CHAPTER SIXTY

Edinburgh

It was nearing midnight, and Garrett shadowed the man as he moved deliberately along Rose Street. The two mingled with late-night pub-crawlers, and every block his target doubled back, pretending to browse restaurant menus and window displays. Garrett turned off Rose Street and moved quickly along the road that ran parallel to the main avenue. He turned a corner at the end of the lane and used a surge of the crowd to conceal his position in a small alcove opposite a chapel. The man suddenly appeared, having increased his own pace, but slowed as he came even with the entrance of the Crown Plaza hotel. Garrett moved from the shadows and into an easy walk behind him.

John Campion sensed the presence a moment too late, and reacted with a muted, "Fuck."

"Careful, old boy." Garrett put his hand on Campion's shoulder and pushed him in the direction of Charlotte Square.

Campion relaxed when he recognized the voice. "So, the prodigal son has returned."

"Fatten a calf and forewarn the brother," Garret replied. "Head to the monument."

The two men continued in silence until they entered the square, which was empty and dark, save for the reflection of lights from Princes Street. When they reached the statue of Prince Albert in the dead center of the park, Campion turned to face Garrett, and hesitated momentarily when he saw the Sig Sauer in his hand. "After your debut on the Royal Mile the other day, I didn't expect you to make it out."

"That's yet to be determined. What is going on?"

Campion ignored the question. "There's been a change of plans, again, but you expected that." He reached into his pocket and produced an envelope and a phone. "New documents, and yet another bloody mobile. You flew in last week, and attended a series of climbing and mountaineering expos in

Cardiff and London, both large enough that no one would be expected to readily remember you. You stayed in South Wales, climbed in the north, and took in the sights along the coast. You leave in one week, out of Birmingham International on a 9:55 a.m. *Scandinavian Air* flight through Copenhagen, to Chicago. Change to *United* at O'Hare, bound for Charlotte."

Garrett took the documents, which included a passport, plane tickets, two thousand pounds in cash, and hotel details in Pembroke and Chelsea. He pocketed the credentials and surveyed the area around them before handing the Sig to Campion.

"Keep the gun, and dump it when you get to Birmingham." Campion began walking back toward Rose Street, then turned. "MI5 know you're in Scotland. I suggest you leave, tonight."

CHAPTER SIXTY-ONE

Scotland Yard
London

Samantha Anderton was late. She had arrived back in London well after midnight, and had been up half of the night putting together her report for Holland, the contents of which were certain to rock the intelligence services of Britain once they were made public. From the damning contents of the safe, it was impossible to know who was involved, and how high at Whitehall the corruption went.

She had just grabbed a coffee and jumped a Tube to Westminster Station, when her phone rang. She informed Holland she was on the way up, and pushed into his office just in time to witness Ewan Healey and her boss engaged in a heated exchange. They calmed down once Anderton entered.

"I'm sorry I'm late, sir."

"Never you mind, sergeant. Agent Healey and I were discussing another matter."

Healey said nothing, and only sat with the customary smirk on his face.

"Have you brought all of our files on the Ahmad case?" Holland asked.

"Yes, sir." Anderton pulled a large folder from her satchel and gave it to Holland, who quickly looked over the contents before handing it to Healey.

"Thank you, Superintendent Holland. We'll take it from here, and let you know what we find." Healey turned to Anderton. "Is this everything?"

She hesitated a moment. "Yes. You might want to take notice of a key we found on Ahmad."

"And?"

"And," Anderton replied, "we've not been able to determine its significance."

"No worries, we will." Healey waved goodbye over his shoulder with the folder as he left the office. "We'll be in touch."

"Prat," Holland muttered after Healey shut the door behind him. "No luck at Cambridge then?"

Anderton pulled a second file from her bag. "You were right. The key was the key. It took me to a facility in Cambridgeshire, where Ahmad kept a safe in a storage container."

"One I'm guessing you entered illegally, opened illegally, and took whatever was inside, again, illegally."

Anderton pursed her lips.

"At least you are consistent," Holland observed, opening the envelope. He looked quickly through the two ledgers before moving to the letter. Holland read it quietly, and then again, before glancing up at Anderton. "Good God."

CHAPTER SIXTY-TWO

Hyde Park
London

Charles Walsingham stood behind a row of lorries parked in front of One Hyde Park. The residential complex, located in the Knightsbridge area of Central London, was billed as the most expensive in the world. He had owned a modest three-bedroom corner flat on the fourth floor for nearly a decade, and with a purchase price of just over twenty-two million pounds, it had been considered an absolute steal at the time. Now, that amount wouldn't even buy a bathroom in any of the higher-end properties. Among the neighboring oligarchs and Near East sheikhs who competed for the most expensive flat on the ritzy block, Walsingham was little more than a *move along, nothing to see here* class of billionaire.

He had acquired the property from a Chinese banker who was under investigation for securities fraud in Beijing and London. A shell corporation based in Rio de Janeiro, which was managed by an LLC owned by Walsingham, purchased the two-bedroom flat a week before the seller hung himself. The wealthy financier could count the number of months he had stayed at his flat at One Hyde Park, but it was a location through which Walsingham had conducted several key business deals, and more than a few influential power brokers had found it a useful haven over the years. Those who lived behind the bulletproof windows protected by security staff trained by British Special Forces had little to worry about from the outside world. Tonight, Walsingham stood beyond the safety of that world, on the fringe of Hyde Park, and waited for Berwyn Rees.

He also stood to lose an empire, and knew the only thing between him and ruin, was a pipsqueak head of section at MI6.

Berwyn Rees exited the Tube at Knightsbridge Station at One Hyde Park. He had been instructed to cross over South Carriage Drive, and walk west. Walsingham would find him. The head of section proceeded quickly through the intersection across from the park, and cursed his own carelessness as he was nearly flattened by a coach that failed to heed the changing light. Rees, who hated being in a crowded, well-lit room with the eccentric billionaire, was now heading to a rendezvous with the man, alone, after dark, and in a near-deserted location.

Meeting in Hyde Park was bloody apropos, Rees thought to himself. Considering the predicament Ahmad's death had put Walsingham in, Rees would likely not be dealing with the philanthropic Dr. Jekyll persona the world knew, and which had earned Walsingham a Knighthood. Tonight, Rees was certain to meet the sadistic bastard with whom he was all too familiar, and about whom he had heard even worse stories.

Rees was beyond cross. Not forty-eight hours after he met with Thackeray at Green Park, who had come from an ill-advised sit-down with Walsingham, Rees had received a call from the financier himself, who also demanded a meeting. He entered Hyde Park and began walking slowly along a path that ran parallel to the main road, his eyes darting between small groves of trees.

"Rees!" The whispered growl sounded more like a command than a greeting.

Rees startled. *Fuck's sake.* He turned and saw Walsingham, partially hidden behind a large oak. "Sir Charles," Rees greeted him as he moved off the path and toward the man.

"Stop pottering around like a twit without a bother."

Rees ignored the reproach and angled to keep the meeting as brief as possible. "This is a considerable gamble."

"Don't lecture me about risk, you little shit. My God, you and your lot have bloody put me in it this time, but good."

Rees bristled. "Put you in it?"

"You damn well know what I'm talking about. It was your job to protect Ahmad. In light of what that lunatic threatened should anything happen to him, I would have thought you'd safeguard the man better than the Crown Jewels."

"I met with Thackeray earlier. He mentioned you two dined on grouse at White's," Rees mindlessly blurted out, suddenly envisioning Walsingham also standing up for him for membership at the club, which would almost certainly guarantee his acceptance.

"What in the blue fuck are you going on about? Did he mention my favorite color as well? My God, man, do you have any idea what is at stake here?"

"Of course, sir."

"Then start acting like it."

"Yes, sir," Rees answered, attempting to suppress his irritation.

Walsingham motioned deeper into the dark grove, and Rees palmed a small caliber pistol in his pocket as they walked. Walsingham suddenly stopped and spun, and grabbed Rees square on his shoulders in a ridiculously theatric gesture. "The letter. Did you find it?"

"I have a copy."

"I don't give a damn about a copy. Did you find the original?" Walsingham drew the question out as if Rees were hard of hearing, or did not understand the danger the document presented.

"Not yet."

"Neither you nor Thackeray seem terribly concerned," Walsingham replied, almost whining. The eccentric financier began to pace back and forth, before he turned, his eyes wild with rage. "If that letter gets out, if it goes public, I will personally splay you out on a fucking pike in this very park. Do you hear me?" Then, almost on a dime, he shifted to a calmer state. "Did you search his office?"

Rees gripped the .22 tighter. "We turned it over. Nothing. The safety deposit box he kept in London has been closed. Nothing at his flat there, nor his cottage in the Lake District—"

Walsingham interrupted Rees. "Why do you have a copy?"

"Ahmad sent it to me not long ago, I presume, to reassure us he wasn't bluffing."

"Where is it?"

"Safe."

"Can I see it?"

"I don't have it with me."

"Then it isn't bloody well safe, is it?" Walsingham snapped.

Rees didn't respond. He wasn't particularly concerned about a fifty-year old letter that contained damning information about Walsingham. He was worried about the financial trail that could be traced to him through Ahmad, scattered among offshore accounts in George Town, Grand Cayman and Zurich, Switzerland.

"What about the money trail?" Walsingham asked, as if reading his mind.

"It's being diverted as we speak, and will soon end somewhere well away from you and Thackeray," Rees answered, thinking of Montjoy. *And kill two birds with one stone.*

Walsingham said nothing, and Rees assumed that he had already discussed the matter with the MP. But the man ultimately wasn't worried about the money, and Rees knew it. He had plenty of it, and sufficient places to go where British authorities would have difficulty extraditing him. But if the letter concerning Walsingham's conduct during the war was made public, and could be corroborated, then there would be no place in the world the famous, much celebrated, widely fêted financial genius could steal himself away to. It was a prospect that delighted Rees to no end on one hand, but if Walsingham went down because of Ahmad, he would damn sure take Thackeray with him, which could potentially involve Rees.

"Very good," Walsingham replied. "I'm very sorry to have shouted earlier, and I ask your forgiveness for my curt behavior."

Rees nodded, aware that Dr. Jekyll would finish out the meeting. "It's not a problem."

"Very well then. There's a good fellow. Find the original, and when you do, notify me through Thackeray." Walsingham put his hand on Rees's shoulders once again, this time in a strangely kind way, as if to assure both men that all would be alright. Rees could only muster a weak smile as Walsingham spun and disappeared into the park.

Rees eased the grip on his gun and began to walk quickly toward the station, looking back over his shoulder several times before he reached the safety of the street.

He continued to brood as he boarded the Underground at Bond Street, one change and four stops up from SIS Headquarters. As he rode the Tube, Rees was well aware of the tight corner that Ahmad's death had backed him up against. He was in the process of extricating himself and pushing Montjoy into it, and although the maneuver was tricky, all the pieces were in place to see it through.

He exited Vauxhall Station, and wearily cleared a series of security checks at MI6. Rees rode the lift to his floor, and at the moment he considered riding back down and heading home for the evening, the doors opened, and he saw a file taped to his office door. He plucked it off the jamb, and unwound the twine that bound the large envelope as he sat down at his desk. Two days earlier, with Thackeray breathing down his neck, Rees had called in a favor with a colleague at Scotland Yard. The photo of the man leaving the Old Provost's Lodge at King's College had so far turned up nothing when compared against all persons with criminal profiles in the massive databases at the FBI, Interpol, and FIND, the UK's Facial Images National Database.

Rees knew that while the new NEC Neoface software was cutting edge, the high angle of the shot, combined with the low resolution of CCTV, and the long hair of the man in the photo, made the likelihood of a positive match low. The Yard had already pared down and ruled out all possible matches for their database parameters, so Rees quietly requisitioned a new search. He requested one that included government employees, limited to American and English citizens, and only those with a direct connection to Oxford or Cambridge. Four hits came back as possible, with three quickly dismissed. Only one remained, though it also had been deemed too low a percentage match to consider.

Rees requested it be sent over anyway, and opened the file to compare the photos against one another. The two were similar, though the one from the database was of a man younger than that taken from CCTV. The biometric markers, which used geometry and texture, including space between the eyes, length of nose, the distance between varying features on the face, and skin color, set the possibility of a match at only fifty-five percent. He could see why it had been dismissed.

Rees was about to trash the file when something caught his eye. He continued reading the specifics of the subject's file, which were enumerated in single-line billet points on the cream-colored sheet.

Subject: Sean Garrett
Age: 42
Height: 185 cm
Weight: 14 stone
Hair/Eyes: Brown/Blue
Place of birth: Damascus, Virginia
Last known residence: Balsam, North Carolina
Citizenship: British and American
Education: New College, University of Oxford
Military: Royal Marines, Special Boat Service, last date of service, 2005
Father: William Thomas Garrett. American, U.S. State Department/Britserv Defense. Deceased 1988
Mother: Laura Madeleine Garrett, née Aldrich, née Montjoy. British. Deceased 1985

"Bloody hell!" Rees blurted aloud as he shot from his chair. He grabbed the sheet of paper and pulled it closer, his attention darting between the photos of Sean Garrett and the name at the bottom of the page.

Laura Montjoy Garrett

PART III

CHAPTER SIXTY-THREE

Fitzroy Tavern
London

Sean Garrett sat beneath the awning of the Charlotte Street Hotel, across from the Fitzroy Tavern, and watched patrons come and go. The world-famous public house had once been well-trafficked by the likes of Dylan Thomas, when it served as the mecca for London's bohemian movement. It had also been the preferred place for Garrett's brother to drink himself silly since his graduate days at university. It was twenty minutes after 6:00 p.m., more than enough time for him to be deep into a well of scotch. Garrett circled to a side entrance, entered, and instinctively turned to his right, knowing where to go. And he was in the seat Garrett expected to find him, as if it were forever reserved as his, no matter the time of day or crowd.

Montjoy saw him and smiled, and beckoned Garrett over with the wave of his glass, spilling several ounces when his elbow knocked the table.

"That's twenty quid you just tipped over, brov," Garrett said dryly.

"No worries. There is a never-ending pour from my man behind the mahogany."

Garrett sat down across from Montjoy, and the two men eyed one another.

"Good to see you, Sean."

"Good to see you're holding up."

Montjoy smiled. *"All's well that ends well—"*

"Assuming it's over, considering what happened at Cambridge." Garrett then added, "a mess, I suspect, your lot created."

"There's a clever lad," Montjoy replied, taking a drink. "It all worked out."

"I'm curious to know what '*it all*' is, exactly."

"Surely a smart Oxbridgian like yourself has pieced it together, the Oxford part notwithstanding," Montjoy, a Cambridge grad, joked.

"I was sent in to gather intelligence from a man that someone on your end decided to assassinate.

I'll give you the benefit that the timing was coincidental."

"It was, purely," Montjoy answered, "though I had no operational control of the plan to eliminate Ahmad, mind you."

Garrett seemed surprised. "But you know who did."

"After the fact—"

"Before I was sent to Scotland?"

Montjoy shook his head. "After, but prior to your making contact with my man in Edinburgh. In any event, I couldn't risk bringing you in too early."

"Or at all, it seems."

Montjoy picked up on the sarcasm. "You must understand, it wasn't my call, in the end."

"Who then?" When Montjoy didn't immediately answer, Garrett felt a measure of irritation building. "Banastre, what's going on?"

"It is complicated," Montjoy admitted, "compounded by the fact that yours wasn't the only operation attached to Ahmad. Several others needed to be managed independent of one another. That, above all, was critical."

"To what?" Garrett pressed, weary of Montjoy's evasion. "Who was running the op?"

"Someone who's walked the halls of MI6 a lot longer than me, and with far more influence."

"Who is he?" Garret asked again.

"Not *he*, mate."

Garrett eyed Montjoy. The revelation was impractical, but his brother's cryptic response suddenly made clear to Garrett what he realized should have been obvious from the beginning. "Bloody hell," he finally admitted. "I didn't see it."

"You weren't meant to."

Garrett shook his head. "I don't believe it."

"Which is why she enjoyed a long and successful career at MI6."

They sat in silence for a moment, and the noise around them ratcheted up as patrons continued to file into the pub, crowding the bar three deep.

"Would you care for something?" Montjoy raised his glass.

"I'll have what you're drinking."

"Club soda."

Garrett was surprised. "I'll take a whiskey."

"Kentucky or Scotland?"

"I'll leave it to you."

"Then I'll order the good stuff," Montjoy joked, as he flagged the attention of the barkeep, gesturing first with one, then two, fingers.

Despite the crowd, the drinks made it quickly to the table, along with a bottle of eighteen-year old, single malt, Talisker.

"Thank you, my good man." Montjoy passed a scotch to Garrett, and gestured behind the bartender. "Patrick, is the room available?"

"Always, sir."

Montjoy stood and motioned to Garrett, who followed him through a small door that exited the main bar area. They walked down a hall to a smaller room with one table and two chairs.

"I've spent my fair share of nights here, sleeping off a long day." Montjoy pulled out a chair. "Cheers," he said, tipping Garrett's glass, but not taking a drink from his own.

Garrett quickly finished his drink, and poured another. "She practically told me, the day I left."

"Did she quote Nietzsche?"

"Of course," Garrett replied. "She cautioned me to remember what he said of monsters and men—"

"*Whoever fights monsters should see to it that in the process he does not become a monster,*" Montjoy finished the quote. "A warning and a hint," he laughed. "As cheeky as ever."

Garrett shook his head, still not fully buying it. "She was a clerk during the war, low level, if I recall mom's account. And after that, MI6, but only administrative."

Montjoy rotated the tumbler several turns in his hands before speaking. "You know what mother told you of grandmother, and essentially that was true, that she was a clerk, and then a staff driver, for the Mechanized Transport Corp, during the war."

"Yes, and then in some capacity in intelligence thanks to grandad's influence."

"She didn't need his help. The MTC was her cover. She served in the SOE for the duration of the war."

"The SOE?"

"The Special Operations Executive—"

"I know what it was," Garrett cut Montjoy off. "I'll assume she was more than just a pretty courier in a skirt."

"Front lines. Dropped into the Netherlands in 1942."

"Wasn't that a blown operation?"

"That would be putting it kindly. *Operation Englandspiel – The English Game.* The Germans infiltrated Dutch resistance early in the war, unbeknownst to the SOE, who continued to deploy agents into landing zones handpicked by the German Secret Police, and relayed through compromised operatives in the Netherlands. Most of our saboteurs were shot by the *Abwehr*, or taken to the prison camp at Haaren. Scores of men and women sent to their deaths thanks to botched procedures and lax security checks. And, good old-fashioned hubris. SIS had its own problems at the time, thanks in part to an assistant to the MI6 station chief at The Hague, a Dutchman who was also working for German military intelligence. After the disaster at Venlo, whereby the same hapless station chief was duped into a trap set by Heinrich Himmler, our entire network in Western Europe was essentially exposed."

"How did grandmom make it through?"

"Pluck and luck, old son. She parachuted in with two others, both of whom were immediately arrested. Grandmother shot two Germans at the LZ and managed to make it into the countryside. She then passed herself off as a Dutch journalist sympathetic to the Third Reich, as she made her way south. Eventually, she rendezvoused with two operatives in Switzerland who had escaped from Haaren, and it was through her that the British learned the Dutch operation had been blown. Grandmother stayed on in Europe, and a year later, was attached to the operation that detonated a section of the heavy water plant at Vemork, Norway, which essentially ended Nazi aspirations of developing the atomic bomb."

"We are talking about the same ninety-year old Scottish woman who's obsessed with making the perfect haggis?"

Montjoy smiled. "In the summer of 1943, grandmother came back to England and picked up right where she left off, but from an office in London. That is the Madeleine Halliwell you know from the photos on the mantel. She met grandfather two weeks after her return, and at the conclusion of the war, was recruited into MI6 because of her SOE exploits. And they didn't stop there. She became one of the first female agents to run her own network, primarily counter espionage and subversion out of West Germany during the early Cold War. When grandfather was recalled and made head of section, she remained point for several stations in Central Europe. By the time grandfather had been appointed vice chief, grandmother had established a highly decorated career in her own right, having become one of MI6's first female senior controllers."

Garrett took another drink of scotch, and wondered how well he knew his own family. Unlike his brother, he had been raised in England and the U.S., which had both helped and hindered his sense of self during those formative years. His father, William Thomas Garrett, had been a State Department official in London during the Johnson Administration. Garrett Sr. had become fast friends with Algernon Montjoy, and his wife, Laura, during his posting, and after Montjoy Sr. died unexpectedly of complications from minor surgery in 1970, Garrett's father married his widow, who had a ten-year-old son, Banastre. By the time Garrett was born two years later, on a summer trip to Virginia, his father had resigned from State and relocated to England, taking a job with a British defense contractor in London.

A sister, Madeleine, followed three years later, and the family split their life between London and Edinburgh. Because his father's work schedule took him frequently back to the States, Garrett would stay at his grandparent's farm in "The Big Valley," in the Virginia Shenandoah. But, every other summer, it was off to Ballachulish, where Garrett found the Highlands as alluring as the Appalachians. During those early years, he and his grandmother became particularly close, and together they would tromp throughout the Glen Coe Range.

Everything changed when Garrett was thirteen years old. He was in Virginia with his father, when his mother—out on a Saturday shopping trip in Hammersmith—was hit and killed by a delivery lorry that had turned the wrong way down a one-way street. Garrett couldn't shake the feeling, and the guilt, that if he had been with her, he would have been able to see the truck, and warn his mother.

Garrett's father fell into a deep stupor, and he moved he and Madeleine to North Carolina. While his sister had a difficult time with their mother's death and the transition, Garrett decided that the only way to deal with everything was to embrace a new identity in America. He excelled in sports and academics, and to fit in, adopted an American accent, which he'd kept ever since.

It was during his junior year in high school that his father, whose health had steadily declined since his wife's death, suddenly died while on a business trip to Boston. And just like that, Garrett's life was thrown back into turmoil. With Banastre recently returned from the Balkans, it was decided that he and Madeleine would live with their Aunt in London.

In England, Garrett continued to excel on the playing field and in the classroom. After scoring in the top 5% on his A-Levels, he was offered a spot at Oxford, where he took first-class honors in economics and management, and broke the record on the university cricket team for most sixes in a single match. After college, Garrett chose to follow in his brother's footsteps by joining the military, and becoming a Royal Marine. Soon after, he was chosen for selection in the Special Boat Service, the elite special forces unit of the British Naval Service.

A career in the military was derailed seven years later, when Garrett suffered an injury to his back while taking part in a nighttime, high-altitude low-opening joint parachuting exercise with Navy Seals in North Africa. He had just been assigned to M squadron, specializing in maritime counter-terrorism, when Garrett was laid up for nearly six months. His release from the hospital was followed by a move to the SBS Reserves, but with the death of his grandmother in Virginia, Garrett decided to leave the Royal Marines and return to the Appalachians. He sold the farm in Damascus, Virginia and moved into his family's home south of Balsam, North Carolina. It was a place he had happily remained, living in the mountains and working as a climbing guide, until a year earlier, when a bomb leveled an Underground line that killed his grandfather, Sir Nigel Aldrich, and put his sister Maddie in a coma.

The thought brought Garrett back to the Fitzroy. "Considering what happened at King's Cross, why bring grandmom on-board?"

Montjoy shook his head. "You're not seeing it, mate. *She* sent you in. It was her show from day one. Grandmother ran the entire operation."

"Which was after what, exactly? This went well beyond Ahmad and the bombing, didn't it?"

"Yes," Montjoy conceded, as he continued to shun his whiskey, watching it slowly mix with the melting ice. "About six months ago, MI5 broke up a terrorist network in Leeds, connected to the same Lake District cell that produced Mohammad Basha. Among the files recovered were correspondences between someone in America and an unknown handler in London, which referenced a series of bombings that were to take place in England and the U.S. I suspected that Ahmad was acting as a go between for mosques in Detroit, Marseille, and London, and needed to find out who the contact was in Michigan."

"Which is why you have the GCHQ. If you're going to use the pretense of preventing acts of terror to spy on everyone, then you damn well better do it."

"If you had any idea of the sheer number of attacks that British Intelligence has prevented in the last year alone, successes that never see the light of day, you might feel differently."

"And unless you can show me where any of those threats were planned by some little old lady from Brighton, or Topeka, don't waste my time." Then it dawned on Garrett. "This operation was completely off the books, wasn't it?"

He watched Montjoy contemplate how much he was willing to disclose. "It was off the bloody bookshelf, mate. I won't go into detail, but I can tell you that Ahmad has been a protected MI6 asset for nearly as long as I've been with SIS. He abused that protection, which ultimately led to King's Cross. After that, the sanction for his death was given the green light. Your part should have ended at Cambridge, with you safely back in the States well before the contract on the professor was carried out. But someone moved the timetable forward."

"Which is why I happened into the middle of it. Your left hand didn't know what the right was doing. You're damn lucky this didn't end up on the front pages of *The Daily Telegraph*."

"Time will tell on that one, but it was a delicate situation to say the least."

"You're not telling me everything," Garrett replied. "What was the primary objective of the op?"

Montjoy eyed Garrett for a moment before speaking. "What I disclose to you now is highest-level clearance."

"No shit, Banastre."

"Do you remember the bombings of the U.S. consulate in Karachi in 2002, and the British consulate in Istanbul a year later?"

"Of course. Al-Qaeda. Scores killed."

"Al-Qaeda, yes, but MI6 was able to pinpoint a portion of the financial backing for those bombings, and a host of other attacks on Western interests in the Middle East during that period, to an individual connected to an investment company owned by a Saudi prince, Al-Ahmed bin Halabi."

"There is no way a Saudi prince was your target. He would be untouchable."

"Quite, and truth be told, he is a good man who is innocent of the entire business. But not so his right-hand man, Nasir Hajjar."

"He was the target?"

"Of the entire operation. Everything else was subordinate to apprehending Hajjar."

"Who is he?"

"Yemeni, from an affluent family. Hajjar serves as head of security for bin Halabi and his company, EuroPenninsula. In his downtime, he funds terrorist activities throughout the Middle East, Europe, and America. MI5 also suspects Hajjar in a number of deaths in England connected to his involvement in the heroin trade. He was educated in London and trained in Jordanian Intelligence. We've tried for a decade to corner him, not even coming close. His relationship with the House of Saud, and his family's position in Yemen, has made it difficult under the best of circumstances. It was grandmother who came up with the idea of using Ahmad's relationship with bin Halabi to lure Hajjar to England. EuroPenninsula is set to sign a very lucrative contract with a North Sea oil company. Grandmother predicted that the timing of the professor's death would bring bin Halabi, and with him, Hajjar, to the U.K., giving us a good chance to finally get him."

"Outsourcing the assassination of high-profile target like Ahmad, and in your own backyard of all places, was nearsighted, by which I mean, absolutely fucking stupid. That aside, my little interruption wasn't the real issue, was it?"

Montjoy shook his head. "The plan to kill the professor piggybacked a secondary objective, aimed at tying up another problematic loose end. The assassin known as David Laurent, the one put on your trail, has operated throughout Europe for two decades, typically at the behest of Middle Eastern interests. We've never known much about him, and truth be told, we've had few issues with who he has targeted over the years. Until, that is, Laurent was contracted to kill Bonar Asquith. Do you remember the MP who was shot in the Underground two years back?"

"So it wasn't a botched robbery."

"Asquith was one corrupt bloke, mind you, but we couldn't have hired assassins running around England offing ministers of Parliament. MI6, through some bloody brilliant grunt work, rooted out Laurent's contact in Albania. It was then, that one of our most reliable assets came into play, a man named Danesh. He is a Saudi National, educated in England. Oxford actually, your neck of the woods. Danesh is also tied to bin Halabi, and has been managing a portion of his business interests in England since the late 1990s. In the aftermath of 9/11, Danesh was rolled up in an al-Qaeda sting, though his connection was tangential. Instead of putting him away, we put him to work. Since then, he's become quite comfortable, and well off, dealing from both ends."

"You ran this asset?"

"No. William Lindsay, now deputy chief of MI6, who was head of Europe Section at the time, oversaw the program that housed Danesh. Danesh was used to employ Laurent under the guise that the contract on Ahmad came from someone in the Middle East. We began to track Laurent's movement once he arrived in the U.K., and it was at this point that we used a professional who's been employed on and off since the tail end of the Cold War. The plan was to eliminate Laurent, in London, making sure to compound suspicion of Nasir Hajjar's involvement in Ahmad's death with forged documents to be left on Laurent."

"Which he failed to do," Garrett observed.

Montjoy nodded his head. "Our man was found with a hollow point in his head behind a hotel near Covent Garden last week. With the botched assassination at King's College, and then at the Savoy, and with Laurent spooked and prepared to go to ground, grandmother had to think on her feet. This is where you came in. You were already in-country, which allowed her to put the Scotland operation together, last minute and quite brilliantly, I might add. She used Danesh once again, this time to lure Laurent to Edinburgh, giving him your photo and the promise to satisfy the second half of the payment if he eliminated his witness."

"Yes, and thank you very much for that."

"Grandmother knew you could handle yourself. Laurent expected someone he could easily control and kill, not a highly-trained SBS counter-terrorist operative with five combat tours and twelve years of experience," Montjoy noted. "In any event, after Danesh sent Laurent after you, he then made contact with Hajjar, using an email address that we had been monitoring, and again purporting to act on bin Halabi's behalf, sent him to kill Laurent. The plan was to get Laurent and Hajjar at the same time."

"A plan so complicated, I might point out, that it had almost no chance of succeeding."

"In retrospect, yes, but we were desperate by that point. After losing the chance to kill Laurent in London, and with him still running around loose in the U.K., we had to amend the manner in which we planned to apprehend Hajjar without the CIA suspecting it was us who set up the professor."

"Which is where, I assume, Deacon comes into play."

"Who?"

"My contact in Edinburgh."

"Deacon—that's bloody rich," Montjoy laughed. "His name is John Campion. Like you, he's got an English mother and an American father. He can also be a pain in the arse who has a difficult time following instructions, so you two have several things in common. He was CIA, but liaised with MI6 for much of his career. John served most of his tours in the Middle East and South America, and was mixed up in the unpleasantness down that way in the 1980s. I've known him almost thirty years, and saved his life in 1994, in Beirut. He was eventually pushed out by Langley, officially at least, and went out on his own, private security and consultation. Damn good at what he did. The kind of old school approach that didn't gel with the kinder, gentler Central Intelligence directive."

"Whose side is he on?"

"His own," Montjoy replied. "From the outset, the CIA couldn't be certain that it wasn't someone from their neck of the woods who was behind Ahmad's death. The corroboration of an

American accent from the two sad sods you battered at Manor House only furthered that suspicion. That Ahmad's CIA handler showed up in London within two days of his assassination, and inserted teams into the U.K. without letting anyone know, confirmed mine. It was only a matter of time until they approached John, especially after your photo and GPS location was dropped into their lap. In the end, I knew he would remain loyal to me, so I used John as a go-between. He was instrumental in handing off the dossier on Hajjar to Langley's team, effectively replacing you as their target. Ultimately, I'm sure he saw himself as against everyone, which would suit him."

"Where is he now?"

"I haven't heard from him since Hajjar was apprehended, which doesn't surprise me."

"And Hajjar?"

"He's been flown to a rendition facility in Eastern Europe."

"I thought those were shut down, after all the negative press a few years back."

"You know better than that, old boy. Shut down from their original locations, but not shuttered completely."

"What does Hajjar offer?"

"He's connected up the al-Qaeda chain throughout the Levant, but particularly in Yemen, a country where we continue to have a limited intelligence footprint."

"And if he refuses to play ball?" Garrett asked.

"Then it's the way of the dodo."

The two men sat quietly as Garrett processed everything Montjoy had told him.

Montjoy interrupted his train of thought. "As I said, all's well. Ahmad is dead, you're essentially in the clear, and Hajjar's en route to an undisclosed location, where the Yanks will drain him of what he knows, and share it with us. As they say, 'the truth will out.' Sunlight has always been the best disinfectant."

"I would argue a hollow point works better," Garrett muttered. Then something dawned on him. "Why was Ahmad protected for so long? Surely his value as an informant did not outweigh the damage he was doing to your interests in England and elsewhere. There is something still unfinished, isn't there?"

"Possibly. I've suspected that the Cambridge operation was about something larger than Hajjar. Something higher up than even I was privy to. A secret the Service has long protected."

"Which you believe to be what?"

"At this point, I'm not certain."

Garrett recognized that he would get little more from his brother. He downed the last of his drink, and stood. "Perhaps the Fitzroy will one day put your likeness up, and make you immortal," Garrett said, referring to the picture of Dylan Thomas that had long adorned one of the pub walls.

Montjoy smiled. *"And death shall have no dominion—"*

"See you in two days."

"Newcastle Station, 2 p.m., Queens Wharf Carpark East." Montjoy lifted his glass as Garrett turned to leave.

Garrett pushed through the door and scanned the bar area. As he walked back toward the pub's entrance, he laughed to himself at the *Reserved* placard that had been placed on the corner table near the bar.

CHAPTER SIXTY-FOUR

Brussels Central Station
Belgium

Brussels was unusually warm for the middle of May, but David Laurent sipped an overpriced American latte nonetheless. Little of it reminded him of a good European espresso, but he admitted that its taste was nothing if not consistent. The much-graffitied Belgique capital, renowned as Europe's most boring city, was not his favorite, nor did he like using Brussels Central, for it was bitterly cold in winter and always seemed to reek of urine in summer.

Like the rest of the continent during the tourist season, Brussels was crowded. That morning, however, Laurent welcomed their sights and sounds, for his own appearance and manner were meant to blend in with the mass of sightseers. In particular, Laurent liked America and loved Americans. He found them, along with the British, to be among the most genuine people in the world, and, much like their coffee, they were always consistent.

The assassin was dressed in jeans, running shoes, a baseball cap, and a golf jacket. He sat with an open travel guide, and had spent the morning watching trainloads of visitors disembark, set to invade the city and cut a swath of selfies and over-tipped servers. The crusaders would conquer Brussels and Bruges, the only places they would visit in Belgium, before continuing on their ten-countries-in-seventeen-days campaign. Hannibal had nothing on these people.

But while he watched and waited, his attention was focused elsewhere. On someone who had beaten him. A man who should have killed him in Edinburgh, but had chosen not to. Human nature dictated that Laurent chalk up what had happened, not to a momentary lapse of skill, but to misfortune. To a turn of luck for his adversary. But Laurent knew better.

He had been bested by someone who had out-maneuvered him, from the beginning. A man like that worked for someone, and that someone would eventually come after him. Of this, David Laurent was certain.

At the moment, Laurent had other issues to deal with. He had to assume his safe house in Austria was compromised, which meant he would lose a cellar of top label wines. It would have to be the south of France for a while. His French was better than his Russian, and St. Petersburg would be too hot and miserably humid this time of year. He would regroup in Nice, and plan his permanent relocation to the States.

A voice interrupted his train of thought. "Don't tell me I've run into a fellow Wolverine all the way the hell out here in Belgium?" The tourist pointed to Laurent's hat.

Laurent turned and flashed a big smile. "Oh how I hate Ohio State," he answered, shifting his vowels in an Upper Midwestern cadence.

The man laughed, loudly, and slapped Laurent on the back. "Hot damn. Tell me you know how to get around this place. It took us twenty minutes to make it from the platform."

"Indeed I do. I was heading to Bruges this afternoon."

"Hey! That was our plan as well. That is, if you don't mind traveling with a big group."

"Not at all," Laurent smiled, extending his hand. "Call me Bob."

CHAPTER SIXTY-FIVE

Secret Intelligence Service
London

Berwyn Rees stood in William Lindsay's office and waited impatiently for the meeting to begin. He suspected his deputy chief had called the sit down to clear the air between his two warring heads of section, and to determine where the running of Ahmad had broken down to the point that the professor was dead, and no one had been arrested and held accountable for the murder. More importantly, there were twenty-plus years of intelligence and assets to maintain, spread between Rees and Montjoy.

Rees welcomed the meeting for a wholly different reason. He had gathered, from Montjoy's own *Dalmatia* files, evidence in the form of documented payouts that the man was connected to an overseas money-laundering operation run through Ahmad. At best, Montjoy would appear to have been negligent in his handling of the professor, having allowed him too much latitude to operate away from SIS oversight. At worst, and if Rees were lucky, it would be perceived that Montjoy was directly involved. Whether SIS decided to take action against the head of Near East operations, or save face by quietly suppressing the allegations and allowing him to retire, was irrelevant. Montjoy would be drummed out of MI6 one way or the other. He and his bloody famous lineage were finished.

Lindsay's secretary knocked. "Sir, Mr. Montjoy has arrived."

"Thank you, Sandra, please see him in," Lindsay replied, not looking up from his newspaper.

Montjoy quietly entered the office carrying a cup of tea. He covered the distance between the door and Lindsay's desk before addressing his boss. "Good afternoon, sir." Montjoy ignored the stupid smirk Rees flashed at him, and sat down opposite the pair.

"Good afternoon, Montjoy," Lindsay responded with his usual detached tone. "Berwyn, if you please."

"Of course." Rees circled Lindsay's desk and took a seat next to Montjoy.

Lindsay remained silent, his head still bent over the results of the previous Sunday's Premier League fixtures, before finally glancing up. "Gentlemen, I have a busy schedule, so you will forgive me if I forego the usual pleasantries. As you are both aware, we are two weeks removed from the assassination of Ahmad, and have little to show for it, other than several rounds of bad press. That is to be expected, of course. God help us if Fleet Street ever began to sing our praises. We should jolly well begin to worry then—" he stopped and eyed both men. It was a habit Montjoy had picked up on early in his tenure at MI6, whereby Lindsay tended to pause mid-flow in the natural rhythm of a conversation. It was a verbal gap that seemed to encourage a response, but Montjoy knew better. Rees, however, had never learned.

"We all think—" Rees began, but was quickly interrupted by Lindsay, who talked over him to finish his own thought.

"I can't say that MI5 or the Yard are any closer to working out what happened. So, I ask both of you, what do we know, or at least, suspect?"

Rees jumped in once again. "As you stipulated, sir, very little. It's an odd thing, I think, that such a high-profile man was murdered so openly, yet here we sit, with bugger all."

"Thank you, Berwyn, for restating the glaringly obvious," Lindsay responded flatly.

"I think the point is well taken, sir," Montjoy suddenly interjected, his muted defense of Rees caught both men off guard. "The assassination of the professor was brazen, and has, not surprisingly, drawn the kind of attention that won't go away anytime soon. The longer this draws out with little or no resolution, the more it looks like someone is hiding something. Or, at the very least, disinterested in finding the truth."

Rees shot Montjoy a quick look. *Nice try, old son.* It was clear that his counterpart suspected what was coming, and was attempting to head it off. Rees would have to spring his trap quicker than expected. "Indeed," he butted back in. "Someone is hiding something. The question is, who, and to what end?" Montjoy said nothing, and Rees continued. "Who had the most to gain with Ahmad dead?"

"Or, the most to lose with Ahmad alive and well," Montjoy replied, this time addressing Lindsay directly.

The deputy chief eyed Montjoy for several seconds, but said nothing. Rees decided to up the ante. "Quite. Who benefitted either way is the key."

"And you've figured this out, I assume?" Lindsay broke his silence.

"I believe so." Rees held up the folder he'd brought to the meeting. "With your permission."

"By all means, though I would caution you to tread carefully."

"Of course, sir."

Montjoy's expression remained unchanged as Rees stood and handed both him and Lindsay several files. Lindsay pulled a pair of reading glasses from his pocket and examined the first document. "What am I looking at?"

Rees glanced at Montjoy, who had yet to give the papers his attention. "Deposits and withdrawals over a period of six years, dating 2003 through 2008, between three accounts at Lloyds Bank."

"Held by whom?" Lindsay asked.

"We don't know, concerning two of them," Rees answered. "Lloyds, of course, will not disclose the owner, short of an official request and inquiry. But, perhaps we don't need to go that route, do we, Montjoy?"

Montjoy looked directly at Rees for the first time. "It's your show, mate."

"If only that were true, *mate*," Rees mimicked.

"Gentlemen—" Lindsay implored.

Rees ignored the plea for civility. "The deposits, all cash, come to just under one million pounds."

"Good lord," Lindsay exclaimed.

Rees turned to the next page of the file. "The second set of numbers enumerate payment to unknown recipients, totaling just over eight hundred thousand pounds."

Lindsay quietly looked over the figures, while Montjoy sat unmoving. Rees allowed his deputy chief another moment before turning to Montjoy. "Anything to add?"

Montjoy looked at Rees, and then to Lindsay.

"Montjoy?" Lindsay asked.

"I would assume the second set of amounts are payments for information, or payouts to assets. As for the deposits at Lloyds, I have no clue what they are."

"I believe they are kickbacks," Rees countered.

"Why do you suspect that?" Lindsay asked.

"Because the recipients of these payments, referenced only by cryptonym, do not match any known assets we cultivated through Ahmad while Montjoy was his handler. Moreover, approximately one week after each transaction, a cash deposit of exactly twenty thousand pounds was made into the third account, one we now know was controlled by Ahmad. At the same time, separate deposits of fifty thousand pounds were put back into the other two accounts at Lloyds, and these same amounts were then withdrawn, on nine separate occasions, approximately a fortnight after each initial deposit.

The total comes to just under five hundred thousand pounds, and there's no record, or indication, of where that money went."

Rees paused, as Lindsay studied the pages in front of him, while Montjoy continued to stare blankly through the window behind the deputy chief's desk.

Lindsay glanced up. "So, what do you think is going on?"

Rees had waited for this moment. "I suggest we ask Montjoy, considering that these documents were found among his own *Dalmatia* files." Rees paused for effect, but neither Lindsay nor Montjoy showed any reaction. "They were scattered amongst rather mundane timesheets detailing Ahmad's movements and contacts between 1999 and 2009. It was pure happenstance that I came upon them as I went back over all files, both mine and Montjoy's, in the hopes of finding any information, no matter how seemingly insignificant, which might lead us to who was behind Ahmad's assassination."

Rees finished, and Lindsay glanced at Montjoy. Rees allowed his own attention to slowly turn Montjoy's way as well, savoring the blank expression he continued to display. Rees knew Montjoy could go one of two routes. He could put up a heated defense, or say nothing.

Lindsay instead addressed Rees. "Impressive, Berwyn. And when exactly did you stumble upon these documents, might I ask?"

"Over the last three days, and there may be more. This is only the tip of the iceberg, I fear. If you give my staff additional time and access, we could more thoroughly backtrack through Montjoy's records, now that we know what to look for." Rees thought about a second set of damning documents he had already planted in Montjoy's files, which he planned to "discover" during a second go-round. Montjoy continued to remain silent, Rees noted. Obviously, he had chosen the latter defense.

"There is one thing that perplexes me," Lindsay said.

"Which is what, sir?"

"One week ago, I took away Montjoy's access to all files related to *Dalmatia*."

Rees startled. "You did what?"

"I removed his security clearance, as per your suggestion at our meeting with the Americans. The restriction pertained to all intelligence, and specifically, to everything connected to Ahmad during the time Montjoy ran him. Moreover, at the same time, I also ordered all files, and I mean every last bloody scrap, documented. It was then that Montjoy officially signed off on *Dalmatia*."

Rees was gobsmacked. He looked over at Montjoy, who still maintained the same bland expression he'd worn through the entire meeting.

"As such, it begs the obvious question, how did these previously unrecorded documents end up in Montjoy's files?" Lindsay asked.

Rees felt a wave of panic welling up, and wondered if it was betrayed by the flush of his face. His mind worked furiously to conjure a way out. When he'd planted the documents several days earlier, it had not dawned on him that Lindsay would restrict Montjoy's access to his own files. "I—I don't know," Rees finally stammered. "Someone in records allowed Montjoy access, against your orders."

"You're suggesting that Montjoy, after losing his clearance for *Dalmatia*, went back into the files and secretly planted incriminating evidence that he himself might be involved in what appears to be a money-laundering scheme?" Lindsay asked.

Rees said nothing.

Lindsay looked at Montjoy. "Anything to add, Montjoy?"

Montjoy looked at Rees and said squarely, "no, sir. As I said a moment ago, it's his show."

Rees fought to regain his composure, and suddenly remembered his discovery a day earlier. "There is something else I've come across that I think you should see," Rees blurted out, searching through his satchel for the dossier on Sean Garrett.

Lindsay interrupted him, "I'm sure that whatever you think you have, can wait. And we certainly don't need to subject Montjoy to any more baseless accusations." Rees began to issue a protest, but Lindsay stared him down. "That will be all Montjoy."

"Yes, sir." Montjoy stood and tossed the papers he had been given into Rees' lap. "Good evening, sir," he said as he turned and left the office.

CHAPTER SIXTY-SIX

London

Robert Riley took a sip of mineral water. "I don't suppose I can expect any kind of believable explanation as to what the hell is really going on."

"I can assure you that these developments are ones we became privy to only since Ahmad's death," Banastre Montjoy replied, as he watched the diverse crowd filter through the upscale cafe in Blackfriars. It was early morning, and everyone, from baristas juggling complicated orders to businesspeople late for work, knew their roles in keeping the rhythm in sync.

"Maybe, but I've got a feeling that you and Lindsay are up to something, especially after our meeting at MI6 last week. Does Moore know what's going on?"

"As much as you've kept William Scott in the loop," Montjoy answered, referring to Riley's boss.

Riley pursed his lips and gave it another go. "What happened to Ahmad?"

"He was assassinated at Cambridge two weeks ago—"

"Damn it, Banastre."

"It is our position that someone wanted Ahmad dead because they discovered he was working for you, or us. The man we believe was responsible, Nasir Hajjar, disappeared from Scotland last week."

"You can shovel that all you want, but we both damn well know that your office used mine to run this little off-the-books gambit. I'd be more pissed if I wasn't running my own op, which I now suspect you were somehow privy to and manipulated from the beginning. Humor me, John Campion was your man the entire time, wasn't he? He fed us exactly what you wanted, including that little bait and switch in Edinburgh."

"I would argue that we both came out in the black on this one."

Riley held up the file that Montjoy had given him moments earlier. "And this?"

"The man behind the King's Cross bombing."

"Is it now—" Riley accentuated mock surprise. "Also conveniently pieced together, just this week, I'm guessing."

Montjoy flashed a faint smile. "And it's the very man you've had under surveillance in Michigan for the last year."

Riley suppressed a laugh. "I won't ask how you know that. Of course, I'm to assume that, like Cambridge and Edinburgh, you're also in the dark as to what's going on in Dearborn, and that you're only the messenger?"

"Just passing it under the table."

"Which means that your end would like to see this," he said, again holding up the folder, "handled informally, without worrying about all those pesky middle amendments from our Bill of Rights."

"Perhaps you should rely on your court system to deal with Hajjar, in the name of equity and due process, of course."

Riley eyed Montjoy. "Lindsay had no play in this, did he? This whole thing was run out of your office. God help you if your side of the water gets wind of what you're playing at. You won't just be drummed out. They'll burn you at the stake."

"I'm the guy who pissed away a career getting pissed, mate. Middle management with the famous grandfather. Everyone knows that."

The comment elicited a muted smile from Riley, who realized he would get nothing further from Montjoy. He extended his hand. "Well done, Banastre. I underestimated you, and I'm guessing a lot of others did as well."

"All in a day's work." Montjoy returned the handshake.

"I have a feeling it will take longer than that." Riley punched numbers into his mobile. He gave Montjoy a nod and put the phone to his ear.

Montjoy tipped his hat as he turned and left the coffee shop.

CHAPTER SIXTY-SEVEN

Ballachulish, Scotland

The Peugeot rolled onto the gravel parking pad. Montjoy switched off the engine as Garrett pulled the Sig Sauer from his jacket.

"No worries here."

Garrett scanned the perimeter of the house. "They couldn't hit an elephant at this distance," he responded, and Montjoy smiled. The reference was to Union Major General John Sedgwick, shot by a Confederate sniper from a thousand yards out at the Battle of Spotsylvania, purportedly while uttering the famous line.

"He was one of the highest-ranking officers killed during the whole of the Civil War, if I'm right."

"You'll be the most senior SIS officer killed in the line of duty, if you're wrong," Garrett replied.

"At least, the first at a small inn in the Scottish Highlands."

"I assume you let grandmom know we were coming."

"I'm quite certain I didn't need to. The woman has a sixth sense." Montjoy pulled himself slowly out of the car, recognizing that his navy days seemed suddenly far behind him. Garrett exited, but kept the semi-automatic drawn. They approached the kitchen door, and before Garrett could knock, it opened.

Their grandmother beamed. "My boys," she said, hugging them both at the same time. "My beautiful boys."

"Grand-mama," Montjoy replied. "I hope you are well."

"If I wasn't, I am now," she smiled, wiping her cheek. "Come in."

"No guests?" Garrett asked as they entered the kitchen.

"I left the entire week open, certain I would see both of you," she replied, accentuating "both."

Garrett loosened his grip on the Sig as his grandmother put a kettle on. "I can assure you we are quite safe here, my dear." She placed her own pistol on the counter, and put four cups on a serving plate. "Why don't you make yourselves at home, and I'll be along in a moment."

Both men moved into the sitting room, which had a small fire burning. Standing by the hearth and holding a photo of Sir Nigel Aldrich, was William Lindsay. If Montjoy was surprised, he did not show it.

"Banastre," Lindsay acknowledged.

"Sir," Montjoy replied, taking note that Lindsay had never addressed him by his first name before.

"And you must be the last-minute party crasher." Lindsay turned to Garrett. "William Lindsay," he said, extending his hand. "I had a look at your file, Garrett. Seems like someone over at SBS thought quite highly of you, particularly the job you did during *Operation Barras.*"

"If they say so, sir," Garrett answered. Lindsay was referencing an operation in Sierra Leone in 2000. Garrett was training in Africa at the time, attached to D Squadron of the SAS, the British Army's Special Air Service, when a militia group known as the West Side Boys took a contingent of the Royal Irish Regiment hostage. He was part of the assault force that routed the rebels and freed the captives.

Lindsay held up the photo he had been studying, which showed Aldrich in an RAF uniform. The deputy chief smiled, reminiscing. "I took this photo. Did you know that? We served together, on more than one front, in more than one war. He saved my life, twice," Lindsay said aloud, but more to himself, "and I'm damn sorry I couldn't return the favor when he most needed it."

All three men stood silent, as the boys' grandmother brought the tray into the room and set it down. "What's done is done, William, and I won't tolerate all this gloominess." She took the photo from Lindsay and placed it back on the mantel. "Now sit, and have some tea."

It had begun to rain, and the sound reverberated off the metal roof of the storage shed behind the cottage. Garrett's grandmother poured two cups, and then touched his hand. "Walk with me, dear."

"Of course."

"Do stay for dinner, William."

"It would be my pleasure, Maddie," Lindsay replied with a slight bow. He watched the two exit through the kitchen door before turning back to Montjoy. "Well done, Banastre. I think it is safe to say that more than a few around Vauxhall Cross underestimated you."

"People see what they want."

"Or at the very least, what they are led to believe. I'm curious. Did you suspect Rees was up to something when you had me revoke your security clearance?"

Montjoy considered the question. "Nothing specific, but I couldn't be certain how deep the Walsingham-Ahmad connection went."

"I dare say you envisioned I must have had something to do with the whole business, considering your tactfully veiled threat during the meeting with Rees."

"Sir?"

"You can quit playing the fool, Banastre," Lindsay admonished. "Obviously, it has served you well, but during that meeting, it was clear you suspected something. You weren't certain who was involved, whether it was Berwyn, me, both of us, or perhaps that I was only covering for him. Berwyn was oblivious, but I picked up on it. A subtle threat, to say the very least."

"I wouldn't know what you're talking about, sir."

Lindsay smiled. "Have it your way. Well played, nonetheless."

"What now?"

"To say the matter is complicated would be an understatement. You may already be aware that Leighton Thackeray is involved, all the way into the silt. Suffice to say, he is untouchable. If anyone went after him, he would not hesitate to bring the entire house down around everyone. He would deny, misdirect, and drag out the inevitable inquiry until it overran and consumed many who weren't even involved. And that would be the point, of course. God knows what he is holding over the heads of people in real power."

"And Rees?"

"The man believes you are somehow linked, through your brother, to the death of Ahmad."

"He's not as stupid as he looks. Will he stay quiet?"

"Berwyn may think he knows something," Lindsay replied, "but he also knows which hand feeds him."

"I'm not so sure about that."

"He'll stay quiet. The identification of Garrett is inconclusive. It will go nowhere."

"And what becomes of Rees?"

"He is guilty of bad judgment more than anything else. Thackeray used him to keep tabs on Ahmad, and Rees made money off of deals through Walsingham. Those were above board where Berwyn's end was concerned, though his myopia allowed him to be pulled indirectly into the illegal schemes that Thackeray and Walsingham were running through Ahmad."

"If you say so, sir."

"In the end, I won't have to demote or drum Berwyn out."

"He might stay quiet for the time being, but he won't go quietly, that I can assure you."

"No, but neither will he agree to work under you."

"Sir?"

Lindsay stood up and walked back to the mantel. "I'm stepping down, Banastre," he said, again picking up the photo of Aldrich. "You're fond of Dylan Thomas? Well, I *will* go quietly into that good night. I don't have long left, and it's time. I've submitted my resignation, and will see the job through June. I've recommended that you be appointed acting deputy chief, and they'll do it. It will be provisional, of course, but I'm certain the interim title will be dropped shortly thereafter."

Montjoy showed no reaction, but he suspected Lindsay caught the slightest hint of a smile. "Yes, sir."

"Don't be modest," Lindsay waved him off. "You've earned it."

"Thank you, sir," Montjoy replied. "A question?"

"Of course."

"You planted the letter?"

Lindsay laughed. "Some might mistake that for an accusation."

"Did you?"

Lindsay put the photo back on the mantel and walked to the window. "What makes you ask?"

"Rees would not have been so careless. And as much as I despise him, he is conniving, which can act as a surrogate for competence, on occasion."

"High praise for Berwyn? Are you feeling quite well?"

Lindsay was stalling, and Montjoy knew it. He could leave it be, or press his deputy chief. "Call it hypothetical praise, sir. Rees would not have wanted the letter to stray too far from him, but nor would he have kept it at Vauxhall Cross. And he certainly would not have entrusted it to some staffer to mistakenly file away."

"No, I should think not."

It had begun to rain harder, and Montjoy would have expected his brother and grandmother to be back already. He glanced at Lindsay. "It was the date, sir."

"The date?"

Now Lindsay was playing the fool. Montjoy decided to up the ante. "Initially, it meant nothing. Until I found the partial letter to Ahmad, linking Walsingham with the Nazis. April 30th. The day Ahmad was assassinated. The same day Hitler killed himself, seventy years earlier. And your man nearly nailed down the hour as well. Ahmad wasn't to be eliminated until summer. You moved it up, why?"

Lindsay said nothing for a moment. "That's quite a leap, Banastre. It could be a coincidence."

"You don't like coincidences."

"I don't believe in them. There is a difference."

"Precisely," Montjoy replied. "The operation wasn't just about Hajjar, was it?"

"Poetic justice, you think?" Lindsay asked. "As we are speaking hypothetically, I would imagine that whomever 'mistakenly' filed the letter where you could get it, must have believed that the time had come to close the books on a very sordid, sad chapter in our history."

"And that person thought I was the man to do it?"

"Clearly, not everyone at MI6 misjudged you, Banastre."

Montjoy said nothing, and Lindsay pursed his lips. "You have to understand, no one was truly innocent during the late, lasting unpleasantness. The war, the Third Reich, the Russians, all of it ran together until it became impossible to determine where one enemy came to an end and another began. The overlap became one gray expanse. Add to the mix a startling lack of desire on our part, or the Americans for that matter, to bring fugitive

Nazis, or their collaborators and profiteers, to justice. You are aware of *Operation Paperclip*. The Yanks completely bypassed the directives of Potsdam and Yalta in order to bring Nazi scientists and engineers to the U.S. after the war. They whitewashed the pasts of these men and women, created fake biographies, and even granted them security clearances. The U. S. government was still paying social security benefits to ex-Nazis until just recently, for Christ's sake. All in the name of progress, and of course, to deny the Soviets access. Ultimately, the Cold War got in the way. It was easier to justify protecting the worst that humanity had produced in order to counter what was created in its wake. It's as simple as that."

"Who is Walsingham? Or, what *was* he, is perhaps the more relevant question."

"What have you pieced together, aside from a date?"

"The accusation leveled against the man in the single page that turned up in my files is cursory, and there is obviously something more. I suspect he was at best a Nazi sympathizer, and at worst, a war profiteer. But I do know that whatever Walsingham and Ahmad were into since the war, we've been protecting both of them."

"Walsingham traded in armaments and peddled information during and after the war, and not always with the right side, so he walked a fine line."

"One that became better defined after 1945, I might add. And more than a few war criminals were tried for less than that. In the end, we knighted and have bestowed countless titles and awards on a man who dealt with the devil during one of the darkest periods of our history."

"You've no idea, Banastre," Lindsay shook his head. "During the war, Walsingham was MI6."

Montjoy was surprised. "And the catch?"

"Precisely that. Thanks to his connections, he helped us round up a host of Soviet spies well into the 1950s."

"What did he do for us during the war?"

"A bit of everything. He was only seventeen when we recruited him, but he became one of our best men in Austria. Because of his family name, he held a sinecure for a steelwork outfit in Berndorf, which provided him the perfect cover and a wide range to travel. He had fingers in pies everywhere. We brought him on in 1941, and he was involved in a string of successful intelligence gathering operations for the next two years. He was one of our top agents, until he nearly blew *Operation Clowder.*"

Montjoy recognized the name. "The more or less unsuccessful SOE attempt to coordinate resistance groups in Austria and Germany."

"Walsingham was very good at what he did, but he was an arrogant little SOB. He was constantly breaching security protocols and going it his own way. A perpetual headache, but he got the job done."

"Until *Clowder.*"

"Before that, actually, in the spring of 1943. Walsingham was put in charge of a highly placed informant in Austria. A man named Roland, a Yemenite Jew of all things, and the nephew of an arms dealer who had lived in Hamburg before the war. Roland gained the trust of several German officers in Vienna, and had somehow acquired blueprints for the new advanced rocket the Nazi's were close to developing. The intelligence reinforced what had been leaked in the *Oslo Report* in 1939, but it was evident the Germans had made significant gains since then. Walsingham cultivated and turned Roland, and convinced him to give us everything he had access to. Several clandestine meetings preceded an exchange set for April of that year, during which time we planned to bring Roland to England. All Walsingham had to do was babysit the asset for forty-eight hours. And what did that daft cunt do? He got into a very public, drunken punch-up with Roland in a bar in the middle of Salzburg. He missed the hand-off, and Roland disappeared. It brought loads of unwanted attention down on our operation, and nearly compromised several others, including *Operation Crossbow.*" Lindsay referred to the Allied initiative to destroy German long-range weapon capabilities.

It suddenly dawned on Montjoy. "Roland wrote the letter."

Lindsay nodded. "Well done, Banastre."

"How did you come by it?"

"Through Ahmad. Roland sent the letter to him, at Cambridge, in 1966. It turns out Ahmad's father and Roland's uncle were business partners in Germany and Yemen during a time when each of them held the ear of the imam. Walsingham's own father, whose parents were Austrian by the way, had formed loose business links with both men before the war, when all three lived in Hamburg. The son picked up where Walsingham Sr. left off after his death in 1947, by which time Roland had assumed the majority of his uncle's post-war interests in Czechoslovakia and Austria."

"And I'd bet a tenner this is where the other penny drops," Montjoy said.

"Roland's father was Ali Abdul Hajjar."

Montjoy recognized another link. "And Roland was Nasir Hajjar's uncle."

Lindsay nodded. "Roland turned up in Tunisia after the war, serving as the front man for a number of outfits running armaments out of the Middle East and into Europe. By that time, Walsingham was on the way to building his empire, and the two had ostensibly linked back up."

Montjoy considered the implication. "Or, never had a falling out in the first place. Did Walsingham orchestrate the pub brawl to cover for something he and Roland were already running during the war?"

"I considered it, but could never prove otherwise."

Montjoy did not like where the conversation was heading. The post-war link with Ahmad was too coincidental. Montjoy could well recall the fall of 1990, and the nine months it took him to cultivate the Cambridge professor into an SIS asset. But hearing what Lindsay now disclosed, Montjoy suddenly viewed that early period in a different light. He saw Lindsay studying him, and his deputy chief voiced what Montjoy was thinking. "You're wondering whether it was you who approached and cultivated Ahmad, or the other way around."

Montjoy did not respond. It was October, near the beginning of term, and he had accompanied his head of section at the time, Geoffrey Charlton, on a scouting trip at Cambridge. They were to meet with a student, a post-grad at Trinity College, who had been recommended as a potential candidate for SIS consideration by Robert Adcock.

Montjoy could still visualize the moment he first met Ahmad, just after afternoon tea with Adcock. He had literally bumped into the professor entering the college, and after a pleasant "pardon me, and have a pleasant day," from Montjoy, Ahmad initiated an extended chat, standing under the clocktower at King Edward's Gate of the Great Court of Trinity College. Montjoy now recognized the irony of the moment, and the inscription of the great clock that marked the exact minute that Ahmad marked him, because now Montjoy was certain that was what had happened. Above them, chiseled in Latin, TRINITAS IN UNITATE RESONAT. *The Trinity resounds in Unity.* He thought of his grandfather, King's Cross, and the connection between Ahmad, Basha, and the bombing mastermind in Michigan, and realized everything had come full circle since that fall day twenty-five years earlier.

More conversations followed the first meet, and almost a year later, Ahmad began spoon-feeding SIS small amounts of low-level al-Qaeda operatives in Yemen. MI6, lacking any real intelligence gathering capabilities in the country at the time, ate it up. Those first, small fish finally beget bigger and better catches, primarily middlemen and mid-level financiers of terrorist activities on the

Arabian Peninsula and in Europe. Then, in March of 2002, six months after 9/11, Ahmad provided British Intelligence with their first wall-hanger, a trophy worthy of display. The target was a high-ranking al-Qaeda commander detained in Beirut, who was slowly drained of reams of valuable intelligence. In exchange, Ahmad was allowed more leeway where his below-board financial dealings were concerned. MI6 gave the man wider latitude to operate, like a middling drug dealer permitted to peddle on the street as long as he dimed out his suppliers. And in the end, Ahmad gave them King's Cross.

Lindsay interrupted Montjoy's deliberations. "You're wondering if it was all worth it?"

Montjoy ignored the attempt to close the topic down. "Where exactly does Ahmad fit into the Walsingham-Roland puzzle after the war?"

"Roland's uncle was a Nazi collaborator before it was considered a war crime. He ran guns between Germany and Yemen before the war, and Roland, through his early connection to the German army, continued the business afterward. Care to guess where Roland lived for several years during that period?"

"Berndorf."

"Within walking distance of the Krupp factory that Walsingham's grandparents owned before the war. Ahmad had finished his studies in England by the time Walsingham and Roland had begun to expand their gunrunning operation. Ahmad was teaching at a university in Saudi Arabia, and his father's prestige allowed the professor to exact a small measure of political influence in Yemen. At that time, the battle wasn't being waged against Western interests, and warring factions throughout Arabia limited the collateral damage outside the region to a minimal amount."

"And was anyone at SIS aware of Ahmad's connections when we brought him on board?"

"Of course. It's the reason we allowed it."

"And no one could foresee the potential blowback?"

"The higher-ups were desperate after so many failed intelligence coups," Lindsay conceded. "Ahmad was our way back into Yemen, the fallout be damned."

"Some consequences are better dealt with before the fact," Montjoy muttered.

Lindsay picked up on his sarcasm. "When you can see them. Of course, at that time, no one wanted to."

"And I can guess why Roland sent the letter," Montjoy said. "Walsingham cut him out."

"Completely, by the mid 1960s, the same year Ahmad took his position at Cambridge. By that time, Walsingham had forged his own contacts, and saw Roland for what he had become, a go-between who did very little but collect a nice paycheck."

"So Roland sent Ahmad, his father's good family friend, evidence he hoped would expose Walsingham, all the while unaware that it was Ahmad himself who became instrumental in completely cutting Roland out?"

Lindsay nodded. "Ahmad was playing all sides against each other, and he did it very well. He used the letter to benefit financially at the time, and thirty years later, as protection. He waited until after Walsingham had been knighted to inform us of the condemnatory information to which he was privy."

"It did more than protect him. Obviously, it emboldened Ahmad, who believed, rightly, he could leverage that knowledge to operate with near impunity, and we allowed it."

"Obviously," was all Lindsay said.

"What happened to Roland?"

Lindsay shrugged, "Whatever happens to men like Roland? He disappeared shortly after he sent the letter."

"Walsingham?"

"Likely. We attempted to locate Roland, without success, but he never turned up. Dead and buried in the sands of Arabia, and long since dispersed by some Persian wind, I should think. Shortly after you came to SIS, Ahmad had linked up with Roland's nephew, Nasir Hajjar, who in turn introduced him to bin Halabi, whose father had known Ahmad's family. By that time, Walsingham had been knighted, and perhaps looking to undo his past deeds, or at least, make some amends for them."

"Or make sure they never came to light. Where does Leighton Thackeray come in?"

"Literally, in 1970. He had been elected MP by then, and linked up with Walsingham shortly after. Walsingham and Ahmad had already been in business together for several years, and Thackeray was able to use his connections and political capital to expand their sphere of illegal dealings, in addition to better insulating them from outside scrutiny. Thackeray brought Rees in with the lure of wealth, but ultimately, to keep closer tabs on Ahmad through SIS. Once Rees became privy to the letter, he recognized that, on its own, it spelled trouble only for Walsingham. Once he better understood the Thackeray-Ahmad connection, Rees could see that he was potentially bollocksed as well. So, he attempted to conjure a way out with the planted documents, hoping to unhook his end and pull you in."

"I won't ask whether this business now gives anyone pause."

Lindsay smiled. "Alexander Pope has always dictated my frame of mind on matters of this nature, and he can speak for me now. '*Whatever is, is right.*'"

"Which *is*, what, exactly?"

Lindsay shook his head. "I'm the outgoing deputy chief of MI6, so I'm the wrong man to ask."

"And Walsingham?"

"I'll leave him to my replacement, but let me give you some advice. Let the dead bury the dead, Banastre. Of those remaining, whom you choose to have punished is your business."

"I'm certain I've never heard the bible interpreted quite that way, sir."

"You'll get used to it as deputy chief."

"At least by the time the interim label is dropped."

"In the end, that is what will dictate its removal, or yours."

"Yes, sir."

Lindsay smiled. "Call me William."

Garrett and his grandmother slowly skirted the ridge that ran along a cove near the cottage. They walked silently at first, his arm around her shoulder. He noted again how much older she suddenly seemed, but had to remind himself that she was ninety, had lost her husband, her daughter, and seen her only granddaughter put into a coma. Garrett felt the weight that had rested on his own shoulders, and imagined the degree to which it must have been magnified for someone on the frontlines. When they came to where the birch trees disappeared into a steep hill down to the loch, they turned and walked parallel on the ridgeline.

"Sean, I am proud of you. I don't know another way to describe how I feel about the entire situation other than that."

"Thank you," was all Garrett said, debating whether he should express his displeasure at being kept on the outside looking in of an operation in which he played an essential part, which included being put on the radar of Scotland Yard, the CIA, MI5, and a professional assassin. He thought better of it, and said nothing.

"From the onset I believed it was important, nay, integral, for you not to be made privy to the primary objective. Banastre argued against involving you altogether, but I knew you could handle yourself. It was I who directed him to bring Langley in at a different place and time than had been originally planned, which meant placing you in the line of fire, even if only for a moment. Please don't hold him accountable. If you need someone to blame, let it be me."

"If I knew what was at stake, I would have killed Laurent."

His grandmother smiled. "*Touché*, I think, is the response you are fishing for." She hooked her arm through his to better steady herself as they traversed a hillock. "Yes, that would have wrapped things up rather nicely."

"Banastre filled me in on your rather unique history, and I must admit, it is difficult to imagine you running around killing Nazis, or running assets out of East Germany between Stasi outposts. It seems from another world."

"It was, my dear, and from another time. Perhaps you are beginning to understand that now, as you approach a place in your life when there is uncertainly whether you have more days in front, than behind. Imagine what it must feel like when any day might be your last."

Garrett made an attempt at levity. "An even one hundred seems appropriate, so you have at least a decade."

The pair stood in silence for several moments, watching fishing boats troll the straightaway between the lochs. "And what happens to you now, I wonder?" his grandmother asked.

"I'm going home."

"Of course you are, but I mean after that. Home as a physical location can be very short-lived."

"I've got my business in the mountains. It's doing well, and I've met someone, a doctor in Asheville. She reminds me of Maddie, and I'll bring her over soon, so you two can meet. What I have learned these last two weeks is that I have no interest in signing on to anything official."

She laughed. "You know your brother well. It won't be long until he calls."

"And I'll answer the phone, we'll have a nice conversation, and I'll hang up."

"Of course you will, dear," she laughed again. They continued to walk along the overlook, ignoring the light rain that had begun to steadily pick up.

"And did you find what you were looking for?" she asked, tugging gently on his arm.

"Redemption, you mean?"

"Whatever you'd like to call it."

Garrett stopped and stared out over the water, the very same that he had watched open up into the void only a week earlier. He thought of his family, dead and gone, and his sister. "No," was all he said.

"Then you must continue to seek it."

"And you?"

"Me?" She put her hands on his cheeks. "My dear, redemption was something I never set out to find. In my profession, it is a luxury one must forego if anything is to ever get done." She patted his chest, and began to walk slowly back to the cottage. "Give it time."

Garrett took one last look over the loch. The rain began to soak through his shirt, and he strained to see the bridge on the far side of the water. He had always, even as a child, viewed the overpass as a gateway to another world. Each time he crossed it and disappeared into the wilds of *A' Ghàidhealtachd,* he felt free of everything that bound him. He imagined in those early years that he had already lived a hundred lifetimes, running through the heather and swimming in the lochs. Perhaps everyone's childhood feels that way in one sense or another, he thought.

Garrett lingered a moment longer as he bid goodbye to his ghosts on the far Highland peaks, for the time being, and turned to follow.

CHAPTER SIXTY-EIGHT

Garrett hugged his grandmother and shook William Lindsay's hand before he and Montjoy walked back to the Peugeot.

"I'll drive," Garrett said, forcing his way to the driver's side door.

"Perhaps I won't see the inside of the deputy's office after all," Montjoy joked, tossing Garrett the keys.

"You putter along slower than grandmom." Garrett started the car and pulled off the gravel pad, wondering if he'd be back sooner than he would have liked, in charge of cleaning out the house and putting his grandmother's estate in order.

Montjoy interrupted his thoughts. "Let's hear the plan again."

"Newcastle to Birmingham to Copenhagen to Chicago to Charlotte. I suspect you've made it as complicated as possible on purpose."

Montjoy smiled. "Enough that MI5 and Scotland Yard will give you no trouble between here and home."

"What will the narrative be out of Whitehall?"

"Ambiguous, for the time being, but along the lines that Ahmad's death was likely a retaliation, and the investigation is on-going. With Nasir Hajjar having gone missing from the U.K., someone in the press will hopefully get clever and connect dots that aren't there."

"And the bombing?" Garrett asked. "You've not told me everything about how the professor was linked."

Montjoy shook his head. "It's not finished."

"The truth will out. That is, at some point in the future and if it's convenient."

Montjoy peered out the window at the rain steadily falling over the unending green fields of northern England. "At least some version of it."

"MI6 is nothing if not predictable."

Montjoy smiled, trying to make light of the comment. "No worries, I plan to be more spontaneous tomorrow."

The two men drove in relative silence for much of the two hours it took to reach Tyne and Wear. They pulled to a curb a half-mile from Newcastle Central Station, and Montjoy moved to the driver's seat as Garrett exited the car.

"Sooner than later, I hope."

"Until then." Garrett turned toward the station, and pulled his collar up against the rain.

CHAPTER SIXTY-NINE

Liverpool Street Station
London

Montjoy stood in the dark by a second-story window covered in grime in a flat overlooking Liverpool Street Station. The small, two-room apartment, sparsely outfitted, was a remnant from when East and West waged war against one another in the shadows, by way of cramped, dingy spaces scattered across Europe. As he surveyed the room, Montjoy supposed that if he ignored the smell of the fish and chip takeaway below long enough, he could pick up the scent of rusted metal, the redolence of spilled blood.

Rain fell heavily, and in the new moon, the residual light cast off the buildings and onto the lane beneath him beset the entire scene with the pallor of a Victorian funeral procession. The backdrop reminded Montjoy that much of what he oversaw, what men like him had long forged, was an endless parade of the dead and dying.

He watched a man in a bowler hat stop beneath an advert for a transport company and shake his umbrella. Montjoy slowly descended a stairwell littered with trash and tinged with dried urine. The cracked tile of the entryway, visible between the buzz of a faulty fluorescent light, was so clichéd of the setting that he laughed in spite of it, before stepping outside.

"Raj."

"Monty," Roger Holland replied. "Good of you to come,"

"Did I have a choice?" Montjoy laughed and patted his old friend on the back. He motioned toward an alley that cut between a pub and restaurant, and the two men moved out of the rain. "How is Helen?"

"Sleeping."

"And Jane?"

"LSE, second year."

"Good heavens."

Holland tamped the bowl of his pipe, and the aroma of sweet Cavendish reminded Montjoy of his grandfather. "Has it been so long since Cambridge, old son?"

Montjoy shook his head. "Too long for those two foolish schoolboys."

"*The exquisite art of idleness*—or what was it all for?" Holland mused, paraphrasing Oscar Wilde.

"Chasing after birds, lest you forget."

"I remember they all loved you, Monty. Everyone has, from the beginning."

"That is about to change, I'm afraid."

"I heard. If the rumors are true, congratulations on the promotion. If indeed, it's a good thing."

"No worse than yours, I should think."

Holland smiled. "Well, enough of that insufferably English habit of polite chit-chat before the unpleasantness. You must know why I called?"

"I suspect."

Holland took a puff on his pipe and pulled an envelope from his coat.

Montjoy opened it and scanned the contents, which included financial ledgers documenting Mohammad Ahmad's dealings, in detail, with Leighton Thackeray and Charles Walsingham. It also contained the 1966 letter sent to Ahmad. It was the original, in its entirety, consisting of three pages that elaborated on not only Walsingham's war-profiteering past with the Nazis, but accused him of using the proceeds from Jewish companies he had acquired illegally and then sold, to fund the seeds of what became his financial empire. Equally damning, was the revelation that Walsingham was an MI6 agent in Austria during the war, at the same time he was collaborating with members of Hitler's High Command, most notably, Heinrich Himmler. Moreover, it detailed a clandestine meeting that Walsingham attended in Cairo, Egypt, in 1946, which served as the springboard for a lucrative money-laundering and gun-running business he ran throughout the Middle East for many years. The author, a man named Roland, also speculated that if he went missing, Walsingham would be to blame.

"Oh my," Montjoy said, in mock surprise, as he finished reading the letter.

"I'm guessing from your reaction that this is not the only copy."

"No, and not the only problem where Ahmad is concerned."

Holland took another long pull on the cherry-colored churchwarden, and blew out a series of small rings, which quickly dissipated as they drifted out from the protection of the awning. The earliest trains had begun to depart the station, and he kept an eye on two men as they shuffled past the alley entrance. "Needless to say," Holland observed, "this type of scandal would lay waste to your little corner of the realm."

"And all the king's horses and all the king's men—"

"Indeed." Both men stood silent for several moments. "Why was it so much easier back then?" Holland asked.

Montjoy considered the question as he watched taxis queuing near a station exit. "Because it was. Those were the days of black and white. There were never any choices to consider, difficult or otherwise."

"And now, nothing but," Holland mused. "Obviously, the very fact that I'm here and handing that over means I've made mine. But it's not me you need to worry about. It was my sergeant who rooted out the entire nasty business, quite brilliantly I might add."

"Samantha Anderton strikes me as the practical and patriotic type."

"She is. Very much so."

Montjoy pulled a card from his wallet. "Let her know that if she's interested, Interpol can wait."

"I shouldn't be surprised that you know that." Holland palmed the plain-looking piece of paper with only a single phone number on it. "Take care, Monty."

"And you, my friend."

CHAPTER SEVENTY

Paris, France
Four months later

B anastre Montjoy sat by himself in Café de Flore, near the corner of Boulevard Saint-Germain and Rue Bonaparte, and a casual stroll from the Seine River. The first time he had patronized the café, a lifetime ago, Montjoy had chosen it as the spot to stupidly fall in love. Foolish, in that it was a nauseatingly clichéd city to do such a thing, and because the target of his affection was a beautiful Parisian university student with brown bangs playing at least two levels above his own. She, bound to stay in the top flight indefinitely, and he, heading toward non-league relegation by season's end.

Yet, here he sat, again, hoping that the attention he sought would not go unrequited a second time.

His coffee was served at the same moment John Campion sat down across from Montjoy. The waiter paused, but Campion ignored him. Montjoy held up two fingers and the young man turned to oblige, stealing a distasteful glance back at the guest who had just arrived. Certainly, not a Frenchman, judging by his dress and displeasing manner, the waiter assured himself.

Campion held fast to his typical demeanor, and waited for Montjoy to speak.

"John," Montjoy said.

"You weren't long up on high and mighty." Campion referred to Montjoy's recent ascension to deputy chief of MI6.

"I have something for you that is of the utmost importance."

"When is it not?" Campion laughed. "But it must be urgent, to root me out. A *Huzzah* would be in order, if it was anyone but you."

"Steady on, or I might take that as a compliment."

"It's as good as it gets, mate."

Montjoy smiled. "Urgent, no, but it is a far more necessary thing that needs to be done now, than at any other time in our past."

"Quite poetic, which I assume comes with the new title, but do us both a favor and speak the plain fucking *Kings*."

Montjoy handed Campion a photo.

"Who is he?"

"That, is a young Charles Walsingham."

"The financier?" Campion examined the aged photo. Walsingham looked barely out of school, and dressed in a smart suit and with a confident smile, it was obvious that the young man was destined for unusual success. Campion was about to hand the snapshot back when he noticed something. He pulled the photo closer, and squinted. "That can't be what I think it is on his right hand."

"It is."

"Some kind of silly schoolboy dress-up, I should think."

Montjoy shook his head. "Unfortunately, no."

"Then I'm all out of guesses."

"Walsingham was a Nazi, and the worst kind, at least for a while."

"A part-time Nazi? That's like being kind-of knocked up. Even pretending that I'm somehow not surprised, the ring can't belong to him. He would have been, what, eighteen?"

"Nineteen."

"Then there's no way he earned it. He couldn't have been an officer and wouldn't have had three years of service. Nor would he have done anything in the killing fields to merit such an honor. He nicked it off some dead *SS* dickhead."

"Strictly *verboten*, you know that."

Campion studied the photo closer, seeking out anything that might betray its authenticity. The ring, the *SS*-Ehrening, better known as the *totenkopfring* by the *Schutzstaffel* who wore them, was one of the highest honors bestowed on an *SS* few. "Unless you show me some corroboration, I say otherwise."

Before he had finished the sentence, Montjoy handed Campion an envelope.

"Bullshit."

"Have a look, and there's more."

Campion pulled four sheets from the envelope. The first three were a letter, the last, a certificate of award presented to Charles Weber. He read over its first two lines.

> *I award you the SS Death's Head Ring. The ring symbolizes our loyalty to the Fuhrer, our steadfast obedience and our brotherhood and comradeship—*

The remainder of the document reminded the recipient of his duty to lay down his life for his country, of the Fatherland's past greatness, and its return to glory through National Socialism. The significance of the Sig-Runes, swastika, and oak leaves was followed by a warning to hold the ring, and what it represented, in the highest esteem. The letter concluded with its closing charge:

Wear the ring with honor!

Campion noted the obvious discrepancy. "This was awarded to a Charles Weber."

"The surname of his Austrian grandparents on the father's side. He was born Charles Walsingham in Reading in 1924, but spent summers in Salzburg until his mother's death in 1933, when his father sent him to boarding school in Austria. He came of age in the shadow of Hitler, and got caught up in the nationalist craze, like so many other teenagers at the time. He joined the *Deutsches Jungvolk,* and spent his time at the training camps at Grödig, in the foothills of the Bavarian Alps. He took the name of his grandparents, not long before he was recruited by the *SS,* trading his single Sig Rune of the *Hitlerjugend* for the double blaze of the *Schutzstaffel.*"

Campion continued reading, and looked up at Montjoy with surprise. "This is signed by both Himmler and Hitler."

"Highly unusual, I know," Montjoy acknowledged, knowing that typically, only a facsimile of

Himmler's signature would have been included. "That both men felt compelled to personally sign it, says something."

"Which was what? Assuming this is Walsingham, what did he do to earn the ring not one year after joining the *SS*?"

Montjoy gestured to the letter. "He turned in a prominent Jewish family harbored by his grand-parents, who were promptly arrested and shot, by the way."

"The entire family?"

"Along with his grandparents."

"Bloody hell."

"Not unusual at the time," Montjoy noted. "Walsingham, as Weber, then turned around, if you can believe it, and donated a large sum of that very estate, which he inherited through his father's bequest, to the Nazi Party."

"I assume this is connected to Ahmad."

"He and Ahmad were business partners."

"The usual postwar trade?"

Montjoy nodded. "Guns and money. The let-ter originated from a wartime business partner named Roland, who hailed from a well-to-do Yemenite family. Walsingham and Roland had collaborated on an arms-running and money-laundering scheme during, and after, the war, until Walsingham cut Roland out. Roland, who was privy to the intimate details of Walsingham's

Nazi past, sent the letter to Ahmad, whose uncle had known Roland's father. For some reason, he believed that Ahmad, who by then was living in England, would be able to help him, and possibly use it to expose Walsingham."

"Why didn't Roland unmask Walsingham himself?"

"Accusing someone of being an ex-Nazi wouldn't gain much traction in the post-war Middle East. Roland did what he thought was the next best thing, and enlisted the aid of Ahmad. And Ahmad did use the letter, but not in a way that Roland envisioned. Foremost, the professor forced Walsingham to go into business with him under threat of exposure, essentially taking Roland's place. Thirty years later, after Walsingham had been knighted, Ahmad disclosed the damning implications of a portion of the letter to SIS."

"What would MI6 care about it?"

"Because Walsingham was one of our agents during the war, and Ahmad has been a protected SIS asset for the last quarter-century."

"Fuck's sake, Banastre," Campion laughed. "You people have stepped in it this time. Let me guess, after they became aware of the letter, MI6 more or less allowed Ahmad to do as he pleased, justifying the decision because of the quality of intelligence he was providing you."

"He knew damn well that we would keep Walsingham's past secret, considering his link to the British government. But Ahmad only gave the first page of the letter to William Lindsay, detailing Walsingham's business dealings during the war. The second portion, the part concerning Walsingham's direct Nazi past, he kept secret, along with the photo. It was his trump card, an ultimate layer of protection. If Ahmad was ever arrested, or exposed, for his illegal activities, he assumed he could leverage the photo of Sir Charles, in all his OBE glory and sporting the *totenkopfring*, as a perpetual guarantor of his safety."

"Clever bastard," Campion acknowledged. "Does Walsingham know the letter is in the open?"

"Almost certainly."

Then something dawned on Campion. "How did you get the photo?"

Montjoy cupped his hands as he leaned forward and put his elbows on the table. "Mohammad Ahmad sent it to me."

Campion leaned back in his chair. "You have my full attention, Banastre."

"It arrived by post, to my home address, not long after he was killed. With it, was a copy of that letter."

"You ran him as an asset. One of many, I might add. Why would he have trusted you, and to what end?"

"I don't believe trust had anything to do with it. Even with the letter, I think Ahmad suspected that his time as a protected MI6 asset was nearing an end, particularly after Lindsay turned him over to Berwyn Rees. It also explains why Ahmad began to defer to Langley. His knowledge of what Walsingham had been became not so much an insurance policy, but a means to settle a score."

"Yours or his?" Campion joked. "And why you? Why not give it to the press? Make it public and go out with a bloody bang."

"I think it came down to either keeping Walsingham's secret, or the man himself, safe. If Ahmad goes to the papers, he reasons, only Walsingham's name is ruined."

"But why risk sending it to someone at MI6 who would have every reason to keep that skeleton, above all others, locked away?"

"In the end, Ahmad knew that we all had scores to settle. It came down to a singular choice."

"He chose retribution."

"Plain and simple."

"But why was Ahmad compelled to go after Walsingham? Certainly, he didn't give a damn about his Nazi past, and the man made him wealthy."

"Because Walsingham had Roland killed."

"Fifty years earlier? Ahmad couldn't have been that bent out of shape about it." Campion shook his head. "Walsingham would have needed to do more than kill Roland to keep that part of his past buried."

"You know what it was like," Montjoy replied. "Europe in ruins, and the Yanks and Russians in a violent tug of war at ground zero. It wasn't difficult for Charles Weber to vanish into the postwar chaos of the occupied zone and for Charles Walsingham to resurface in England, not only as a survivor of the bloodbath, but an MI6 agent who took it to the Nazis behind the lines."

"I assume you want it to look like a suicide?" Campion asked, as he stood.

"*Attempted.* And however you choose to stage it, make sure he is unconscious, but alive, when first responders arrive."

Campion eyed Montjoy warily for a moment. "That will be a first, but I suppose you have your reasons."

"And John," Montjoy added as Campion turned to leave, "make sure these ledgers, and this photo, are found near Walsingham."

Campion settled back into his chair, his tongue pushed into his cheek as he studied Montjoy closely. "I don't need to point out the guaranteed blowback which will follow. The Swiss won't sit on this, and when it hits the papers—"

"Heads will roll back home."

"Right off the Cliffs of Dover, including, maybe yours. You better damn well be sure of what you're doing."

"Well aware."

"You'll be circling the drain at SIS."

"Perhaps."

"This will create a major embarrassment for the British government, who will have to choose between being clueless, or being part of a cover-up where Walsingham's Nazi past and their knight-hood are concerned, as well as put MI6 where it hates to be, on the front pages."

"The Service has weathered far worse," Montjoy responded. "I want Walsingham to suffer for as long as he has left, and Leighton Thackeray to burn."

"I should have guessed that Ichabod Crane-looking tosser was involved."

"There are others."

"And if that fire fans out of control?"

"Hopefully it will, sufficient enough to engulf those close to it."

Campion said nothing for several moments. "Alright. Enjoy your peace and quiet, which should last for all of one whole week." He stood and pushed in his chair. "Ta, for the coffee."

"Always my pleasure."

Campion laughed. "I doubt that."

"Don't. Of them all, you saw what we do for what it is, and for that, I've always admired you." Then Montjoy added, "and so did my grandfather."

Montjoy saw the corner of Campion's mouth began to turn upward, before the man caught himself. "Sod off, Banastre," he said as he turned and left.

Montjoy smiled, knowing the departing shot to be one of affection. "And you, old friend," he responded, with Campion already out of earshot. Montjoy finished the last of his coffee and held up the empty cup in a somber toast. To his mum, his grandfather and sister, a career revived, and the ghost of a girl in a flower dress sitting across from him thirty-five years earlier.

CHAPTER
SEVENTY-ONE

Dearborn, Michigan
October 2015

Youssef al-Zahrani waited impatiently for the white walk symbol to flash at an intersection near Fairlane Town Center. At least once per week, he traversed the seven mile round trip from his mosque in Dearborn to enjoy the one Western indulgence he allowed himself on a regular basis, a chocolate dipped soft serve from Dairy Queen. The imam would often see how slowly he could consume the treat, and how far he could get before the cone began to melt and he was forced to finish it off quicker than he liked. Today, the heat of an early fall evening guaranteed he wouldn't even make it to Ford Woods Park.

By the time al-Zahrani reached the park, many of the weekend games had finished up. A few families still loitered at the pool, but most of the others were in the process of packing up and leaving. He was already late for a meeting with Aabis al-Adheen, and decided to cut directly through the wooded green space, rather than take his usual route, an access road that skirted a nearby neighborhood.

Al-Zahrani needed to clear his head, and think. Their success in London had been, regrettably, only partial, for two of the three bombers had failed. The first, at the London Eye, was the result of cold feet. The young medical student they had recruited and cultivated over a two-year period suddenly had second thoughts, and promptly turned himself in to the nearest constable. The other, scheduled to detonate himself in the lobby of the National Gallery at Trafalgar Square during a formal reception, suffered no such reverse of conviction, only a failed battery cap. Instead, the Qatari-born travel agent living in Coventry, panicked, and ran from a pursuing police van straight into the path of a lorry navigating the roundabout outside Charing Cross Station, which subsequently navigated right over him.

Only Mohammad Basha had succeeded, on the Piccadilly Line, killing thirty-seven people and wounding seventy more. One other casualty they had not anticipated was Mohammad Ahmad, a Cambridge professor who had facilitated contact between al-Zahrani's mosque in Dearborn, and one in London, which ultimately produced Basha. It would take months, if not longer, to organize another reliable channel through which to coordinate future attacks in the U.K. and Europe.

Tonight, al-Zahrani and al-Adheen would meet to discuss the final planning phase of four separate, simultaneous attacks that were to take place in America. Since their success, and failure, in London, al-Zahrani had begun to rethink his overall strategy. Though past bombings in New York, Madrid, London, and elsewhere had seemed to turn the Western establishment on its head, the effect was only temporary.

Al-Zahrani had come to realize that most Westerners tended to compartmentalize their worldview, and saw themselves as ultimately disconnected from the death and destruction that happened to someone else, in large urban centers somewhere else. The damage was too minimal, and the locations were simply too removed, to maintain any lasting hold on the psyche of these people. As a result, the two men had decided to alter their tactics. Instead of bombing famous sites in great cities, they would strike terror in the heartland. By killing ordinary Americans in their most trusted places, the message they wished to send would resonate for a generation to come.

Four locations had been chosen. A minor-league baseball game in Greenville, South Carolina, a mall in Omaha, Nebraska, a restaurant in downtown Austin, Texas, and a college building in Colorado Springs, Colorado. In two months' time, Middle America would be awash in its own blood.

Al-Zahrani quickened his pace, and noticed a lone man moving slowly between a set of picnic tables. He was wearing the traditional white Muslim *throbe* and checkered *ghutra* and *eagal*, and reading a book as he walked. The imam did not know the well-kept disciple, but expected that he would recognize and acknowledge al-Zahrani as they passed, as he was wearing his traditional cream-colored *bisht*, which signified him as a man of importance. Al-Zahrani nodded as he passed the young convert, who suddenly smiled at him, a look he took as one of admiration.

Soon, that same acknowledgement would reverberate throughout the Muslim world, the imam thought to himself.

"*As-salamu alaykum wa rahmatullahi wa bara-katuhu,*" the man said, using a longer form of the greeting.

"And may the peace, mercy, and blessings of Allah be upon you, my young friend," al-Zahrani replied.

The man suddenly shot out his arms in greeting, and moved to grasp the imam's shoulders, who was slightly taken aback by the informal and intimate attempt at contact. In a low voice, Tre Ward assured him, "don't worry, you'll still make your meeting with al-Adheen."

Al-Zahrani was momentarily confused, wondering if al-Adheen had sent the young disciple to escort him to the rendezvous. It was at that moment that he registered the flash of a double-edged knife and felt successive thrusts into his sternum, collapsing his lung and piercing the aorta of his heart.

Al-Zahrani strained to call for help, but found he could make no sound. Ward moved in to complete the hug, patting the man heartily on his back to finish the gesture, as he scanned the surrounding area. Dusk had made the two men virtually invisible to the few people who were still scattered far across the park. The SOG operator propped the slumping body against a tree, and emptied out al-Zahrani's wallet, tossing it next to the body. He placed the book, a copy of a now blood-soaked Koran, in the dead imam's hands, and left him in the repose of a man resting and reading peacefully, as evening fell over Dearborn Heights.

ABOUT THE AUTHOR

William Hunter has a PhD in history from the University of Cambridge. He has lived in Switzerland, Germany, Scotland, and England, and now resides in the mountains of North Carolina. *Sanction* is his debut novel.

Website: www.williambhunter.com

CPSIA information can be obtained
at www.ICGtesting.com
Printed in the USA
LVOW11s2322130318
569789LV00001B/138/P